A MAGICAL
RECKONING

MAGIC AND MISCHIEF – BOOK ONE

N. R. HAIRSTON

A MAGICAL RECKONING / N.R. HAIRSTON
1st paperback edition 2017.

Cover Design by Lou Harper
Formatted by Adam Poe

Published by Fire Ink Media, LLC

For my kids, who has always believed that mommy could do it.

To my mom, whose nonstop support made this possible.

Five Stories of Supernatural Betrayal

By Any Other Name

Rye must risk her life to save her best friend and fellow Scope agent from the drug runner bent on draining him of valuable skunk oil. Having skunk DNA herself, she'll do anything to shut down the illegal operation and get her friend back, but putting her trust in a stranger may lead to an unexpected tryst, as well as the ultimate betrayal.

I Was Asked to Kill Him

Delia is a pacifist who never wanted to kill her boyfriend, Greg. In a world full of powerful beings, she'll do anything to stay under the radar. She paid her debt to society and only wants to get back to a quiet life – but Greg isn't finished with her yet.

Pear Town Ruckus

A game of Spades is all that stand between telekinetic Leah and paying her rent this month. When fellow card player, Xavier offers to be her partner, she's delighted, that is until she finds herself fighting for her life in Pear Town, a place even cops dare not enter.

Belle of the Ball

All Kerry wants is to go home. Swept away from her hopeless existence into a life of strange luxury in an alternate universe, Kerry isn't convinced her luck has changed. As she discovers the ugly truth buried under the world of opulence and indulgence, she also discovers that she may not be as helpless as she thought, which is good, because what they have planned for her is a fate worse than death.

A Gathering of Succubi

In a race against the clock, Kia only has twenty-four hours to discover which of her fellow Succubi is killing humans. All supernatural beings are under the rule of the powerful First Families, who have laid down their mandate - find the killer, or all Succubi will suffer the consequences.

BY ANY OTHER NAME

ONE

The Scope agency buzzed with eager officers, all putting in extra hours, desperate to make a name for themselves. Scope only dealt with major and specialized crimes. Which meant if you solved the right case here, it could put you miles above your pay grade. None of that mattered to me, though. The only thing I wanted after the day I'd had, was to go home, have a nice bath, and unwind. I should have known it wouldn't be that easy.

Drena, who'd been on the force a few years longer than me, shut down her computer and turned my way, brown curly hair falling in her face as she did so. "You catch that fly boy, Rye?" she asked, inquiring about the case I'd been working on for the last couple of days.

I picked up my bag and tossed it over my shoulder. "Yeah, found him at the top of Estes, sent Garrett to bring his ass down." Estes was one of the tallest buildings in our town.

She laughed, a victorious grin on her face. That was the thing about Drena, a win for one of us, meant a win for all. It's what made her such a great agent and one of my top mentors. "Guess he didn't know we had a dragon on the force."

I nodded, pleased with myself. "I guess not."

Jerald, who had fly DNA, had escaped to the top of Estes, thinking my skunk ass wouldn't be able to catch him. Too bad for him, my buddy Garrett had only been ten minutes away. Garrett had dragon blood, enough said.

On my way home I stopped by Mia's, my favorite pizza parlor. They had the best food in town, and Scope agents got a ten percent discount. No better place to eat, if you asked me. Since I'd missed my lunch chasing Jerald around, I opted for a large, extra anchovy, double pepperoni, triple cheese pizza.

My mouth went dry as the delicious smell of garlic and sauce filled up the car and made it impossible for me to wait. As soon as I came to a stoplight, I flipped open the box and dug in. Hmmm. The cheese was so damn gooey that half of it slid back into the carton. I loved when it did that and hurriedly snatched it up. So what if I burned my tongue and the roof of my mouth? It was worth it. Fresh pizza, straight from the oven, was always worth it.

The only thing I needed now was a six pack and my night would be complete. I pulled up to EZStop, the convenient store around the corner from where I lived. I made sure to finish off the rest of the slice before getting out of the car.

Beer in hand, I came out of the store, and stopped cold, taking in the sight before me. My passenger door was open, and a tall, well-built man, who looked to be around twenty-eight, with shaggy hair, and clothes that looked like they hadn't been washed in about a century, stood eating his heart out.

"Hey," I shouted, dropping my bag, and tackling him to the ground.

He'd been so focused on the food, that he hadn't even seen me coming. "Please don't spray me. Please don't spray me." He placed his arms in front of his face as if to protect himself from my toxicity.

I let him go and stood. "I'm not going to hurt you, you idiot, but what the hell do you think you're doing?"

"I was hungry." He said it like that was supposed to explain everything.

I crossed my arms and leveled him with a blank stare.

He had the nerve to look sheepish, his eyes straying anywhere but to me. I counted to three, promising myself I wouldn't strangle him. After the day I'd had, the only thing I wanted was to go home and relax. The last thing I wanted to do was deal with a food thief. I decided to go. "Just take it. I'll get myself another."

He grunted, and then quickly jumped to his feet. "But I came here for you! Your name's Rye, right?"

I took a step back. "Who are you?"

He stared longingly at the pizza box. The slice he'd been eating was now ground into the road.

I waved my hand toward the car, letting him know that he could go ahead and get another piece. Why the hell not? Something told me my night was already ruined.

He didn't answer my question, just snatched up another slice, and crammed it in his mouth. It was disgusting to watch, and I turned my head, trying to give him a bit of privacy. "I'm not going to take it from you," I thought I should let him know.

His jaws worked overtime, as he tried to talk through a mouth full of food. "Do you really think I can understand you like that?" I asked.

He swallowed the rest and pointed across the parking lot to where I'd dropped my bag when I'd first come out of the store. "Can I have one of those beers?"

"Oh sure, how about a foot massage while we're at it. Maybe some peppermint tea?"

He smiled as if I was serious. "I'll take one of those square chocolates on my pillow, and I much prefer backrubs. I don't much like my feet being messed with."

I suppressed a chuckle, not wanting to give him any leeway. "Look, dude, what do you want? It's been a long day, and that spot in front of my TV's calling me."

His features turned grave, and I felt the mood shift from playful to alarming in an instant. He reached into his pocket, and pulled out a long silver chain, with a shiny skunk foot on it. My heart caught in my throat as I stared at the item in front of me. "Got this from a skunk named Cam. He needs your help."

I snatched it from him and ran my hand over the cool metal making sure the inscription was still there. I'd given it to Cam for his birthday last year, and as far as I knew, he hadn't taken it off since. The first thing I did was call Cam's phone, but of course it went straight to voicemail. Shit.

My hand shook as I placed the chain in my pocket and readied myself for what I was about to hear. "Where is he?" I asked, my voice barely above a whisper.

"Drake has him."

My eyes went wide and I had to lean up against my car for support. That was absolutely the worst thing he could have possibly said to me. Drake ran one of the biggest drug operations this side of the hemisphere. I'd been working his case for the last nine months and was just starting to make progress. He'd come on the scene three years ago, and had been relentless in hunting down his top competitors and taking them out, whole crews at a time.

Skunk oil was his top moneymaker, and he needed skunks like myself and Cam to get it. Taking the fat from the lateral glands in our backs, and then heating it past the boiling point, made for a product consumers were willing to pay thousands for.

I shuddered as I thought about it. The whole process was painful, and it often took days for our bodies to replace what had been taken. It ranged from us being unable to get out of bed because of the pain and loss of energy, to being completely paralyzed for months. A real fear for anyone with skunk DNA.

The oil had a ton of healing properties. People put it on their skin to protect from the cold and they also used it as a moisturizer. Got a cold? Rub it on your chest, throat, and nose, to relax the airways and break up the mucus. People with arthritis, or broken bones, found it especially useful, as it not only healed them but also took the pain away.

Men rubbed it on their penises and could orgasm for hours. Women did the same with their vaginas and had the exact same results. It was even used as a contraceptive in some circles.

Heat it to a certain level, and it would get you high as a kite, so high that you wouldn't come down for days.

Kidnapping was a crime punishable by jail time, but kidnapping those of us with skunk DNA and forcibly removing our oil, was a death sentence. If the perpetrators were found guilty, they would spend the rest of their lives in jail, with no chance of ever tasting freedom again.

I turned back to my new friend. "What's your name?" I

didn't want to keep calling him dude.

"Jax, and I barely got away. Cam was being held down at the time. I couldn't save us both."

I immediately grew suspicious. "You're not a skunk. What did Drake want with you?"

He wiped sauce off his hands and onto his pants. "No, I'm not a skunk, but I can do this." He picked up a slice and raised his hand over top it. The pizza shook and wobbled and then a small dollop of olive oil popped onto his finger. "See? I can reach into your glands and pull the fat out, undiluted, and completely intact. Not many that can do that and Drake knows it."

I watched him wide eyed and impressed. I'd never seen anything like that before. I bit the inside of my jaw hard, trying to suppress the fear steadily rising in my gut. The only thing this did was add even more profit and efficiency to the whole skunk oil business. "How many of us does he have?"

Jax pushed the pizza out of the way and took a seat on the passenger side. "I don't have an exact number. Besides, he didn't keep us all in the same place."

Shit. I took a deep breath and steeled myself for an answer I may not have been able to deal with. "How was Cam when you left? Is he ... did they ... is he still alive?" To even have to ask that question hurt me more than words could describe, and I readied myself for his response.

He nodded, and I closed my eyes in relief. Cam was... well, Cam meant everything to me. He was my best friend, had been since we were kids. There was nothing we wouldn't do for each other, and there was nothing that was going to stop me from finding him and bringing him back home.

Cam already knew I'd tear this world apart just to keep him safe. For now, I needed information. "How long have they had him, and how did you escape?"

"They kept us in cages." He swallowed hard. "Drake's lackeys would take me out, three, four times a day to extract the oil. I'd never seen Cam before, but when they came to get me this last time, he was on his knees, his hands in restraints. The silver chain was at his feet, and they were taunting him with it. Saying stuff like, 'If Rye could see you now she'd have the whole Scope team here,' and holding the chain up, asking 'Didn't Rye give you this? Holy shit! What would she say if she saw me holding it?'"

He stopped talking and took a breath. "Drake had a phone call and stepped into the next room. That left only two men guarding myself and Cam. I took them out easily, but before I could get to Cam more men came. So, I snatched the chain up and promised him I'd find you before I escaped."

They probably kept him chained not only to hold him in place once the pain hit but also to control the thiols, which would sometimes shoot out when we were being drained.

Thiols was what those of us with skunk DNA used to protect ourselves against would be attackers. That awful inhuman smell could clear a room in seconds, as well as choke the life out of any adversary. We could also turn it sweet and have you groveling at our feet. That one we didn't use often, because it caused a breakdown that left us without thiols for days, until our supplies built up again.

Right now, I felt it racing through my veins in a quest for vengeance. Someone had taken my best friend, and they were damned sure going to pay. I turned to Jax because there was something in his answer that just didn't sit well with me. "So, you just left him there? Saved your own ass and left him to rot."

He ran a hand down his face, fingers resting on his lips before he answered. "If I'd stayed, I wouldn't be standing here with you now, and you still wouldn't know where Cam is."

I didn't understand everything that was going on, but for now, I wasn't letting Jax out of my sight until I could find out more. He had information about Cam's whereabouts, and so I'd be damned if I was letting him go.

I picked up the bag I'd dropped and got in on the driver's side. Jax dropped into the passenger seat and closed the door. I waited until he hooked his seatbelt. "If you're lying, or aided in his capture in any way..."

He ignored me completely, and instead of answering, popped open a can of beer and took a big gulp. "Ahhh." He wiped his mouth with the back of his hand. "This is the good stuff. You did get my favorite."

Incredulous, I stared at him. "Did you hear what I said?"

He drunk down some more. "I heard you."

I shook my head and started the car. "Okay then, let's go."

I walked through the door of my small three-bedroom house, placing my keys on the counter.

Jax stood off to the side as if waiting for me to tell him what to do. Well, he needed to get cleaned up before he did anything. "I'll find you something to wear." I searched through the closet in the guest bedroom and was able to throw together a decent shirt, pants combo.

While in the back, I called Scope to let them know what was going on. I had them put agents on my house in case Jax wasn't who he said he was, and I let them know that we needed to assemble a team to find Cam.

I walked back up the hall to find Jax was still in the same spot I'd left him. "Second room on the right. You should find everything you need in there. Get cleaned up, and then we can talk." He caught sight of the clothes in my arms and smiled. "Oh, goody. I'll just take these." I handed the stuff over and then walked into the kitchen to tidy up.

The pizza had grown cold, the beer lukewarm. I placed them both in the fridge and pulled out a piece of baloney instead. Cam couldn't stand the stuff, and holding it in my hand now, only made me think of him more.

I wiped my eyes and walked back into the living room. Just the thought that he was out there somewhere, alone and being hurt, left a hollow feeling in the pit of my stomach.

I tossed the baloney in the trash and took a seat on the couch. The only thing on my mind was Cam, and getting to him as quickly as I could. To do so I needed to be at my best, so I figured we'd get a decent night's sleep here, and then head out first thing in the morning.

Jax came back up the hall about twenty minutes later, freshly scrubbed and clean shaven. He'd blow-dried his hair, and black locks reached almost to his shoulders. I tilted my head to the side as I stared at him. He looked good, and I knew under different circumstances, well let's just say the night would have ended on an entirely different note.

He sat beside me and placed one of my throw pillows in his lap. "You know what we're doing? Because I don't."

I turned weary eyes toward the ceiling, taking a moment to gather my patience. He sounded like we were discussing a school project, instead of trying to save my best friend's life. "Remember how to get back to where you were held?"

He raised an eyebrow. "You think Drake and the others are still there?"

We were going there either way. "They probably left behind some clues. They always leave clues behind."

His eyes shifted to the floor. "If you say so." He didn't exactly sound convinced.

Before I could respond my doorbell rang. Jax leaned over and peered out the window. He pointed outside. "Do you know him?"

I pulled back the curtain. It was Drew. One of my late-night friends. I'd promised him money for a new pair of shoes. "I got this."

"Hey, baby." He wrapped arms around me the moment I opened the door.

I pushed him away. "Not now. I'm busy."

He started to argue but stopped once he saw Jax. His jaw tightened, and his voice came out hard and accusing. "Busy? That what they calling it now?"

I glared at him, because now really wasn't the time. My best friend was missing and he wanted to play the jealous card. I riffled through my purse and pulled out eight twenties, thrusting them into his hand. It was time for him to go. "You would've gotten more if you hadn't acted like an asshole."

His eyes went wide, voice indignant "You got another dude

in here and I'm the asshole?"

I opened the door. "I'll talk to you later." He stared at me hard for a second then turned his attention back to Jax.

I let out a slow breath, trying to keep my cool. I needed him gone. We had so much to do, and he was only wasting time. Anyway, he knew who I was. He was acting like a boyfriend and I didn't have one. A couple of friends, yeah. But a boyfriend? Never.

Jax got a little more comfortable on the couch and spread his arms out. "We were just having pizza and beer. Her treat. She is generous, isn't she?" He sounded mocking and from the glint in his eyes he knew it.

Drew's nostrils flared, but I pushed him out the door before anything could happen. "Catch up with me in a few days. We'll have a good time. I promise."

Jax watched me closely after he was gone. "You do get it in, don't you? I like a woman who knows what she wants."

Ignoring that completely, I pointed down the hall. "Guest room is second door on the right. The sheets are clean and the bed is made. Try to get some sleep. We pull out first thing in the morning."

I was almost out of the living room, but at the last minute I turned back toward Jax. "I don't know you, and right now I don't trust you. The only reason that you're here is so that I can keep an eye on you while we give my team time to get everything together to move in on Cam's location. Don't make me regret it. Oh, and if you come out of your room, alarms will sound. Just something for you to think about."

TWO

The department had an abundance of undercover cars at its disposal, and so I'd decided to use one of them, rather than go on my own.

Jax sat on the passenger side. The expression on his face was inquisitive.

I paused from putting the key in the ignition and turned to him. "What?"

He let out a chuckle that said he couldn't believe I was even asking. "You know what. Where's our backup? Or are we just going to take Drake and his army on by ourselves?"

I started the car. "Are you saying you couldn't do it?"

He licked his lips and sat up a little straighter in the seat. "I'm saying I'll damn sure try. For what he did to me, to Cam. For the pain you're feeling right now. I'll kill him." He sounded so sincere.

I started the car, not really wanting to examine why his words hit me the way they did. "Yeah, well, we got back up. They're following closely behind. They'll be there if we need them."

"You sure? Because I'd be happy to take him and his whole crew out by myself. With your help, of course."

He smiled at me and something dangerous flipped over in my stomach. I cleared my throat. "I'll keep that in mind."

We drove about three hours before pulling over for a food break. Neither of us had eaten breakfast, wanting to get to Cam as quickly as we could. It'd been a bad idea and both of us should have known better. We couldn't fight on an empty stomach and right now the hunger pangs were ripping me apart.

I parked at a "Heel to Boot" steak house and got out. "We can eat here."

The nonchalant smile on his face said it didn't matter to him one way or the other. "Food is food. I eat everything. Never tasted something I didn't like."

I didn't even bother to acknowledge that with an answer. I waited until he got out of the car and then locked the doors. We'd kept up a constant chatter all the way here, covering a broad range of subjects. He was easy to talk to, and the conversation flowed effortlessly between us.

"We need to get this to go. We don't have time to sit down and eat," I let him know.

The place we stopped at was full. I never ate at a restaurant with an empty parking lot. If no one was eating there, there was probably a reason.

"I want a steak," he said, voice flat and serious.

Here we go again. "Okay…"

He waited for me to figure it out, and when I didn't, he went on. "You can't eat a steak on the road. In a car." He shook his head. "It just ain't right."

He was being purposely irrational, but it still got a slight chuckle from me. "Okay. We'll eat here, but we have to hurry. I want to get to Cam as quick as I can."

The waitress sat us at a booth in the back, one of the only empty seats in the whole place. I ordered a T-bone, with a baked potato and broccoli on the side. Jax ordered a T-bone as well, plus a ribeye, New York strip, and a myriad of different sides and desserts.

I was sick just watching him. "You're not going to eat all that."

He cut off a chunk of his T-bone and dipped it into A1 and then ranch. "Watch me," he said, shoving a forkful into his mouth.

I had more important things to worry about than Jax's food

choices as my mind once again turned to Cam. Pressure built behind my eyes, but I took a deep breath trying to expel it. I wouldn't cry. Not here and not now. Cam deserved better than that. "I'm going to the bathroom," I said after I'd eaten a little over half my meal.

Jax had eaten everything and was now demolishing a large bowl of ice cream. He was all solid muscle, and I wondered how he could stay that way and eat the way that he did. I'd never met anyone with his unique ability, so maybe that tied into his metabolism or something.

He hardly seemed to know I was there, eyes so focused on the food in front of him. "I'll be right here," he finally said.

I'd just washed my hands and exited the restroom area when a hushed voice called me back.

A young woman, with straggly brown hair, and whose clothes were more off her than on, stood by the exit doors just behind the kitchen. She waved me over.

I checked back to where Jax sat at the table, licking his fingers, and drinking a glass of water. I turned back around. "What do you want?" She didn't seem to be here to eat.

Her eyes blinked at me, big and scared as she pointed toward the back exit. "They got that boy bad. I'm afraid they gonna break his legs. They got 'em on the ground. He a skunk. One of your kind."

I hung my head low. I didn't have time for this, but damnit, I couldn't leave another skunk in the lurch. Sometimes it pissed me off how easy it was to target us. Sadly, this wasn't the first time I'd run into something like this, and probably wouldn't be the last. Still, I knew to stay on my guard as many of us had been trapped this way as well.

I'd never been taken and was pretty sure I could handle myself, so I'd step out real quick, and then Jax and I could get back on the road.

One of the things that hurt us was that we were so easy to identify. All those with skunk DNA had black bushy hair that curled at the ends, with a large white stripe down the middle. Nothing we could do about it. We couldn't dye it. I'd tried many times, as had others. Not believing our parents when they'd told us that our hair could never be changed.

We could cut it all off, though, and some skunks did. I just hadn't reached that level of extreme yet, but I damn sure wished Cam had. Especially if it meant it kept him safe and out of harm's way.

I caught Jax's eye and gestured to let him know I'd be right back. He gave me a thumbs up and then shoved half a pie in his mouth. I couldn't help but laugh just a little. What in the world was I going to do with this guy?

The hot summer sun hit me the moment I stepped out the door. It was so damn humid that my clothes were starting to stick to me. I swept the sweat from my brow and walked to the dumpster where a bunch of guys were gathered with sticks. Except... I turned to the girl. "Where's the skunk?"

She pulled out a small baton, her face now hostile. "Right here, you stinky ass bitch." She made a move to punch, but I saw it coming and ducked. Before she could try again, I delivered a hard uppercut to the side of her face.

She flew across the concrete, landed hard up against a car, and then fell to the ground. I wanted to question her. Find out what her game was, but a bat to my knees dropped me in an instant. What felt like a firecracker exploded through my legs, and hot, raw pain took my breath away.

By now my adrenaline was flowing, and I was more than ready to rumble. I loved to fight, something few knew about me, but found out quickly enough once they'd challenged me.

The guys with sticks closed in on me. One dragged his on the ground, a menacing look on his face. Another repeatedly beat his into his right hand, looking cocky and self-assured. The other two simply held theirs at their sides but kept a steady pace with their partners.

I breathed thiols at the one dragging his bat. His eyes bugged out of his head, and he grabbed at his throat as it became harder and harder for him to breathe.

I still had the other three to deal with and they were coming straight at me. I aimed thiols into the eyes of the one who was beating his bat. His hands flew to his eyes and he let out a howling scream. "I can't see. I can't see. Fucking skunk bitch blinded me. I can't see."

I cracked my neck and turned to the other two. "Still want to try me?"

Pissed now that I'd already taken out three of them, they both charged me, yelling and screaming all the awful things they were ready to do. I bombarded them with more thiols, I didn't know why they thought I wouldn't.

Before I could direct it though, cold metal wrapped around my neck, cutting off my air supply. My arms windmilled in front of me as I tried to break free. I couldn't breathe. Damnit. I couldn't breathe.

"You punch like a bitch, bitch." The woman whispered in my ear, her breath coming in short spurts from the effort it took to choke the life out of me. I should've hit her harder, or at least made sure she was down for the count. A costly mistake on my part.

The men were still caught in the thiols, but without me to control it, it soon dissipated, freeing them up to come at me. "Gonna take you straight to Drake. He knows what you're up to," the guy on the right said.

My body started to give and I realized I wouldn't be able to fight them off much longer. One of the guys punched me in the face, rocking my head back and causing my eyelid to split open.

Blood rolled down my cheek, but there was nothing I could do about it. I knew backup usually traveled thirty to forty minutes behind, but I thought they'd had time to catch up.

The chain grew tighter and I wondered how many skunks they'd trapped this way. Was Cam one of them? Were these punks the reason he'd been captured?

I couldn't think on it any longer, as my vision blurred, and my head felt like it had rocks in it. I was losing focus. I knew I was choking, but I couldn't remember why. All I knew was that I needed to break free. I needed…

I heard a loud grunt, and suddenly the pressure was gone, and I could breathe again. Relieved, I fell to my knees, rubbing my hand across my throat. There would be a burn mark there. I could already feel it forming. I coughed, and then winched. My mouth was dry as hell, and blood dripped from my lips.

I was wetter than I should have been, and from the smell, I already knew why. I turned to see Jax holding the woman's spinal cord in the grip of his hand, a furious look on his face.

"There's two more," I tried to warn him, my voice scratchy and barely above a whisper. He nodded to where the two guys had decided to cut their losses and were now running in alternating speeds down the street.

I allowed myself to breathe a little easier. "What took you so long?" I asked before I passed out completely.

When I came to, I was on a hard mattress, and my whole body burned like fire. A small lamp sat on the table by the door, its light low enough not to be distracting.

Jax sat beside the bed, his hands steepled in front of him, eyes intense and focused.

"Water," I said, hoping I was loud enough for him to hear.

He jumped up immediately, relief all over his face. "Hey. You're alright." He placed my phone in my hand. "It's been ringing. I told Drena and the others where we were. But I didn't tell them everything. I didn't know what you wanted me to say."

I nodded and then took a glimpse around. The room had one small, black mini fridge in it. Jax opened it and pulled out a bottle of water. "Figured you'd want this when you came to. I got it out the soda machine. Put it in there to keep it cold for you." He sat on the side of the bed and opened it for me, pulling out a straw from the nightstand and sticking it in there. I was impressed and appreciative of his foresight.

I tried to move, but he placed a hand under my head and raised it slightly.

"Thanks." I could only drink a little at a time, but he was patient with me, letting me go at my own pace and sip as I pleased. "Enough." I finally said, after I'd had my fill.

He sat the bottle aside and leaned over top of me. "What can I do to make you feel better?"

"Skunk oil. My back." I hoped he understood what I was asking.

He gave my hand a squeeze. "You sure?" he asked, his voice barely above a whisper.

"Do it," I managed to croak out.

"It's going to hurt a little," he said softly.

I let out a breath. "I know."

Grabbing an empty water bottle that he'd probably had earlier, he gently rolled me over and waited until I nodded okay before he began.

It started off slow but quickly sped up. It was a painful process no matter how you did it, and I found myself gripping the sheets to keep from screaming out and injuring my throat even more.

I clenched my teeth as a good deal of the liquid in my back was removed. As he did his work, and the pain worsened, I did end up sticking the covers in my mouth and biting down hard on them.

A tear rolled down my face as I thought of how this was being done to Cam daily, without his consent, and likely as violently and painfully as they could get away with.

A small bit of thiols leaked from my hands, but not enough to do any harm.

Finally, Jax announced he was done. He turned me back over and tried to give me a reassuring smile. "Be right back." He made a dash for the bathroom and came back with a wet cloth in his hand. He sat back on the bed and began to wipe the sweat from my face. "I don't know how to do this," he confessed.

I figured he wouldn't. Most people either shot skunk oil straight into their veins or took it in little pills that their drug dealers made for them. Unless they were using it for sexual purposes, which was a whole other case altogether. "Just rub it all over me. Specially my neck, ribs, and face."

"Can I use this?" He held up the already damp rag. I nodded to let him know that that would be okay.

He carefully poured some on the washcloth and began a smooth massage of my neck. It was warm and soothing, and I could already feel it rocking me to sleep.

My eyes grew heavy as Jax continued to rub the liquid all over my body.

Somewhere in the back of my mind, I noted that I must trust him just a little, to be able to surrender so completely in his presence.

We decided to stay the night at the hotel. Drake had sent those thugs after me, which meant he knew we were coming. How he'd known what route we'd take I didn't know, but I wondered if he had people spread out on all likely paths.

A scary thought, while I was still incapacitated on the bed.

We agreed that we hadn't been alert enough. From here on out there would be no more separating. Wherever Jax went, I went, and vice versa.

There would be more coming for us, and after this failed attempt, I expected them to triple their efforts.

THREE

The next morning saw me fully healed and ready to get going.

"Know any backroads?" I asked once we'd settled in the car.

He raised an eyebrow. "If that's what you think is best." He didn't sound too confident about it, but he didn't try to fight me, so maybe he trusted my judgment. "Take a right at the light, and follow that street to the next light, and then turn left."

I turned the car to the right, hoping this would keep Drake supporters off our backs. We didn't have time to stop for a fight every couple of miles. Cam needed our help, and I was determined to get to him as quickly as I could.

Energy flowed through me, and if not for the urgency, I wouldn't really mind letting off a little steam with a good street brawl. That's the thing about skunk oil and why it was in such high demand. The effect was almost magical and it made you feel like you could take on the world.

My knuckles tightened on the wheel. I couldn't wait to catch up with Drake and those who had hurt Cam. "How many people does Drake have around him on a daily basis?"

Jax thought about it. "About ten powerful strong guys, alert for anything. Drake pays them well, and the way they troll under him is almost fanatical."

I thought about Cam being constantly brutalized by these men and felt myself choke. "Are they abusive?" I finally allowed myself to ask.

He let out a breath as if he knew the answer would bring me pain, and he was doing everything he could to avoid it. "They can be," he answered after about thirty seconds.

I gripped the wheel harder, not even caring about the trickle of tears falling down my cheeks.

Jax turned away from the window and touched me on the arm. "Hey, hey, now, none of that. Cam is going to be alright."

I knocked him away. "Stop being nice. It's freaking me out."

He threw his hands up. "Hey, you don't get dibs on freaking out. Cause seeing you being choked to death freaked me out."

He sounded serious, and I spared him a quick glance before turning back to the road. I exhaled lightly. "She didn't choke me to death. I wasn't dead. Skunk oil can't bring you back to life. You'd do well to remember that."

He smiled and changed the subject. "Gonna thank me for saving your life?" He held up a finger. "I think I broke my pinky in the process."

He was so damn outrageous. But somehow, he hit my humor button just right every time. "Yeah, well, sorry about that. You should have rubbed some skunk oil on it when you had the chance."

He stared at the finger and then ran his hand across it. "Some dripped on it while I was getting you well. It's all good now."

"You want me to thank you for that too? For the oil healing your finger?"

His voice took on a low rumble and he turned in his seat. I kept my eyes on the road, not wanting to see the look on his face. "Thank me for taking care of you when you couldn't take care of yourself? No. Never. You don't have to ever thank me for that."

He said it with so much damn conviction and passion that I almost ran off the road. "Yeah, well," I cleared my throat and steered the car back onto the road. "Thanks for all that. You could have taken advantage and you didn't. So...."

He smiled brightly, but I could see the teasing in his eyes. "Are we best friends now? Is that what's happening here?"

My mind immediately turned to my true best friend, and just

like that, my mood soured. "Let's just focus on where we're going, okay," I said shortly.

He turned in his seat. "I wasn't trying to upset you. Just wanted to see you smile again. I like it when you smile. It's nice." He said the last part so low that I barely heard him.

"This one time," I started to speak then had to stop to catch my breath. "This one time, I was working a case. The perpetrators had me surrounded, four of them. Before we went in, we'd thought it was more like forty. We'd heard the message wrong." I shook my head, thinking about the way Cam had come blazing through that door. "Do you think he waited for backup? No. He came crashing in anyway. He didn't give a damn what happened to him. He came for me. He always came for me. So I'm not going to let him down."

"That's all nice, but how many times have you done the same for him? I'm pretty sure you've shown him your loyalty on more than one occasion. I'm sure he knows that you're coming for him. Try to take comfort from that."

I laughed, but it was hollow and empty. It felt like every part of my soul was dying and the only thing that could make it better was finding Cam alive and well. "We have each other's back." I hit the wheel hard with my fist, and more tears flowed out of my eyes. "How did I not even notice he was missing? If I'd been searching for him sooner--" I stopped unable to keep talking.

Jax's voice was soft when he spoke. "Were you busy with a case?"

The guilt hit me right in the chest. "Yeah, chasing down a freaking fly," I said, disgusted with myself.

He laughed loudly and it was a beautiful magical sound that I decided I liked just fine.

At Jax's direction, I turned off the main highway and onto a street made of gravel. A yellow and white sign warned me to watch out for falling rocks. The hillside was lined with them. I gripped the steering wheel tighter, imagining one of them tumbling down and crushing us to death.

"What are you thinking about?" Jax asked after I'd been quiet too long.

I gave him a small, sad, smile. "Nothing really. Just trying to keep my mind from what we might find here." The image of Cam's lifeless body, staring up at me through empty sockets, had chills running down my spine.

"We're probably not ready to be crushed to death by giant rocks. Still have the skunk oil if we are, though."

I pretended to scold. "I already told you, skunk oil can't heal the dead."

"Why you got to shoot down all my efforts to comfort you, Rye? I'm trying to step up to the plate here."

I kept my eyes on the road. It was narrow and I feared we'd go off the side if I lost focus for too long. "You're impossible," I said in a way to keep our easy banter going.

His voice turned serious in an instant. "I don't have to be. Maybe I'm a little more than you give me credit for."

I swallowed hard, not liking the direction this conversation was headed. "I only know what you show me," I said lightly, hoping he'd leave it there.

Of course, he had to push it farther. "Or maybe you just refuse to see?"

I shook my head at his weighted statement. This wasn't a conversation I was ready to have. "How much longer until we get there?"

He pointed to the right. "Take this turn."

We'd been driving for a while, only passing a handful of cars here and there. I took the exit he told me to and went down another dark road. Driving in the car, this road was rough. I could only imagine how hard it must have been on foot. "How the hell did you make it out of here?"

"I walked." He said it like it was the most natural thing in the world. "Once I got to the main road, I was able to hitch. Did that a couple of times until I made it to your hometown."

We finally arrived in front of a medium-sized building set far back from the highway. The place appeared deserted. The parking lot was empty and the only sound was the idling of our car. I cut the engine, my hands still on the wheel. "How do you want to do this?"

"We need to act with caution. I don't think anyone's here, but we should assume there is."

I squinted at the massive, looming structure. "So we just walk in?"

His face said he didn't care one way or another. "I mean we can creep if you want to. If you like creeping. We can creep."

He seemed so damn serious that I couldn't tell if he was fucking with me or not. "Let's go."

We got to the door, but couldn't open it because of the sizable padlock holding it together. I was just about to use my thiols when Jax squinted his eyes, and a loud boom sounded, catching me completely off guard. I jumped back as the lock erupted from the inside out, bits and pieces flying everywhere.

I knocked a few shards out of my hair and turned to him with a scowl. "Maybe a little warning next time, asshole."

He smiled ruefully. "My bad. Gotta admit, I'm full of surprise and excitement." One glance at my sour face had him clearing his throat and straightening. "And now is not the time for that. Sorry."

The door swung open, and we walked into a vast open space. No one was here now, but it was clear they'd left in a hurry. Chairs lay sprawled across the floor. Two coolers held nothing but dirty water and looked like they hadn't been used in days. I picked up a portable hot plate from the table and turned it over in my hand. "Did they actually cook on this?" I asked.

Jax, who'd being busy kicking blankets out of his path, spared me a quick glance. "I guess. I never saw it, but then again, I was only brought out for one purpose." He went on with what he'd been doing, and I stood rooted to my spot.

His words hit me like a sledgehammer, and I stayed stock still, trying to wrap my head around what he'd just revealed to me. Finally, I placed a shaky hand on the table in front of me, watching his back as he searched the floor for clues.

He'd been a victim too, yet somehow I'd allowed myself to forget that. I'd been so caught up in Cam that I hadn't even stopped to think about the shit that Jax himself had been through.

He hadn't complained once, not even when he'd had to turn around and head straight back to the place of his torture. I stared at him in awe, not sure I'd be able to keep it together under such circumstances. He went about his business, oblivious to the eyes boring into the back of his head.

I stared at him a moment longer until a spot on the floor called my attention away. I squatted to get a better look. It was blood all right, and I pulled out my to-go-kit, forcing myself to believe that it belonged to anyone but Cam.

Gloves firmly on, I sucked up a bit with my syringe and dropped it into the DNA testing kit. It only took a second for Cam's smiling face to pop up on the screen. A closed fist to my mouth, I took a few breaths, trying to control my emotions. I should have expected this, yet somehow I'd allowed it to knock me off my guard.

Jax placed a gentle hand on my shoulder, and I leaned into his touch, grateful for his support. I sniffed, and cleared my throat, coming to a stand. "I have to call this in. We need to se-cure the spot. See what clues we can find. Maybe we'll get a beat on their next location."

I placed a call to my shadow team, to see how close they were. They said they'd be able to reach us in about thirty minutes, and I didn't feel there was much more we could do without more supplies.

I could still see the spot with Cam's blood and I tried not to think about what that meant. Was it the result of a blow to his face, or maybe a small cut or wound?

Had it been bandaged? Had his injuries been properly tend-ed to? Or had they been left to fester and get infected? I ran a frustrated hand through my hair and tried not to scream. This whole thing was driving me insane, but I bet that was nothing compared to what Cam was going through.

The air was stuffy to the point that I couldn't breathe, and suddenly I had to get out of there. "Look, my team will be here soon. I'll turn the air conditioner on in the car and we can wait in there."

He followed me to the door. "You mean I'm not going to

be your dirty little secret anymore? I actually get to meet your friends?"

I smiled at him acting like a dork, which I knew was his goal. "I just want to make sure the site stays secure until they get here. Come on."

He followed behind me. "You didn't answer the question."

"That's because I didn't realize it was a question."

The afternoon sun smacked us dead in the face, but it was the state of my car that really caught my attention. It sat on all fours, the wheels ripped to pieces. My hood was open, with wires scattered all over the place.

I walked with caution, not sure what I was ready to encounter. Someone was doing their most to keep us here. The question was why. "Who could have done this?" I whispered, trying to form some type of picture in my mind of what to look out for.

Jax measured his steps until he was the one leading the charge. "I told you about his numerous guards. It could have been any one of them."

"Let's--" That's all I got out before a blow to my back knocked me to my knees. I rolled to the side, taking most of the fall on my left arm.

I tried to get up, but a hard punch to my face knocked me back again. Pain exploded in my left jaw, but I shook it off, knowing I was in a fight for my life.

Trying to get some kind of traction, I snatched up a handful of my assailant's hair. I pulled as hard as I could, yanking the person's head back and using it as momentum to bring me to a sitting position. Once there, I opened my mouth and used my thiols to cut his eyesight, at the same time choking him from the inside out.

He fell to the side gasping for breath and screaming. I pushed him away and came back to my feet. My eyes immediately went to Jax. He had one hand around the throat of a man, while his other hand was draining the sweat out of a different guy. The woman he squinted at, and she dropped, grabbing her splitting chest and screaming.

I started that way but was blocked by two solid bodies. They stood side by side, one male, and one female. The man had a blade in his hand, and he stuck out his tongue and ran the knife across it, staring at me the whole time. The woman had a sneer on her face, but no weapons that I could see.

I cracked my neck. If they wanted to do this, we could do this.

The man laughed, knife bouncing from hand to hand. "We knew you were coming. Saw you from miles away."

"Then you should have been prepared for this." I dropped to the ground and knocked him off his feet. The girl came at me, but I was ready and delivered a kick square to her face. The guy swung on me, knocking my head back and splitting my lip.

I spat blood from my mouth and wiped the excess away. "That all you got, boy?" They charged me from either side and I ducked, causing them to rip into each other instead. That gave me enough time to blow out some thiols and drop them both to the ground choking and gagging.

I stepped over their bodies and made my way to Jax. He still had three on him and was doing everything he could to hold his ground.

I used thiols to take out two. Jax flexed his hands, and the last one's organs exploded out of his body. Blood and tissue rained down on us in the most disgusting way possible.

I pulled gook out of my hair and wiped slime off my face. "Really?" I asked, my voice terse. "Always the dramatics with you. Damn." I swiped more gunk away. "Where can I clean up?"

He seemed apologetic, but not really sorry.

"What?" I asked, once I saw that he couldn't meet my eyes.

The reluctant look on his face told me I wasn't going to like what he had to say. "I don't think they have running water here. We pissed in buckets and drank out of water bottles."

"How did you wash up?"

He raised an eyebrow like he was surprised I didn't already know. "Did you see me when I first arrived? Did you smell me?"

I didn't even want to think about it, but I did remember. He'd smelled like he hadn't had a bath in weeks and I guess he hadn't. "Just come on." I waved him toward me.

"Where are we going?"

"There are two coolers in the building. They had water in them. I'll use that as best I can."

His voice held uncertainty. "That water was green. You sure you want to bathe in that?"

I stared at him hard. It was his fault I was covered in this gunk in the first place. I turned my eyes away and took a deep breath, because I did realize I was being a little unfair. "Well, what do you suggest then?" I tried to make my voice light, not wanting him to know how irritated I was.

He pointed behind him. "Crossed a small river when I escaped. You can't see it from the road, but it's there."

After doing a careful check of the perimeter to make sure no one else lurked around, I gestured for him to lead the way to the water.

We walked for about five minutes, still on guard for any more of Drake's team, before the air began to cool and a small river stretched out before us. I had nothing to change into, but it really didn't matter. The sun was so damn hot that it wouldn't take long for our clothes to dry.

I stripped down right in front of him, modesty never being a problem for me.

Jax gave me the once over, a lazy smile on his lips. "You could at least buy me dinner first, Rye."

"I already did. Twice." I dipped my toe in the water, trying to gauge the temperature. It was a little cool, but not as cold as I thought it would be. I slipped inside. "I've bought you dinner twice. When are you going to start putting out?"

He stood before me completely naked. His chest broad, and his abs hard. Under different circumstances…. I shook my head. Now was not the time for that. I turned away and set about washing my clothes as best I could. A huge splash had water smacking me hard across the face. "What the--" I turned around just in time to see Jax spring up from the bottom of the river.

"What?" he asked, once he took in my irritated expression.

"We're not at the beach."

He actually had the nerve to look chastised. "I know that."

I rubbed my pants together, and then fanned them out. "Then why are you doing freaking somersaults off the bank?"

He dipped back under, and then came up right beside me. I jumped a little, then cursed myself for letting him affect me this way. "Why do you care what I do, if I'm not bothering you?" The heat from his body acted almost like a magnet, pulling me closer, and making me want things that I knew were best left alone.

My pants slipped from my hands, and he came even closer. We were only an inch apart now. His breath tickled mine, his voice low, rough, and filled with longing. "What do you want, Rye?"

I felt myself quiver. I wanted this, wanted him. Bad. Maybe more than I'd ever wanted anyone, and for that reason alone, I knew I couldn't do it. Still I came closer. We were touching now, bodies lined up perfectly against each other. His hand shook, as he reached out to pull me against him. I melted into his arms, my mind fighting me to break it off, my body responding with raw need.

He gripped me tighter, his lips meeting mine in a rushed kiss that turned frantic in a second. "I want you," he mumbled, kissing down my neck and around my shoulder.

"Shut up." I raised his head and guided his lips back to mine, exhaling softly when they touched again. He tasted like the coffee and donuts we'd gotten on the way here, and I'd never loved that flavor more. I wrapped my legs around his waist and then guided him to my opening.

"I don't have any protection."

I squeezed him tighter. "It's up to you. I can always heal myself, and I am clean. I'm tested every couple of months."

He kissed me again. "Me too," he mumbled against my lips.

I slipped him inside me and gasped. He felt so fucking good that I could easily see myself getting lost in him. "Fuck." I winded my hips down, trying to get as much of him as I could take. I wanted it all. Damn he felt good. "Take it. It's yours, for now, so take it."

His thrusts sped up, his breath coming in short spurts. "Damn, Rye." We kissed furiously as if any minute this could all be taken away. "Didn't... know... it... could... be like this... didn't know..."

I matched his rhythm, throwing my head back and trying hard to get to that climax I felt building in my stomach.

He snapped his hips faster and I felt like I would die from pleasure. How the hell could something feel so good?

We kissed again, this time, more demanding than the last. "Don't... want... this... to... end... want... to... stay... inside... you... forever." Soon we were both grunting and coming and it was the best thing I'd ever felt in my life.

Our lips inches apart, our breaths mingling, I whispered the words that had been on my mind the whole time. "Next time we use the oil." Remember what I said about it extending the orgasm in men and women? He did, because he shuddered against me, and suddenly he was coming again, holding me tight and kissing my neck the whole time.

Once he was done, he laid his head in the crook of my neck, breathing hard, and repeating my name over and over again.

My whole body tingled, and the only thing I wanted was to curl up in a ball and go to sleep. I was boneless and didn't care who knew it. I placed a soft kiss on his shoulder and then detangled myself from him.

He beamed at me as if I rose the sun and hung the moon. "C'mere."

I went willingly into his arms. "What do you want?"

He grinned that crooked smile again. "You gonna give it to me?"

I chuckled lightly. "Depends on what it is?"

"Can I get a new pair of shoes?"

"You--" I punched him in the arm. "Yeah, you can get some shoes, but you got to work for them."

He grabbed me around the waist and dipped me in the water. We both went under and came back up wiping our faces.

A loud voice sounded from the bank, causing us to jump apart. "Am I interrupting?" Drena stood there, hands on her hips, expression unreadable.

I turned to Jax. "She's with me," I said before he could react. Seeing her there brought everything back to me. Cam. Cam was still out there waiting for me to find him. I kissed Jax again, feeling nothing but affection. "Thank you. For allowing me to forget for a minute."

I got out of the water and didn't look back. My clothes were still dripping, but I put them on anyway. They felt icky and wet, but I figured they'd dry eventually.

Drena watched me with blatant disappointment. "What?" I asked, feigning innocence.

She scoffed, and marched in front of me. "Just come on." I took a quick peek behind me and saw Jax coming out of the water and putting his clothes on.

Three trucks and two SUVs had joined my car in the parking lot. Drena handed me a set of keys. "Here take these."

I pushed the lock button trying to see which one I'd be driving. "Find anything yet?" I asked, walking over to the blinking lights of the black SUV.

The fat that Jax had drained from my back was taking its effect, and the fight we'd just had only made it worse. The skunk oil helped, but it didn't replace the fat that had been lost. I was tired and knew if I didn't find somewhere to rest soon, I wouldn't be any use to Cam or anyone else.

Drena shook her head, going back to my original question. "Haven't been here long enough. But we did catch up with the last two from the steak house. We're going to try and flip them, see what they know."

Jax finally joined us, and I decided it was time to go. "Let's get our bags. We're going to change vehicles."

Drena refused to acknowledge his presence. "Already taken care of," she said to me alone.

She was pissed, and she had every right to be. I was supposed to be working a case, not having sex like some teenager on spring break.

"These our new wheels?" Jax asked, as a way of breaking through the tension.

We needed to talk. What happened between us had been nice, but as long as Cam was missing, I couldn't let it happen again. "Get in," I said by way of an answer. The first thing we needed to do was find a clean hotel room. These clothes felt grimier by the minute, and the only thing I wanted was to get out of them.

Drena had her phone pressed to her ear. "Not so fast." She walked over, a finger raised in the air.

I held my breath, hoping she'd found something that would help us find Cam.

She scribbled on a piece of paper and then thrust it into my hand. "One of the steak house guys is talking. He gave up three addresses. Probably more places like this one here, so we need to be careful. It could be a trap."

I read over what she'd written. The closest one was still a couple of hours away. "I'll check them out. What's your tail like?"

"We won't be far behind."

FOUR

The car ride to the hotel was silent, my thoughts focused completely on Cam. I gripped the wheel tight and thought back to that floor with his blood on it. My mind swam in several different directions and for the first time since this whole thing started, it really began to sink in that I might not find him alive. A sob rose in my throat, but I fought it down. Cam needed me. Tears weren't going to help anyone.

The room we rented had a separate bath and shower. So Jax took the shower and left me with the bath. By the time I got out, he'd already changed into fresh clothes and had ordered room service. The smell of garlic, green peppers, and onions filled the air. I licked my lips. I didn't care what it was. I was eating it.

"I didn't know what you wanted," he said from his spot on the floor.

"You don't have to sleep down there." I pulled the portable little tray over to the bed and took a look. It held a container of baked spaghetti, with copious amounts of cheese. I inhaled deeply, taking in the smell. Two pieces of garlic bread lay wrapped in foil. I opened them and put one piece on my plate. Under another tray was a tossed salad, and then, under another was sweet potato pie. All perfect, except there was only enough for one. "Where's your food?"

He'd been laying on his back, but came up to a sitting position. He stared at me for a full twenty seconds, but didn't say anything. He turned eyes toward the floor and then mumbled something so low that I could barely hear him.

"Jax?"

He exhaled as if I was forcing something on him he didn't want to say. "I just thought I'd eat your leftovers or something."

"Why?"

He didn't answer, but his eyes never left mine. It took a moment for it to sink in, but when it finally did, I look at him curious. "Jax, where do you work?"

His eyes said he had no idea where this was going. "Albright Enterprises," he answered uncertainly.

My eyes widened. Albright was one of the top defense agencies in the country. How the hell had it taken me this long to know that he worked there? "So you're with the government?"

"Yup."

"How come you never said anything?"

His expression never changed. "You never asked. Why are you now?"

Was he serious? "Cause you'd rather starve than let me take care of you." I stared at him incredulously. "You make more money than I do. You can't get to your cash right now, so let me help you. Let me do it for Cam, and what you did for him. Fuck what people think."

He shook his head. "I don't care what people think about me. I never have."

"What then?" If I sounded exasperated, it's because I was. I really didn't understand his reasoning.

"I don't care what people think," he repeated. His eyes bore into mine, two pools of heat, slowly ripping me apart.

My breath hitched as the meaning of his words sunk in. "I don't think that, Jax," I said softly. "I'm not really ready to buy you a pair of shoes. It was a joke. One we both enjoyed. Remember?"

"Yeah, but that was right after we'd, you know."

I smiled at the memory. "Yeah, I know. Look, after this is all over you're more than welcome to pay me back for everything." He smiled, and my heart lifted knowing we were on good terms again. "Except the steak house," I added. "The department had to come in and pay for that."

He laughed, easing the rest of the tension out of the room. "We skipped out on the check, didn't we? You've made me a criminal! What will my superiors think?"

I put my hand to my chest, pretending to be scandalized. "What will mine think? Oh wait, they paid for the check. We're fine." I threw the hotel phone at him. "Get you some food." He ordered five times the amount he'd gotten for me.

We spend the rest of the night discussing how we'd go about approaching the next three addresses. He stayed on the floor and I curled up in the bed, willing myself to believe that Cam was still alive, and we wouldn't be too late.

The first place was empty in a way that said no one had been there in weeks. The second had leftover food and a few over-turned chairs, but besides that, nothing. We didn't make it to the third.

It was well past two in the morning by the time I pointed the car toward the last location. Jax sat on the passenger side. He'd steadily tapped on the window for the last ten minutes and I was just about to go insane. "Stop!" I finally shouted, not able to take it anymore.

He looked startled, and then he put his hands in his lap. It seemed like it took some effort to keep them there.

"What's wrong?" I asked.

He seemed conflicted. "Something about this seems off. I don't like it."

"You think it's a setup?"

He ran a hand down his face. "How long did it take for Drena's team to catch up with the two from the steak house?"

I saw where he was going with this. "You think they met up with Drake first? Maybe got directions on what to say?"

His answer was slow. "Maybe he'd already instructed them

on what to say. Just in case they were caught."

"Then he knows we're coming. Maybe we should--" Boom. Before I could finish my thought, a large truck slammed into us and sent the car spinning.

"Hold on." I fought with the wheel, trying to keep us from going off the side of the road. "Grab my phone, speed dial two and let Drena know what's happening."

We skidded onto the curb. Shit, Drake wasn't going to make it easy, but I should have known that. I'd just gotten the car back on the road when the hood was ripped away, causing it to go spinning again. We weren't going to make it out of here without a fight.

I eased down to third gear, slowing the car enough to regain control. Once done, I stopped driving, cut the engine, and turned to Jax. "We gotta do what we gotta do."

He pulled me close. "Just you and me? I like those odds. Haven't failed us yet." He kissed me hard, and then pulled back. "We can do this," he whispered.

"I know," I said, stepping out of the car.

Three figures met us in the middle of the road. Drake, Tec, and... Cam! My eyes froze on my best friend. He stood tall, shoulders thick and broad, black hair the same length as mine. I exhaled deeply, my eyes shining. I could hardly believe it. Cam was alive and unharmed. Everything was going to be okay now.

Without even thinking about it, I jumped into his arms and squeezed him as hard as I could.

I could hear Jax in the background, calling my name, trying to stop me. I didn't listen. Jax could wait. Right now, the only thing I could see was Cam.

He gripped me tightly and spun me around, a big smile on his face. "I'm okay, I'm okay." He gave me a light kiss on my forehead and then released me. "I knew you would come. Told them you would always come for me. Once I saw him take the chain, I knew there was a good chance he'd go to you, and you'd come. So, we had to be prepared."

"I saw your blood on the floor," my voice cracked as I thought back to that moment. Somewhere in the back of my mind I wondered what he needed to be prepared for, but I pushed that away, too happy to be in his presence.

Jax appeared by my side, face hard, body alert. "Pretty sure he knows that." He stood like a tightly wound spring, ready to pop off at any moment. "The more I think about the time before my escape, the more I realize just how at ease Cam was. Other skunks, they'd be shaking and scared. None of that from him. In fact, thinking back, the taunting about the chain seemed more like friends jeering each other around a table of beers.

I wondered if Jax had hit his head. "Why would you think that? He's the one who was in restraints, remember?"

Jax's expression softened as he talked to me. "To control his thiols. Rye, you've been talking and hugging him for the last three minutes and neither Drake nor this other guy have made a move to stop you. Why do you think that is? Think about it." He said that last part with a little more force. "They had a big shipment due, I heard some guards talking. That's why I thought they'd found Cam and brought him in, because I'd already drained every other skunk there dry.

"I had no idea he was in on the whole thing. The only reason he probably gave his oil was because if he hadn't, they never would have made their quota."

Drake and Tec were being eerily silent. Even now, they stood by watching all this play out, but doing nothing to intervene. That wasn't right. Shouldn't they be running or trying to rip us apart? I whipped back around to Cam, who hadn't move from his spot, his eyes and face unreadable.

My voice shook, as I asked questions I never thought I'd have to. Not to Cam anyway. "You don't...? It's not...? You don't work for him, do you?"

He stepped back rather cockily and something inside me broke, as I knew his next words would change me forever. "No," he said, and I sagged in relief until he began to speak again. "He works for me."

Everything in me froze. I tried to move, but my body felt like lead. My mouth opened, but no words came out. I hadn't heard him right. I couldn't have. Cam couldn't... He wasn't...

My knees buckled and vomit erupted in my mouth.

A strong arm wrapped around me and kept me from hitting the ground. Jax. He pressed me to him, and I held on for dear life. At least someone was still on my side. "Don't give him your pain," he whispered. "He's not worthy of it."

I wanted to argue with him, and I started to do just that. I opened my mouth to tell him that he didn't know Cam the way I did, but then the reality of the situation bore down on me, and I let out a large sob instead. Now wasn't the time to fall apart and I knew that, but Cam, my Cam. I just didn't understand.

Knowing that my crying helped no one, I took a moment to compose myself, and then turned to Jax. "How long have you known?" I asked, my voice laced with acid.

His grip tightened, but there was a gentleness in his tone. "Not until I saw them here. They didn't behave like enemies. Something just seemed off about the whole thing."

I allowed myself a glance their way. Cam now stood between Drake and Tec. "I don't want to hurt you," he said. "I just want you to understand."

I ran a disbelieving hand down my face. What was there to understand? "You don't really expect me to be okay with this?" I asked. "Because that's what it seems like you're asking." I tsked at his audacity. "I think you know me better than that."

Cam took a couple of steps toward me, and Jax pushed me behind him as if I needed his protection. Annoyed, I stepped around. "I got this. I don't need any help."

He nodded. "I know you don't. It was instinct is all."

I stared hard at my best friend and realized I'd probably never really known him in the first place. Because the Cam I knew wouldn't do this. The Cam I knew didn't think like this. "Cam," I said, my voice low, my tone pleading for him to help me understand.

The hard line of his mouth went slack for just a second, and I thought I'd gotten through. Then he spoke, and my heart broke all over again. "Drop the case, Rye, and we can both leave here unharmed."

The pressure behind my eyes was too much and a few tears

slid down my face. I started to wipe them away, but then said, fuck it, he caused them, so let him see them. "I love you. Actually care about you." I pointed to Drake and Tec. "They don't give a fuck about you. Yet you sent your minions to kill me. To stop me from reaching you. How could you do it?"

Not even a blink. "I knew you could take 'em."

He hadn't known shit and his words set off a firestorm in my blood. Half the oil he used probably came from his own body. They objectified us enough; to have another skunk do it was disgusting. "You sell yourself like a whore," I spit. Not really meaning it, but too damn mad to take it back.

His voice was hard as stone. "And you fuck like one. Buy any one of your special friends something pretty lately?"

I wouldn't let him distract me. Which I was sure he was trying to do. "I like my men a certain way. I won't be shamed for it. What does that have to do with you turning on your own people?"

His chest rose, and his face contorted into one of such furious rage that I had to step back to keep my composure. "My people." He sounded like he had a mouth full of rage. "You mean the same people who let my mom die instead of giving her the skunk oil that would have saved her life? Are those the people you're talking about?" A cloud of thiols flooded around him, feeding off his energy and managing to appear as menacing as he did.

I chose my words carefully. "That's not true, Cam, and you know it."

His mom had been a Scope agent. One day she and three other skunks had come under fire. They'd fought hard, but Cam's mom had taken a hit to the gut and upper shoulder.

Cam said they should have taken skunk oil from their backs to heal her. All involved put in their official reports that there hadn't been time. To stop meant to die, and none of the four had made it out of there unscathed. Sadly, Cam's mom had been the only casualty. Cam had wanted the other three brought up on charges. It didn't happen, and not one skunk in our community stood by him. They'd all agreed that it was better to have one dead skunk, than four.

I let out a breath. That had happened when we'd been teenagers, still in high school. The fallout had been terrible.

For three months straight, I'd held him while he cried. Every night he'd climb into my window, and every night I'd make room for him in my bed, offering whatever comfort I could.

He'd gotten therapy after that, and I'd thought he'd come to terms with it. I guess he hadn't. I closed my eyes, my mind in turmoil. What the hell kind of friend had I been, that I'd never seen his pain? Especially since I was sure that this confrontation was something he wanted.

He could have called me at any point and told me that he was okay and not to worry. Yet he hadn't, and I had to think that this was why. He was hurt, angry, and tired of holding it all inside.

"I'm sorry," I said, and I meant it. "You weren't okay and I should have realized that. I… I don't know what to say."

My words bounced off him like a spring. "You didn't want to see. No one did. My mother died in the gutter like a rat and not one skunk gave a damn. Including you."

I shrunk back with a shudder. He might as well of had hit me with a sledgehammer, it would have hurt less. "Fuck you." I could hear the tears in my voice and knew they matched the ones rolling down my face. "Fuck you."

He seemed undaunted. "Back off the case, Rye. You don't have enough to prove it's me now, but if you keep going… Well, let's just say I'm not willing to take that chance."

I blanched. "You really think you're making it out of this intact?"

He came to his full height. "I'm trying to offer you grace. I don't want to hurt you unless I have to."

I lunged for him, but he spun, landing a hard blow to the right side of my face. Jax leapt into action and the two fought head to head, toe to toe.

I rose from the ground and saw Tec and Drake try to make a move for Jax. I used my thiols to knock them back, then went for Cam, knocking Jax out of the way.

Cam cracked his neck, and we began a slow circling of one

another. Thiols crackled between us, but since we were both of skunk descent, it was no different than breathing.

He could still catch these hands, though. This was going to be a straight up, no holds barred, bare-knuckled, street fight. I waited for an opening and then slammed my elbow straight into his face, followed by a quick uppercut. His lip split and he stumbled back with a grunt. I tried it again, but this time, he caught me with a left.

My jaw exploded, but I didn't have time to dwell on it. I kicked at his head, and he grabbed me by the foot and spun me around. I went down hard on my side, pain ripping through my whole body. I stopped for a minute trying to breathe through it and check on Jax at the same time. He was doing just fine. He had Tec's eyes in his hands and Drake on his knees in an invisible choke hold. Satisfied that he was okay, I turned back to my own fight.

I was on all fours now, and Cam grabbed me by the head and slammed it hard into the street. "Told you to let this go." He grunted. "Why won't you just fucking listen?"

I blinked hard, trying to clear my vision. My head felt like It had just been put through a blender, but I knew I had to push the pain down in order to stay in the game. I kicked his legs out from under him and then flipped it so that I was on top. I began to rain down relentless blows on his face and body. "How could you? How could you do it? You're as much skunk as I am. How could you!"

I picked up a rock and smashed him with it. "Send your people to kill me. Did you really think it would be that easy to take me out?" I was shaking with anger and that's all he needed to get the upper hand.

He elbowed me in my face, and I fell off him and hit the ground. He started to climb on top of me, but headlights appeared, stopping us both.

Drena and the rest of the backup team hopped out of their cars. She ran to Cam and myself and pulled us apart. She seemed more confused than anything. "Why are you fighting each other?" she demanded.

I pointed at Cam, trying to catch my breath. He didn't wait around for me to find it. Instead, he snatched up Drake and headed for the trees that lined the side of the road. They went right past Tec, but he was dead anyway, so nothing they could do there.

"Get him," I yelled, finally finding my voice. Too bad no one knew who I was talking about. As far as they were concerned, Cam was still an agent and we now had Drake in custody so everything was fine.

Jax knew better, though, and he made a mad dash to stop them. One of my crew intervened, grabbing Jax and throwing him to the ground.

"Get off him." I ran to where they were. "We need to stop Cam. Drake works for him. They're in this together."

Drena's eyes told me how unsure she was, and I turned to her in a rage. "I'm not joking! Why do you think we were fighting?" Cam had been an agent for years and had never shown the slightest sign that he was crooked, so I understood her reluctance, but I needed her to trust me on this.

Jax came to his feet, sparing a scowl for the agent who'd tackled him, before turning to us. "She's not lying. He ran our car off the road." He pointed to the smashed-up mess that was now minus a roof.

Drena's eyes still held skepticism. "Are you sure?"

I closed my eyes and tried to have patience. "Drena, come on. This is Cam, I'd never lie on him."

She nodded, as if that thought hadn't crossed her mind, and then turned on her heels. "Spread out, but for now we'll continue to approach agent Cam with honor and respect. Until proven otherwise, he's still one of us." It was the best I was going to get, and so I let it slide.

Jax walked with a limp. His face was bruised, right eye swollen, and knuckles raw. He was still standing, though, and that's what mattered the most. "The last address?" he asked.

I shook my head. "I thought we agreed that was a trap?"

He seemed conflicted. "What if it's not? Maybe he just saw that we were close and decided to head us off, get us before we got him."

I turned to Drena. "We have to get there before they do."

She raised an eyebrow. "You really think they'd go back there?"

I was almost sure of it. "It could be the base of their whole operation. They're not going to just leave all that stuff for us to find." I think that's why he stopped us before we reached the last address. He had too much to lose if we found it.

"They're on foot," Drena said.

I gave her a frank look. "This is Cam. He's probably got cars waiting on every corner."

"Right." She left half the agents in the field and the rest of us went by vehicles. We drove lights flashing, foot to the floor, disobeying all traffic signs, in an effort to make it there before Cam did.

A big metal warehouse sat at the end of a dead-end road. A few cars were in the parking lot, and we jumped out knowing we were in for a fight. A pile of metal dog chains lay discarded next to an old chain fence. I picked up two and wrapped them around each knuckle. I wanted to fuck him up and I was willing to use any means I had to do it.

I didn't wait for the others. Running to the front of the building, I used my thiols to break the lock and then kicked the doors apart. A frenzy of activity was taking place inside. Dozens of people loaded up trunks, unplugged equipment, and rolled up mats. I caught sight of Cam over by a huge desk, hurriedly stuffing some papers into a manila envelope.

I ran straight for him. He turned when he saw me, but I slammed him in the face before he could react. His head snapped back, and blood flew from his mouth and nose.

I pounded him relentlessly, the metal chains on my fist making a clinking sound every time they hit. Someone grabbed me by the hair and yanked my head back. I flipped the person over, but the distraction had been enough for Cam to get his bearings.

He spat blood out of his mouth, then leaped toward me, arms raised. I didn't move quickly enough and he snatched up a handful of my hair and forced me to the ground with it. He leaned over me, face in a snarl, eyes hard and unforgiving. "You think you can beat me, little girl? Think I'm one of the men in your harem?"

He began to drag me by my hair. Panic rose in my throat as I clawed desperately at his hands and arms, trying to free myself.

"Didn't want to hurt you." He sneered. "Wanted to keep you out of it, but you just couldn't leave well enough alone, could you? Just had to keep digging." He paused and when he spoke again his voice had a little more steel in it. "So here we are. I guess I knew this day would always come."

The air was thick with the smell of blood, sweat, and other bodily fluids. All around us the fight raged on, and I knew I would have to find some way to break his hold on me.

I dug my nails into his hands, but still he held on. "Gonna teach you a lesson," he grunted. "Gonna drain you dry. You won't be able to move for months."

He dragged me to the back of the warehouse, away from the rest of the fight. An examination table sat by a workbench, full of medical supplies. This must be where they extracted the oil.

Something dark and disturbing weighed heavy on me, as I thought of all the helpless skunks that had no doubt been brought here against their will. Did he drain them all dry? Everything in me wanted that answer to be no. Draining a skunk completely, left us paralyzed for months, sometimes even years, depending on how long it took for us to build the fat back up.

He tossed me on the table. My back hit hard against the cold metal, but I refused to show pain on my face. I wouldn't give him the satisfaction.

"You should feel lucky," he said, holding me still on the table. "Anybody else do this to me." He pointed to his battered face, "I'd kill 'em."

He picked up a small silver device. I didn't recognize it, but I would bet that's what they'd been using to drain the fat.

He turned it on, and the harsh mechanical sound was like a death sentence to my ears. Fuck that. I wasn't going out without a fight. I used my thiols to knock the supply bench over. It clanged to the floor, and Cam jerked his head to see what the commotion was. That was all the opening I needed.

I wrapped my legs around his neck, got a good grip, and then flipped him over. He hit the floor hard, and I jumped on top of him and begin to pound his face. "You, selfish, sonofabitch. I would have done anything for you! Anything!" With each word, I hit him harder. "You would do this to your own people! They degrade us enough! How could you?" I grabbed him by the shirt. His eyes swam to the back of his head, and I knew he was seconds away from passing out. Disgusted, I let him go and stood. I removed the chains from my hand and used them to tie him to the table.

I turned back toward the fight, aiming to get back in, but noticed that Cam's crew had been crushed. Many sat handcuffed and gagged on the floor, waiting for transport to the local holding cells.

Drena's breath came hard as she surveyed the room, making sure there were no stragglers lurking about. Her hair was in disarray, but other than that, she seemed fine. One of the perks of having turtle DNA was the hard shell. When she chose to use it, nothing could touch her. "Backup is already on the way. From the amount of skunk oil here, we're pretty sure this was his main base of operation. I'm going to check around."

I scanned the crowd for Jax. I needed to know that he was all right. He must have seen me first, because by the time I caught sight of him, he was already headed my way. He still walked with a limp, his clothes were all but torn off him, and his right arm hung at his side. "You okay?" he asked, once we were in speaking distance.

I shook my head. "I should be asking you that."

He ran a bruised hand through his hair, which was already doing a good impression of a distorted bird's nest. "Come on. Let's go secure the scene."

We walked until we came to a set of steps that led down to a basement. The smell hit me halfway there. Urine, blood, vomit, and human feces stunk up the air and made me want to hurl. Jax's eyes met mine, and I was sure we both feared what we were about to find.

Cages. At least forty of them covered the entirety of the floor. Each one had at least two people in them, most of skunk descent. Dirt covered their faces, their bodies rail thin.

Some lay on the floor of their cages, others just squatted. The hair on most of them hung loose and limp, and their eyes… Their eyes almost took my breath away, as most were lost, empty, hollow sockets, that said they never expected to be rescued, and had accepted the fact that this was their life now.

The ones who weren't of skunk descent must have had unique abilities as well, in order for Cam to be interested in them.

Jax let out a breath and squeezed my hand. "I'll go get help."

"Thank you," I croaked out, not sure I could say much more.

My whole body shook, and I had to lean against the banister to keep from falling over. What the fuck was wrong with Cam? Why would he do this? Was it self-hatred? Or did he just despise every other skunk in the world this much? I shook my head, wondering how had I'd been so blind?

Jax came back, Drena and a few other agents behind him. Drena stopped at the bottom, mouth opening and closing. "Oh, my… this is…" Her voice filled with horror, and she gaped at me as if begging me to tell her this wasn't real.

I turned away, not able to meet her eyes or anyone else's.

Jax came behind me and wrapped his arms around my waist, engulfing me in his warmth. I let out a slow breath, and closed my eyes, grateful for the support. "They've been locked up long enough," he whispered.

I nodded, and with our combined powers, we began busting the locks off the cages. Drena and the others joined, and soon all those imprisoned were freed. Drena pulled out her phone. "Medic was already on the way. I'm gonna tell them to send extra."

Relieved that it was finally over, I collapsed against Jax. He caught me so that I didn't hit the floor, and then lifted me into his arms. I wrapped my arms around his neck. "I'm not a damsel in distress," I said, my breath coming hard, my chest rising and falling. "I don't need you to save me."

He wiped a few strands of hair out of my face. "Good. Then

I'll just put your ass back down. You're heavy."

My grip on him tightened, and suddenly I burst into tears. The last couple of days had been horrific, and now I felt like it was all hitting me at once. "Take me home," I said, my face in the crook of his neck. "I can debrief later, for now, just take me home."

He kissed my cheek. "Okay, Rye. I'll take you home." Drena threw him her keys, which was her way of saying we were free to go.

The parking lot was filled with agency cars and medic trucks. Everybody was abuzz because the infamous Drake had finally been taken down. I knew some were surprised to see Cam handcuffed and being loaded into the back of a medic truck. But that was a conversation for another day. For now, it was enough that we had them.

Jax put me in the car and closed the door. "Let's get you home."

He stayed with me that night and went home the next day. Some of the fallout had spilled over into his agency, so he needed to get back to work right away. We'd parted as friends, and promised to look each other up, whenever we got the chance.

Once the victims had been debriefed, we were able to find Cam's last three spots and shut them down.

For Cam himself, he wasn't talking, and neither was Drake. They were both recovering in the prison wing, Cam under police protection.

It had taken weeks to process, but finally, we were satisfied that we'd gotten everything we were going to get. The skunk oil had been logged in as evidence and then administered to those who'd been held against their wills, getting them back to health quicker than any stay in a hospital would have. It was their oil anyway, he'd stolen it from them, so it was only right.

FIVE

Drena and I had been neck deep in paperwork for weeks, and tonight finally marked the end of it. I left the office feeling good that it was over, but not sure how to move on from Cam's betrayal. It would take a while, and so for now, I decided to just take it one day at a time.

Once home, I pulled a can of chicken noodle soup out of the cabinet and reached for a bowl. It had been a long night and that's all I had the energy to fix.

My doorbell rang and I set the soup aside and peeked out the door, hoping it wasn't Drew, or any of my other male "friends" for that matter.

Jax stood on my porch, a pizza in his hand, and a six-pack under his arm. I opened the door, smiling. "What are you doing here?"

He gave me a quick kiss on the cheek and then stepped inside. "I wanted to see you." He put the pizza and beer on the table. "You don't have company, do you?" he asked, glancing around.

I got plates out of the cabinet.

He shook his head. "Who eats pizza off a plate? Put them back, we're grubbing straight out of the box."

I shrugged. "Fine with me." I put the plates away.

He took out two beers and put the rest in the fridge. "If you try to get glasses I'm leaving. I'm just telling you that right now."

"Drink beer out of a glass? I would never," I said, pretending to be scandalized.

He pulled me onto his lap. "I hope it's okay that I stopped by. I did try to call first."

I looked at my phone over on the counter. I'd turned the power off at the office so that I could focus on getting some work done. I just hadn't turned it back on yet. "I don't know, depends what you got on this pizza. You did get the right type of beer, so there is that."

He flipped the box open. "Oh, that wasn't for you. It's my favorite drink. I told you that."

Hmm, the smell from the anchovies, double pepperoni, and triple cheese pizza made my mouth go dry. I licked my lips and then pinched off an anchovy. "Yeah, I guess you can stay."

He hugged me tight. "Really? I would have thought you wanted your canned soup over there."

I ignored him and stood. "Be right back." I made a dash down the hall and came back with the game, Four in a Row.

I sat back in his lap and picked up a slice, the cheese sliding off the side just the way I liked. I threw it in my mouth. "Hmmm. Good stuff."

He bit into his own piece. "Are we really ready to play Connect Four?"

I set the game up, giving him red chips and me black. "It's called Four in a Row."

"A rose by any other name."

"Oh, shut up." I grabbed him by the face and kissed him hard, his lips tasted like pizza sauce and garlic, and so I kissed him again wanting to get more of it.

He kissed me on my neck. "You trying to have your wicked way with me?"

I dropped the first game chip into the slot. "Nope, just trying to distract you so that I can win the game."

He pulled me closer, at the same time dropping one of his red ones in. "Two can play that game."

Turned out to be the best round of "Connect Four" I'd ever played.

I WAS ASKED TO KILL HIM

ONE

He wanted me to shoot him. I looked at Greg and wondered if he'd hit his head. "You what?"

He placed the gun in my hand and pointed at his chest. "Straight through the heart." He said it as if we were discussing a day at the beach.

He stood about six feet tall and had blonde hair that he usually kept tucked behind his ears. It was out of place now, and my fingers tingled wanting to put it back in its proper spot, anything to avoid discussing this nonsense. "I'm not shooting you." I tried to give the gun back, but he turned on his heels and walked out of the room.

I watched him go, then closed my mouth around a sigh. That was weird. No other word for it. I looked at the cold metal in my hand and wondered how things had turned south so fast. We'd just eaten a nice dinner, and instead of dessert, he'd decided to top it off with this shit.

Still shaking my head, I poured two cups of coffee and took one in to him. He looked up at me and smiled. "Thanks, babe." He pulled me onto his lap, his hand tight around my waist. The coffee sloshed to the side, but since it was mostly made of water I managed to pull it back and keep it in the cup.

That was the only thing I had going for me, controlling, changing, and refiguring water. It was all I knew how to do. My sister, Lena, was telepathic and she had the power of telekinesis.

We were close, and unlike the kids at school, she'd never tried to make me feel bad about only having one power, or having a dumb useless one that no one else had or even wanted.

That was a long time ago. I'd grown up a lot since then and though I'd never learned to love my power, I had come to own it. It was a part of who I was and there was nothing I could do to change that.

It wasn't long after I'd come to truly accept myself that I met Greg. Right now, we were three years going strong and I couldn't be happier. Not that we hadn't had our problems in the past, his wandering cock being one of them. I shook my head at that thought. That all was behind us now. I snuggled more into his arms. No more problems. I'd be willing to put our love up against anyone or anything.

He kissed me behind my ear. "Do this for me, babe." Do what? Shoot him? I put my coffee to the side and sat up. "What the hell is wrong with you? I'm not going to shoot you and if you keep talking like that, I'm going to call someone to take you off to the looney bin." I was only halfway kidding.

His grip on me tightened, and he rubbed his head into the side of my neck, giving my shoulder a few quick kisses to help drive his point home. "I need this, Delia, please, babe. Please."

I gasped out loud, couldn't help it. He'd said, please. A word I'd never expected to hear spill from his lips. He'd never said it before. Well, he'd never said it in my presence anyway, and certainly never to me directly.

I laughed unbelievably, probably because I'd convinced myself that he didn't even know the meaning of the word. That laughter was quickly cut off when I realized what it meant that he was saying it now.

Assisted suicide, that's what it really came down to. Instead of dismissing it, I needed to ask myself why he was asking in the first place. I cradled his face in my hand and then kissed him softly on the forehead. "We're going to get you some help, okay. I don't think you're well."

He chuckled in a way that said I just didn't get it. "Delia, babe, listen." He removed my hands from his face but didn't let them go. His eyes held a seriousness that I rarely saw there, and though his next words were comical, his voice was hard and stern. "I am immortal. I can't be killed. If you shoot me through the heart I will rise again."

I wanted to hit him. I really did, for wasting my time, and for scaring the shit out of me. At the same time, I was relieved nothing serious was going on and we could get on with our night.

His next words dashed any hope I'd had for a good and easy evening. "I'm not joking."

He wasn't joking and I'd had enough. I tried to detangle myself from him, but he held on tighter, unwilling to set me free. This only pissed me off more because, really? "Let me go, Greg. I'm not playing."

He reluctantly released me and I stood, staring down at his hard, unblinking eyes. "I'm going to bed." I truly didn't give a damn what he did at this point.

He stopped me before I was halfway down the hall. "If you don't do it, then you'll never see me again."

I turned back around. "Well, if I do, you'll be dead so..."

His face stayed cold and hard. I took a step back as reality set in. He was really serious. He actually wanted me to kill him. I pulled my phone out. No more talking. He needed help.

Greg shook his head. "Sure you want to do that?"

"You're not giving me much of a choice." It took everything in me to keep from outright shouting, but I did raise my voice a couple of levels. Silently chastising myself, I took a deep breath and tried to regain control of my emotions. "What would you have me do, Greg? You're not making much sense."

His face softened. "I need this, Delia. I really want to share it with you."

My frustration reached its breaking point. "Share what!? You're not making any sense!"

Tears flowed freely from his eyes now. He got up and came to stand in front of me, lovingly touching my face. "Baby, please."

I felt as if I was caught up in a sadistic nightmare and would awaken at any moment to see that everything was normal and my boyfriend didn't want to end his life.

He didn't even try to wipe his eyes. "I am immortal. I can't be killed. Shoot me through the heart and I will rise again." He put his hand under my chin and raised it until we were eye to eye.

I wiped his tears away. All the years we'd been together and I'd never seen him cry. Not once. My phone weighed heavy in my hand. I had to make that call and it gutted me to my core. I loved this man, but he wasn't well and I had no idea how to help him.

He wrapped his arm around me and pulled me closer. "This will open up a whole new life for us. I can take you home now. Let you meet my family. Our love can grow. We can get married and everything. Please let me show you what I can do." He seemed so sincere.

By now I was crying too. I lay my head on his shoulder. "We're going to get you some help," I whispered.

He eased me off him and held my face in his hands. His eyes flashed blue and everything in me came to a standstill. Something was wrong. Images of us together, married, with kids, flashed through my head. I tried to move, but my feet stayed glued to the spot. I tried to cry out, but the words froze in my throat.

Greg was talking, but my head was so fuzzy, I couldn't make out a word he said. His voice moved at a rapid fire pace, and I wondered if he was even trying to make sense. The language sounded foreign and I was sure I'd never heard him speak it before.

I tried to move again, but to no avail. Everything felt murky and wrong. He was doing something to me, but for the life of me, I couldn't figure out what it was.

Images of me shooting him and then us living happily ever after plagued me. I had to break out of this haze. I didn't want this, didn't want to do this. Something had a strong and I... couldn't... I... couldn't break free.

I picked up the gun and fondled it.

His eyes flashed again and suddenly everything became clear. I had to do it. I had to shoot him. It was the only way. If I didn't, then he would die anyway. Only he wouldn't come back to life. I needed him to come back. I had to do it.

My voice spoke almost on its own. "How long will it take you to come back?" Somewhere in the back of my mind, I was screaming, but for some reason I couldn't seem to get through to that part of myself.

Greg got a huge smile on his face and his speech became a little more excited. "It depends. Sometimes it only takes moments and sometimes it can take over two hours. Just be patient and know that I'm coming back to you."

He was coming back to me. All I had to do was shoot him and everything would be okay. Shoot him, he'd come back, and everything would be fine. I only needed to pull the trigger.

Greg had to be killed, that was the only way. I nodded my head. I'd do it. I had to do it. I didn't have a choice. I nodded again, letting him know that I was with him. I would do this for him, for us.

His eyes lit up again and he pulled me closer, giving me a sweet kiss on the lips. "Do it," he said, his mouth soft against my own.

Sweat dripped from my brow. I had to do this. That was the one thing I could see. I had to shoot Greg. I didn't really have a choice.

My hand shook so bad that I had to take a second to compose myself. I pointed the gun at him. It was the only way to save him. The only way for us to be together. I had to save his life. I had to shoot him and then we would be so, so happy.

His eyes took on a wild look, light blazing out of them and straight into my pupils. "Through the heart," he said, reminding me.

I nodded. This was the only way because Greg said so, and of course, Greg was right. I pulled the trigger six times. There. It was done.

Greg crumbled to the floor and blood pooled around him. I was so excited as I stood there waiting for his return, that I almost jumped up in down with glee.

My eyes felt glazed, as I started to plan for our future. I wanted to go to his hometown and meet his family. I wondered what color our wedding would be. After three years of waiting,

I'd say it was about time.

Blood flowed around my shoes, but I couldn't care less. I almost felt like falling to the ground and covering myself in it. I thought about what I would say when I met his parents, his sisters, and brothers. I thought of us starting a family together. Unfortunately, it only took a minute for it all to come crashing down.

Someone must have heard the shots and called the cops because they only knocked once before rushing through the door. I must have looked insane. I was standing over his body, smiling, and plotting like an idiot.

"Drop the gun!" I heard one of them shout. I was startled more than anything else, but I slowly placed it on the floor. As soon as I did, they surrounded me. They put me in cuffs first and then started to ask me questions.

I was still smiling, ready for him to come back to life. I couldn't wait to see the look on their faces when they realized they had to let me go.

I looked around the room. There were eight of them. "He's not dead. Wait one minute and he'll come back to life," I tried to explain.

"What happened here, ma'am?" one of them asked me.

I looked at Greg's body, willing him to wake up, but in the back of my mind, I knew it could be two hours before that happened.

"Did you shoot him?" A different cop asked me.

I felt like kicking Greg until he woke up. I figured I might as well be honest with them. They'd see for themselves in a moment anyway. "He's not dead," I said to the skeptical cops. "He's immortal. He can't be killed. Wait one minute. He'll be back again."

"Get her out of here," I heard a new voice say. He had on plain clothes and looked to be around thirty. Tall with red hair and bright green eyes, he turned so that he could address me directly. "My name is Detective Leon Kravis, and I'll be talking with you shortly." He put on a pair of gloves and then used his telekinesis to float the gun to his outstretched hand and bag it.

The cop who'd been holding me tried to lead me away. "Uh-uh!" I screamed, my heart beating so fast, I thought it'd jump out of my chest. I had to make them understand. "He's immortal! He will come back to life. Wait and see." By now I was frantic. If he'd only breathe again everything would be all right. He didn't though, and they wouldn't listen. Instead, they led me away.

TWO

They buried him while I was still in jail. I still believed he was coming back. I hated the thought of him being underground, all closed up, unable to breathe. There was a trial. They found me mentally incompetent. Let them tell it, I didn't know what I was doing. They wouldn't listen. Even after I told them, I knew exactly what I was doing. He was immortal and he couldn't be killed.

Instead of jail, it was the sanatorium. I spent five years in a place where fear and unpredictability ate away at your soul until there was almost nothing left. Five years. That's how long it took me to realize I was wrong. I'd killed him.

He'd used his powers of persuasion on me and I'd had no defense against him. I didn't know why he'd wanted to die or why he'd wanted me to do it, and I accepted the fact that I would never know.

Once free, I tried to rebuild my life, to forget about Greg. He'd hung me out to dry. He had to have known I would go to jail for his murder and he hadn't cared. Why involve me at all? That's what I just didn't understand. Why had he needed me to be the one to pull that trigger?

I'd been out three months when I saw him again. I was at the mall doing a little shopping and just enjoying being able to come and go as I pleased. No one telling me when to eat, when to sleep. I could walk where I wanted, and talk to whomever I pleased.

He spotted me before I spotted him. He was with a woman

and three small children. He smiled at me, walked right up looking happier than I'd ever seen him. "Delia, hi, gosh, it's been a couple of years since we last saw each other. I think you've met my wife, Amber. So, these are our kids: Mitzy here is four, she's the oldest. Little Greg junior is three, and our baby Catharine is two."

Boy was he gushing with enthusiasm, moving his hands around all excitedly and acting as if we were simply two old friends showing off baby pictures and reminiscing about the good times. "Didn't you get married too? You have a little girl, right?" he went on.

I might would have said something, might would have answered one of his questions, if only I could breathe. If only I could make my brain work. Hard as I tried, I couldn't connect the dots. How had he come back? When had he come back to life? What the hell was he babbling about?

I tried to inhale. He thought I was sick. He reached over and tried to help me. I didn't want him touching me.

I stepped back a few inches. "I'm fine, just trying to catch my breath. It's still hard for me. It's been five years. You know I just got out of the mental hospital about three months ago for killing you."

He laughed and looked at his wife. She didn't share his amusement. "Honey, you know she's just picking with us. It was only three years ago that we saw her at the Christmas party the Jacks family had. She was with her husband then."

His wife smiled as if she remembered this imaginary event. "We had a good time that night. How is your husband, Delia? He's a contractor, right?"

These people were crazy, or maybe I was crazy, or maybe this was all some sort of sick dream and I was still locked up in that place.

"Is this real?" I asked them.

Amber looked down at her fur coat and then back at me, surprise written all over her face.

This was too much. "I killed you," I said looking at Greg. "I shot you through the heart six times."

He and his wife shared a worried glance and then he reached for his phone. "What's your husband's number? I think it may be a good idea to give him a call."

Rage bubbled in me like a volcano. I looked around the mall at the mountain of shoppers happily chattering on their phones and talking back and forth to the people beside them. They had no idea that my world was slowly falling apart and I wanted to keep it that way. I didn't want a scene, to lose control, and have everyone call me crazy again.

Taking a few calming breaths, I turned back to Greg and his wife. "I don't have a husband. I've never been married. I don't have kids." I resisted the urge to add, 'I wanted all those things with you. Thought I'd have all those things with you.' Because as much as I may have wanted them before, I didn't want them now.

What I wanted was some clarity. What I needed was someone who remembered as I remembered. I walked over to a bench and sat down. They followed me.

Amber grabbed Greg's hand. "Is there anyone we can call for you?" she asked me.

I held up one finger and pulled out my newly acquired cell phone. I'd only had it about two weeks. At the time, I'd thought it a splurge but now I was glad I'd made the decision to buy it. I called Detective Leon Kravis.

He'd come to see me when I'd gotten out, gave me his card and, told me to call him if I needed anything.

Well, now I needed something. As soon as he answered, I told him I was having another episode, and he needed to come quickly.

"Was that your husband? Would you like us to wait until he gets here?" Greg asked.

I put my phone back in my pocket and tried to make my voice speak above a whisper. "That was a friend. I think he may be the only one who can help me. He said he'd be here in about ten minutes."

They seemed relieved, and both took a seat beside me. The kids sat on the opposite bench.

Mine was a strange case and I guess that's why the detective had reached out when I'd first come home. Either that or he didn't really agree with my freedom.

I saw him the moment he walked in, scanning the crowd, and walking fast. I guess he didn't want me killing a bunch of people in the mall and then screaming about their immortality.

The second he spotted us, he stopped moving and his eyes slightly bugged. This time it wasn't me he looked at. It was Greg. Confusion mixed with disbelief crossed the detective's face. Wasting no time, he hurriedly picked up his phone, talked for a little bit, and then walked over to us.

He stood in front of Greg, almost boxing him into that one spot. "Who are you?"

Greg looked at his wife and then to me before he answered. "My name's Greg Grant."

Leon shook his head. "Greg Grant is dead. I handled his body myself. He was killed five years ago by this lady right here. Now who are you, because I don't remember him having a twin."

Amber snatched her phone up, shooting death glares at the detective and myself. "I'm calling the real police and I'm reporting you both. This isn't funny."

A commotion started as a crew of policemen made their way toward us. Leon stood with his hands behind his back, watching their approach. Once they were close, he looked at one of the officers and then pointed to Greg. "Arrest him on suspicion of fraud."

Greg looked at me as he was asked to stand up. "Delia, what is this about? I've got my family here. What are you trying to do to me? I was good to you."

Amber began dialing her phone again. "I'm calling my mom to get the kids and then I'm calling our lawyer. Don't worry, honey, we'll get this straightened out."

After the police led Greg away, the detective turned to me. "Do you have any idea what's going on, because if I find out that you've been lying to me--"

Pissed that once again I'd been unfairly accused, I cut him off. "I was the one who called you. He came up to me and started talking nonsense. I felt like I was still locked up in that place." I wrapped my arms around myself, visions of cold nights alone in that hospital invading my mind and making me shiver.

Leon watched them leave, a thoughtful look on his face. "Maybe you never belonged there in the first place. Come on, let's get down to the station, see if we can figure this thing out."

Sweat broke out over my skin, and my voice trembled when I spoke. "Am I going as a guest, or...?"

He put a hand on my arm to reassure me. "As far as I can tell you've not done anything wrong. Come on, we'll figure this out. Hell, I'm as stumped as you are."

Once we got to the station, I looked around for Greg's wife and lawyer, but apparently, they hadn't arrived yet. The detective led me into a room in the back. Greg was already there, with two officers guarding him. They left when we came in, shutting the door behind them so that only Greg, Leon, and myself remained.

Kravis was the first to speak. "Your wife's gone now, so stop the bullshit."

Greg exhaled deeply and sat back in his chair. "Well, I guess I'll explain."

Leon used his telekinesis to fly his gun out of its holster and into his hand. He held it by his side, as if not sure if he would need it or not. "Make it quick." His voice came out clipped, his gaze hard and steady. He and I both took a seat at the door, blocking the exit.

Greg smiled and looked up at me through his eyelashes.

I shook my head. If he thought that disgusting smile was still able to charm me, he had to be delusional. "You set me up," I accused, the words like acid on my tongue.

He didn't even try to deny it. "I did."

Leon's head jerked up and he leaned forward in his chair. "How did you do it? How are you even still alive?"

Greg crossed one leg over the other. "Oh, I really am immortal. I can't be killed, not by you anyway. Which is why I need your help."

My head began to pound and I started a slow massage of my temples, trying to get a handle on it. I'd never been so confused in my life.

The way things were going I almost wished I were back in that hospital. At least there, things made sense. As ironic as that may seem.

I turned to Kravis for clarity, but he looked as confused as I felt. Good. At least I wasn't the only clueless one in the room.

Greg sat patiently waiting. He had to be beyond deranged if he really thought I'd do anything to help him. "You took five years of my life, mind warped me without my permission, and now you think we should just be friends?"

He clasped his hands together on his lap and spoke in the most nonchalant voice I'd ever heard. "I did it to make you stronger." He cocked his head to the side. "It doesn't seem to have worked, though."

I sat on my hands, sure I'd start choking him if I didn't. He smiled as if that action alone proved his point. "Most people who'd spend five years locked up would come out fighting." He shook his head in disgust. "I don't know what I expected from you."

Leon's fists curled and his stare hardened. An angry buzz floated around him, but I needed him to keep it together until we found out more. Cops never liked playing the fool, and so far, Greg had duped us both. "You really want to spend the rest of your life in jail? Start talking."

Greg let out a laugh that ended in a smug grin. "You really think your jail can hold me?"

Leon gave him a thoughtful look. "We have cells that block power. You're not going anywhere, so you might as well tell us what the fuck is going on."

Greg's eyes flashed bright, and Leon shot him in the arm before he could start his mind control. Footsteps sounded, and Greg's phone begin to squawk. "That was me, we're fine. You can see from the interview window." He hung up the phone and a few seconds later the footsteps receded.

Greg slumped over in his chair, hand on his arm, blood leaking from his wound. "You hit me!"

Leon held his hands up. "I told you I would. Now talk."

Greg turned to me, accusation in his eyes, and hatred on his face. I turned away, not knowing what to do with that. Did he really blame me for his own stupidity? How was it my fault he'd decided to set me up for murder?

He cleared his throat and ran a hand through his hair. "Your bodies are made up of fifty-seven to sixty percent water. Where I'm from, which is a different universe, if you haven't figured that out yet, we're seventy-five to eighty percent water. My country, Langunda, neighbors the country, Kelm. Their bodies, the Kelm, are seventy-eight to eighty-three percent water." He said it like that explained everything and we could all go home now.

"Fascinating." Leon said. "Now what does that have to do with you faking your own death?" His brows drew in tight together and he sat up a little in his chair. "And who's in your grave?"

Greg laughed as if any of this shit was funny. "Oh, come on. No one's in the grave. I mind warped the undertaker and grave-diggers. It was a closed casket for a reason. I should know, I stood off to the side and watched, in case I needed to whammy someone real quick."

Leon listened, nodding his head the whole time. "So you were telling the truth about being immortal. Okay, I'll give you that, but why'd you leave her to rot? That's the part I don't understand."

"Cause he needed me locked up," I said realizing that he hadn't messed up at all. Everything had gone exactly as planned.

Greg clucked his teeth at me. "I know that face, Delia. Think you've got this all figured out?" He shook his head. "You don't."

Leon pointed his gun again. "Well then, explain it. So that we can both understand."

Greg's jaw clenched as he looked at me. I took a moment to think back on our relationship. Had he always had this level of disdain for me, or was this a new development? His voice came out hard and scolding. "I've never met someone so afraid to fight in my life." He shook his head, incredulously. "I did everything I could to force your hand." His fingers tapped the table in front of him. "Yet, no matter how bad I treated you, no matter how fucked up, you never tried to fight me. Remember when you got your pocketbook stolen? How about the time you were jumped in that alley? Even then, you wouldn't defend yourself."

My hands shook, wanting to throttle him. If he kept talking he would soon get what he wanted, as it was, it was taking everything in me not to grab Leon's gun and shoot him again. "You set all of that up?"

I'd been scared to leave the house for weeks after both incidents, and here he was smiling like a proud parent. My eyes flew to the detective's gun and Leon shook his head and put it back in its holster. I wasn't going to really use it, but I guess he didn't know that.

Greg sat watching, a big smirk on his face. "Sending you to jail was a last resort."

I grind my fingernails deep into my skin, trying to keep my composure. "Because you thought it would make me fight?"

"I had no idea they'd send you to a sanatorium. Not that it made any difference. You still wouldn't fight." He huffed liked I'd ruined all his life's ambitions. "I waited at first, you know. Just knew you'd finally make a move." He looked like he couldn't believe things hadn't worked out exactly as he'd planned. "Then I got tired of waiting, figured I'd catch up with you whenever you got out."

A fire roared in my belly as I stared at him. "I never ripped anyone apart, so you deserted me and ran away?"

He gave me a blank look. "I would have saved you. Gotten you out of there. Had you been like any normal person and at least tried to fight."

My hands balled at my side. The fucking gall. Who did he think he was, playing with my life like that? "So, let me get this straight. As soon as I'd started beating people up with my powers, you would have scooped in and saved me? Then what? Did you really expect me to fall back into your arms as if nothing had happened?"

The smug look on his face was answer enough. "You would have."

Conceited bastard. "Why, Greg? Why go through all this?" I really wanted to know the answer. He'd set up this big elaborate scheme, with the sole purpose of making me fight. I shook my head. Apparently, he'd been setting shit up since the first day we'd met. But why?

"Because I needed you in my world."

"Why not ask me to come?"

"I needed you prepared for battle. I'd been working on you for three years. I got tired of waiting."

"Why not mind warp me?"

"Well, that only lasts for so long. Would have had to keep doing it. Which would have eventually turned your brain to mush. Who could you help then? No. I needed you there on your own. That was the only way this was going to work."

I thought about the amount of water he said his people carried and slowly things began to click in place. With my power, I could hurt them, control them and that's what he really wanted.

Detective Kravis apparently came to the same conclusion. "So, because you're a coward, you thought you'd use her as an assassin?"

The look on Greg's face said why not. "She can control water. Which means she can rip our bodies apart. Be a while coming back from that. Long enough to take over a whole country in fact."

I felt my fingers twitch. "Not real smart letting me know how to dispose of you."

His laugh said he thought that was preposterous. "Like you'd ever even try. Kelm has been planning to overthrow us for a while now. We have agents working both sides of the coin. We're not strong enough to hold them off. Their forces are twice the size of ours. Their current leader, Yama, wants peace, but his second in command, Bale, well he's been whispering in ears and making plans against us for years. We have it on good authority that one of his first official acts will be to take over Langunda."

Kravis asked what I was thinking. "So why don't you take them out first?"

He tapped his finger. "We don't have the manpower."

Something he hated to admit, judging by the look on his face.

"So why doesn't Bale get rid of this Yama and take over?" Again the detective and I were on the same wavelength.

"There are things worse than death. Bale would never be recognized as the true leader if he was to ever raise hands against the current leader. That's not how things work there. Besides, we are immortal. Time means nothing to us. We've known Bale's plans for the past twenty years. I searched for ten before I finally found someone with the ability to control water. Watched you for two before I approached."

I felt sick to my stomach. The shit he'd gone through to deceive me. How much pain could have been avoided, had he been honest with me? "Why not tell me that? Why take me through all of this?"

He looked at me as if I'd just asked him to fly to the moon. "Knowing that's the only reason I'd talked to you, would you have really helped me? I wanted to get to know you first, but the better I got to know you, the more I knew you would never come fight for us. Then I started to push you, things like the robbery and the beat down." He held out his hands. "Still nothing. This last attempt was my final effort, and well, we see how that turned out." He acted like I was one of the greatest disappointments in his life. How could I not have seen this before? Was I really that dumb, or had love blinded me to all his faults and shortcomings.

Still, he'd come back to our world. A married man with kids. That brought me up short. Where was his wife? She'd said she was calling their lawyer and coming straight over. I found it strange that she hadn't made it here yet. "Where's your wife?"

He deflected the question. "Mind letting me up so I can stretch my legs a bit?"

Leon snorted. "Not a chance. Now keep talking."

He exhaled loudly as if telling us the truth was some big burden. For him it probably was. "Amber's not my wife. The kids are trained agents. All are from Langurda. Everyone there's willing to help. We need you, babe. But you must be willing to fight. You have to."

I swallowed hard, trying to control my emotions. The sheer

audacity of this man. "I'm not helping you," I said as firm as I could. "Me against a whole country. Does that really make sense to you?" I looked at Leon. "Does it make sense to you? I mean you do think this is as irrational as I do, right?"

Kravis looked as if he couldn't believe I'd even bothered to ask. He pointed to Greg. "The only question is why doesn't he see that? He really seems to believe that one untrained fighter can take on a whole army. I may need to order a psych eval. He could be suffering from delusions."

Greg looked completely unfazed. "Seventy-one percent of the earth's surface is water. There's not a person alive whose body's not composed of the stuff. You could rip it all apart if you wanted to, yet you won't even try."

My mouth went dry at the thought, that had never been what I'd wanted. "That's… That's not what my abilities are for," I stuttered. Just the thought of hurting others with my powers left a cold lump in the pit of my stomach. I could never do that, and I didn't feel as if that was something to be ashamed of.

He looked at me with disgust. "Oh yeah, yeah, you use it to keep your coffee warm and your food hot. Most people use stoves for that."

It was true. I used my powers for daily mundane things because that's what they were made for. My mom had always instilled that into me and my sister. The path to least resistance was the best one to take. Violence was never the answer. There was always a better way. So, no. I wouldn't help him defend his country from someone who wasn't even currently threatening it. I shook my head. "Not my fight. I'm not getting involved."

Leon nodded his approval and then stood, "She's given you her answer and I'm placing you under arrest." He took out his cuffs.

"Whoa, whoa, whoa," Greg raised his hands. "Under arrest for what?"

Was he even serious? I didn't even give Leon time to answer before I started naming off his sins. "How about illegally mind warping me? Or, I don't know, how about the fact that I spent the last five years locked up for something I didn't do? That good enough for you?" My voice shook with anger and I didn't care. I wanted to rip his eyes out. This man was vile, and the fact that I'd once loved him sickened me to my core. "You really don't believe you did anything?"

His chin jutted out like it used to when he'd done something wrong, but wanted to convince me he was right. "I was acting on the orders of Bebbi. Langunda's top ruler." His voice lowered and turned into a growl. "You can't judge me and your laws can't hold me." He made a move for the door and Leon used his TK to sling him across the room.

Greg hit the wall and crumbled to the floor. He only stayed down for a second, before he was back on his feet. His eyes flashed blue and a stream of light came from them aimed toward our heads.

He missed us both. Leon waved his arm and slung Greg again. This time, when he fell, he began to chant, and his eyes flashed like before, when he'd tricked me into shooting him.

My mind went back to that time, five years ago. I tried to take a breath, as my hands shook, and my pulse raced. Five years of my life taken away because this man didn't know how to take no for an answer.

Years of him pretending to love me, pretending to care. All so that he could use me. Get what he wanted, and then discard me like yesterday's trash.

Sweat dripped into my eyes. Who did he think he was? I'd mourned his death. For years, I'd been haunted with the belief that I'd killed the man I loved.

My eyes started to burn, but I couldn't bring myself to care. For the first three months in that place, I'd cried day and night for a man who only saw me as a pawn.

I'd trusted him. More than I'd ever trusted anybody in my life. For me, that was huge. My body began to tremble and the whole of my insides started to rumble.

They'd put me in a straitjacket when I'd first arrived at the sanatorium, locked me in a padded room for days. I felt the rage building, could feel the storm brewing.

Slowly I came to my feet, the water inside me boiling with

my anger. "Nst, est, grol," I said, speaking in my mother's native tongue. Using the water inside me I began to rise in the air. "Nst, est, grul, grol."

The whole building began to shake, chairs fell to the side, the table flipped over, and Greg shrank back in fear, nothing but pure terror on his face. Leon's mouth hung open, and he looked from me to Greg as if expecting one of us to have an explanation for him.

Inside I cracked. Everything slid to the side and then I shattered completely. I opened my mouth and angry breath flew out of it like the wind. It screamed, hollered, and tore apart everything in its path.

Greg and Leon were both caught up in my whirlwind. Flipping and turning, no ground beneath them, they both tried desperately to find something to hold on to.

Lips moving, they were trying to talk to me. It was all moot. I couldn't see past the force of my wind and the violence of my own anger. Using the water in his body, I brought Greg closer. I snatched him by his shirt, his face mere inches from my own. "Nst, grul, mui, grol." It came out as a howling scream and I watched with horrific satisfaction as his face broke from the fear.

I wrapped my hands around his neck and forcibly slammed him to the ground. My attention focused only on him, the chairs fell, the wind stopped, and Leon hit the ground with a grunt.

Straddling Greg's hips, I raised him up by the throat, his eyes locked with mine. "Nst, grul, grol!" All I knew was pain. "Nst, grul, grol!" All I felt was rage. I smashed his head into the floor. "Nst, grul, grul." Blood splattered across my face and I heard his bones crunch.

It had no effect on me and I smashed him again, my hands choking the life out of him. "How dare you!" My scream turned into a howl and the wind began to whip again.

The chairs, table, and Leon rose in the air and started to spin. I stayed right where I was, holding Greg down and squeezing as hard as I could. The water boiling in me heated my hands and burned through to his neck. The smell of charred flesh filled the air and still I kept squeezing.

I could hear the officers on the other side of the door banging and trying to get in. I heard a loud boom and knew they were trying to break the door down. I pushed Greg away and he slid across the floor. My hair flew in every direction and with my arms outstretched, I rose in the air again. I flew the door open and the policeman on the other side began to sway as the wind lifted them.

I howled out my pain. "Nstee, yee, ghu!" and then dropped them all to the floor. Bodies fell all around me as I busted out the doors and disappeared into the night.

THREE

Leon came for me three hours later. Images of what I'd done plagued my mind and I curled up on my couch wanting nothing more than to sweep it all away.

Often when we got mad, my sister and I would speak in the language we'd both learned as kids. My mother was from the Isles of Ria, powerful people known for their superior abilities and peaceful attitudes.

I balled my fist into my stomach, hoping to dull the ache I felt there.

How ashamed would my mom be of me now? I'd let her down and with her mental powers, she probably already knew what I'd done.

I picked up the phone to call my sister and then dropped it, not wanting to hear the disappointment in her voice. The doorbell rang twice and then Leon was banging and yelling my name.

I dragged myself to the door and opened it just a peek. He busted in, stumbling through the threshold. "You really think I'm ready to talk to you through a hunk of wood after the way you showed off today?"

I clambered back to my place on the couch and swallowed hard. "Did I hurt anyone?"

He shrugged. "Few bumps and bruises. I told them he'd put the whammy on you again."

I didn't deserve his protection. "Thanks," I said, barely able to look him in the eye.

He took a seat on the table in front of me. "No problem, but mind telling me what the hell all that was about?"

I pulled my covers tightly around me. "I lost control."

He nodded. "You speak the language of the Isles."

"My mother is from there," I said quietly. "They live there now. Her and my sister."

He shook his head in disbelief. "Never thought I'd see a person from the Isles behave that way."

I blanched and then hid my face in the corner of the couch.

He tapped me on the shoulder. "Oh, come on now. I didn't mean anything by it. I liked it. You really gave him what for."

I turned my head slightly. "It's not how we do things."

"Well, I wouldn't encourage you to do it again, but I understand."

I sat up and folded my legs under me. "Did I hurt him badly?"

His laugh was laced with disbelieve. "She asks as if we're talking about the weather."

"He can't die. I think we've established that," I said dryly.

He started to nod then caught himself and stopped. "Still. But, no. He's already healed and sitting in a cell. Probably won't be there for long, though."

Probably not. "Why are you here?"

He stood. "Just doing my job."

I walked him to the door. "Well, you can go back and tell them that I'm not in the process of killing anyone."

I went to turn the knob, but something on the other side, knocked me back, causing me to stumble and almost fall.

Amber rushed inside, eyes blazing and hand raised. Leon lifted her in the air and used his TK to throw her across the room.

Her hand never wavered, and falling backward, she still managed to chant. We were lifted and sucked into a black swirling portal. Darkness surrounded us as we tumbled and flipped, hitting hard when we finally came to a stop.

We landed in a watery cell and quickly came to our feet. The water wasn't exactly to our knees, but it was well past our ankles.

Some had made it inside my ear, causing a switching sound. Yuk. I hated when that happened, and quickly used my powers to remove it.

I did the same for Leon. He looked at me, mouth opened a little, then nodded a thanks.

His clothes clung to him, soaking wet. "What the fuck was that?"

The cell we were in sat inside of a large room that looked like a police station of some sort. There were many people walking back and forth, but no one paid us any attention. Most of them were dressed in red and blue uniforms and didn't seem to notice the water under their feet.

Leon took out his cell phone. "Not used to being on the other side of the bars." He ran a hand under his collar and his voice came out a little stilted. "Got to call the station. My boys will get us out of here."

Well, apparently, he hadn't been paying attention. Amber had sent us tumbling into Langunda. I knew that as sure as I knew anything. I waited quietly for him to come to the same conclusion.

He frowned at his phone, then knocked on it a few times. "It didn't get wet. It was deep inside my inner coat pocket when I fell."

"Look around." I waved my hand about. "Any of this look normal to you?"

His eyes took in the water, the people dressed in uniform, and the way they were all walking through the water as if it meant nothing. "They need a good plumber?"

"And we need to get out of Langunda and back home."

His head snapped around, taking a closer look at our surroundings. I saw the exact moment that reality set in, panic, then steel resolve.

Relief flooded me. That would make this so much easier. Someone willing to take charge and get us out of here.

He wiped a hand down his face. "So they're going to make you help? Whether you want to or not."

Well, not exactly what I was looking for, but I could work

with it. "Can't you just sling the doors open and get us out of here?"

He peered at the bars over, a thoughtful look on his face. "I can try." He put his phone up, took a few steps back, and then raised his hands. The bars rattled and shook, but stayed firm in their spot. He tried again. Nothing.

Shit. Heat rose from the back of my neck to my face and hands. The room started to look smaller and the walls began to close in.

I took a deep breath and then another. What were we going to do? I wanted to call out, but if the people on the other side were ignoring us, then they weren't hurting us, and that was still important.

I looked at Leon. "Try again." My voice sounded like it had when I was a nine-year-old child and the kids at school wouldn't stop teasing me about only having one power.

The fact that my power was useless only sweetened it for them. "I'm going to tell my mama." I'd cried, only to have them laugh even harder. I came from a family of pacifists. There was no real danger in me telling my mom.

I had anyway. She'd come up to the school and talked to some of the other parents. They'd promised to have a word with their kids and even punish them.

Whatever they did didn't work, as my tormentors had come to school that next day and were a hundred times more vicious.

I shook the unpleasant memories away. I was older now, stronger, and in control of my own destiny. I wouldn't go down so easily this time. "Well then, let's come up with a plan," I said to Leon.

He chuckled with disbelief, and then looked at me as if I'd grown three heads. I pulled my shirt tightly around me. "What?"

His tone was incredulous. "Are you really that scared of your own ability? After the way you behaved in my holding room? Really?" His eyebrows drew together and he looked truly confused.

He was no help at all. We were going to be in here for the rest of our lives. I gasped out loud in an effort to control my panic. The walls started to get closer again. I took a seat on the bench and drew my legs under me. It felt like I was suffocating.

I took a deep breath and then another. That didn't work and so I took more. Soon I wouldn't be able to breathe at all. I wrapped my arms around myself trying to curl into a tiny ball and disappear. All I wanted was to go home. Why couldn't I go home?

Leon's voice cut through my haze. "Delia, I need you to stay with me now. I can't do this on my own. I need your help, okay?"

I blinked away the blurriness to see him staring down at me. He took a handkerchief out of his pocket and handed it over. "You're sweating bad. I'll try the bars again."

I took the folded white cloth and wiped my face, pushing damp hair out of my eyes and tucking it behind my ear. It had to work this time. It just had to.

Leon held his arm out, and again the bars rattled and shook but didn't give an inch.

"You're not strong enough," Amber said. She walked into our line of sight, Greg at her side. His face was all healed, and he walked without limp or affliction.

I jumped up, and Greg stumbled back as if I meant him harm. I blinked at him, stunned, and knew his newfound hesitance around me would take some getting used to.

Amber stared at him for a good hard second, then turned back to us. "All you have to do is help us and you can leave."

"Why is the floor wet?" It was a very silly thing to say and I had no idea where it'd come from.

She ignored that completely and looked at Greg. "Five years in a mental institution and this is the best we get? No fight at all. She has to do better."

He nodded. "Let me try." His eyes flashed blue and he began to chant under his breath.

My whole body began to tremble because I knew what that meant. He'd make me do something I didn't want to do again. Make me behave in a manner that my mother and sister would never forgive me for.

Make me spend five years in a place that ate away at my soul and left me an empty version of who I used to be. He'd… no! I started to scream, and scream. My arms stretched out and using the water in my body I began to rise. I wouldn't let him hurt me again. I couldn't.

The water below began to tremble, my hair stood straight up, and the only thing on my mind was freedom. Still in the air, I held out my hands, making the water bubble and hiss as I raised the temperature in it. Steam started to rise, but since that was made of water too, I swiped it away, remembering to keep it at bay next time so as not to distract me.

"Delia!" Leon. I cooled the water on our side of the bars but left the rest burning, still keeping the steam from rising.

All around us, uniformed people scrambled, jumping up on chairs and desk to get away from the scalding. I wasn't letting them off that easy.

They meant to hurt me. Every one of them. Force me into something against my will, and be damned how I felt about it.

Well, I'd show them exactly how I felt about it. With the water at my mercy, I created a tidal wave that I hurled out in every direction.

The force of it knocked the bars away and I wasted no time snatching Leon up so that we could get the hell out of there.

The water rose even higher, and Greg, Amber, and the others went down, arms flapping, and screams turning into bubbles as the water pulled them under. Keeping Leon and myself in the air, we fled the room.

There was a door down the hall and to the right. Once back on solid ground, we ran for it. Leon and I both used our abilities to knock out anybody who got in our way.

A frantic voice sounded down the hall. "Stop them." Amber.

Without me directing it, the wave must have receded. Amber and Greg, both soaking wet, sprinted our way. I kicked the door open, Leon using his powers to back me up. It flew off its hinges with no resistance it all.

We kept running. Darkness and water surrounded us. It was night here, yet boats and other such water equipment rode up and down the street. The wind chilled me to the bone, my clothes clinging to me.

I looked at the unfamiliar surroundings, panic starting to set in. "What do we do?" I asked Leon.

He grabbed me by the arm. "We keep moving." By now Greg, Amber, and many others were right behind us. Leon threw them back and we ran in a different direction. They were still close until a blue motorized boatcar knocked them out of the way.

"Get in!" A voice from inside yelled. "I'm from Kelm. I was sent here to get you."

Knowing full well it was probably a trap, we hopped in anyway, leaving Greg and the others in the dust. "Thank you," I said to our mysterious benefactor.

She nodded. "I'm Klenaya, but no more talking until we get to Kelm. There, Yama will explain everything."

Okay then. I sat back in my seat and finally allowed myself to take a breath. Then I remembered who the Kelm were, and what they had planned for Greg's people, and I started to panic all over again.

I looked at Leon, sure that he was thinking the same. He waved his hands in a way that told me to chill out and wait. I nodded and turned back around. I could do that. I could wait and see.

We rode through the water for a while, then Klenaya told us to buckle up and we went flying. I tried not to scream as I was flattened against my seat. Too scared to breathe, the only thing I could do was hold on until we finally came to a screeching halt in front of a large white palace.

It looked like something a queen and king would live in, and it was probably big enough to fit a whole country inside. Lights shone down on it making it bright and showing off its spotless shine.

Klenaya cut the engine and got out. "We've had our eye on you. We knew the Langunda would make their move, now that you're no longer in the take away."

Leon and I got out as well. "What's the take away?"

"Where you were for the last five years."

Oh, the hospital. Okay. I gave her the side eye. Greg had said the Kelm were plotting to take over his people. They didn't seem hostile so far, but I knew better than to trust them too much.

We got on an elevator that quickly took us to the top floor. The water was a little higher here, but still barely past our ankles. The room Klenaya led us into was solid white, and a pair of miniature toy boats floated our way.

Two men sat on the floor with controllers in their hands. They yelled and jabbed each other as they twisted and turned the devices from side to side.

Oh. I think I was more surprised than anything when it finally dawned on me that they were racing. I quickly stepped aside, not wanting to impede anybody from making it to the finish line.

"Children!" Klenaya hissed at them and then turned to us and smiled.

The guy on the right looked to be about twenty-one and favored Klenaya so much that I caught myself doing a double-take to make sure I hadn't missed something.

They both had tanned colored skin, with bone straight blue-green hair that hung loosely around their shoulders, with bright purple eyes, which seemed to lighten without notice every couple of seconds.

She pointed at him. "My twin Kyle. And our father, next in line for ruler of Kelm, Bale. Aren't we in such good hands," she said sarcastically.

A scream erupted from the floor and Kyle jumped up, dancing, and hopping across the room. "I got it, dad. I got it. First world champion, you'll never catch up."

I looked at Leon and his face read my emotions exactly. What the hell kind of people were we dealing with here?

The other man was older, a little on the short side with a bald head. He came to his feet with a smile. "Nice to meet you. I'm Bale. This is my son, Kyle, and I guess you know Klenaya."

Klenaya sighed loudly. "I already told them that."

"No harm in telling them again," he answered right away

and then looked me over. "Let's go in here."

We followed him into a spacious room with black and gold walls, water covering a matching floor. A large table sat in the middle with about twenty chairs around it.

It looked like something one would expect to see in a castle, and it smelled like peaches and berries, probably because of the multiple fruit bowls sitting atop the table. I looked to Leon, who seemed as impressed as I was.

Bale bid us to have a seat and then left the room.

Back a moment later, he walked behind a brown-skinned man, with shoulder-length purple hair. I knew before even being told that this had to be Yama.

He was regal in his manner, and every step he took was laced with authority. He stopped moving when he got to my seat. "You ever make it rain?" His voice was smooth like butter.

Talk about being hot under the collar. I fumbled with my fingers, anything to keep his piercing gaze off me. "I... I... don't know how."

He looked at the water on the floor and then back to me, a small twinkle in his red eyes. "Sure you do. And when it rains, you control everything." There was no answer to that, and so I said nothing.

I expected him to take a seat at the head of the table, but instead he opted for hanging off the side. "Do you know what tacium is?"

I shook my head. "Never heard of it. Why?"

He picked up an apple out of a nearby basket and bit into it. "It's the reason that you're here. Hasn't anyone told you already?" He looked from the twins to their father, then turned back to me. "Tacium is the life blood of this realm. We use it in our food, drinks, clothing, all material, every building. There is nothing here that doesn't have a bit of tacium in it."

I couldn't help but wonder why. "What does it do?" Because it had to do something. If not, then why use it in the first place?

He took another bite of the apple, then proffered his hand as if to offer me some. I shook my head no, and he went on. "Tacium makes us immortal. We can still be hurt, but we'll always heal, and we'll always come back to life."

I nodded my understanding and he went on.

"We lose the tacium, we lose our lives. We can only last three, maybe four days without it until we're weakened to the point of being immobile. It's been that way for as long as anybody can remember. It's all we've ever known."

Well, that explained a lot about Greg and his miraculous recoveries. From the sound of it, they were addicted to the stuff. Still, I had no clue what that had to do with me. "Okay?" I said, as a way for him to go on.

He popped a few grapes in his mouth. "The only place tacium grows is here in Kelm."

Of course it is, but no, wait a minute. "Why are you trying to take over Langunda then? If you're the ones with all the tacium?"

Yama raised a brow, an amused look on his face. Bale sat up with a stir. Klenaya looked confused, and Kyle laughed out loud.

Yama gave each one of them a stern look, then turned back to me. "Lies roll off Langunda tongues like honey in the wind."

Huh? I shook my head; sure I'd get a headache if I tried to understand what he meant.

Leon grunted under his breath, which probably meant he didn't get it any more than I did. "So you control the purse strings?"

Yama shook his head. "It's not that simple. We buy and trade with many other countries. Not everything grows here." Another bite. "Not everything we need is made here. Each country has goods unique to its landscape and climate, so it works out for everyone."

"Langunda?"

"Made some bad investments, bad trade deals, and have been looking for a way to pull themselves up for the last twenty years or so. Then they found you."

Leon snorted, and all eyes turned on him. "Look," he said, holding his hands out in front of him. "I ain't saying you're lying, but twenty years is a hell of a long time to wait to rob someone."

Yama chuckled as if this was the silliest thing he'd heard all day. "And time means what to a man such as myself? Twenty years is no more than a couple of hours when you have all the time in the world."

That was my cue to get the hell out of there. "Leon and I don't have all the time in the world, so if you would just open up one of those little portals for us, we'll gladly be on our way."

Bale sat with his hands folded on the table. "What makes you think they're not there waiting for you?"

Leon nodded. "I'm almost certain that they are. Probably got people staked out at the station as well. Think about it, Delia, you really believe they're going to let you go that easy?"

I slid a slow foot across the floor, not at all liking what I heard. "So, what do we do then?"

Yama pulled up a chair, placed it beside me, and sat in it backward. "You stay here until we can neutralize them. I've already been in touch with a few other countries, alerted them to the situation. The majority of them should be here by morning." He put the chair back and stood. "Until then, accept our hospitality and know that we mean you no harm."

It wasn't only up to me. I turned to Leon. He thought about it for a minute, then begin to negotiate. "We can stay, be kinda pointless not to, but let's have a look at this here tacium that's causing such a ruckus."

Klenaya bounced up like a spring. "How about I take you where it grows? Give you a look at it up close and personal?" She seemed eager to leave, or maybe she really liked riding.

Leon sure seemed keen to go. "Coming?" he asked me, rising to his feet.

Of course I was coming. What the hell else was I going to do?

Yama smiled as if he was used to Klenaya's flights of fancies, and at this point, it was just inevitable. "Take your brother with you, please."

She glared at him like he'd slapped her. "Cause I'm the one who needs a babysitter."

Yama shook his head and smiled at her in an almost fatherly manner. "I never said it was you who needed watching."

Her grin was filled with glee. "Why yes, Yama. I'll gladly

keep my brother on a chain today."

He clicked his tongue at her and walked out of the room.

We arrived in what looked like the opening of a cave. Men dressed in blue and green uniforms surrounded the place and all the entrances.

If tacium was as important as they'd said, then I understood the precaution. What I didn't understand was making yourself dependent on something that may one day dry up and kill you anyway.

What would they do if the tacium suddenly stopped growing? It seemed like a heavy price to pay for the promise of everlasting life.

We stepped out of the car, the air so suffocating that it almost hurt to breathe. I wiped the sweat from my face and followed behind Klenaya.

When we were a few feet away from the cave entrance, she stopped suddenly and whipped around, her voice urgent and hushed. "Don't make any sudden moves and stay close to me or Kyle. Got it?"

We nodded our agreement, and she allowed us to walk on.

The men at the mouth of the cave were dressed in the same blue and green uniforms as the others, and stood talking and laughing about something, but straightened the moment we walked up. "Klenaya, Kyle, your father alerted us to your arrival. Remember to stay together and don't touch anything."

Her gaze shifted to Leon and myself as if we were naughty kids whom she'd already warned multiple times to behave.

"Geez, you'd think they had liquid gold down here or something," Leon whispered to me.

The caves were as wet as everything else, and the sound of sloshing water could be heard everywhere we stepped. Clouds of dust crowded in on us, sending both Leon and myself into unstoppable coughing fits. Kyle and Klenaya walked without affliction as if they did this every day. As far as I knew, they probably did.

"You think gold is more valuable?" I asked Leon.

He thought about it for a second and then shook his head.

"Unlimited resilience, immortality? Yeah, I get it. Was just trying to say something to lighten the mood, you know?"

I got it, this place was dirty, depressing, and I could feel it pressing in on us. Every few minutes the ground would shake and rumble, and I just knew we were going to have a cave in. I tried to keep the annoyance off my face, but it was hard. I hadn't wanted to come down here in the first place.

Overhead, lights shined down on us, making our steps a little steadier than they otherwise would've been.

We walked for a bit until we came upon more men and women dressed in uniforms. With eyes intent on their task, they used telekinesis to shake cave walls open. "Does the tacium protect us from a cave in?" I asked as the ground trembled around us.

"No," Kyle answered. He rubbed a hand through his hair. "Really think I'd risk all this if it wasn't secure?" He shook his head. "I think not. They've been doing this for years. Nothing to worry about there."

I'm glad he had so much confidence. I, on the other hand, didn't share his optimism. "Yeah, well, I think I'll stay on my guard just in case."

He chuckled, as if I was being silly, and walked on.

Once the workers broke through the walls, they brought out a blue powder substance and loaded it into the many miniature boats circling the cave.

Tacium. So that's what it looked like. That's what had made my life hell for the last five years. I kind of wanted to reach out and run my fingers through it. Considering they'd probably be chopped off if I tried, I decided not to risk it.

In the next room the tacium was loaded onto a table and then packaged twenty to a boat.

Kyle's eyes shone as if all his dreams lay in this damp, sad, cave. "So what do you think?" He really seemed to want to know. Did he expect us to be amazed? He sure looked like he did.

I bit my lower lip and tried to keep my cool. I couldn't be in a good mood because none of this was fun for me. "Stunning. Fabulous, can we please leave now?"

His face fell hard, and I felt like an ass for taking away his shine. "I'm just tired, Kyle. It's been a long day, right, Leon?"

Leon, apparently seeing the situation for what it was, readily agreed. "Yeah, buddy. This really is an impressive setup you got going on here. But I think I've seen enough. Wanted to know what all the fuss was about, is all."

We arrived back at the white building in time for dinner. Leon and I were served a good meal and then showed to our separate quarters. An armed guard was placed on each of our doors, and that helped me feel a little more secure.

I was still a little nervous and ended up doing more tossing and turning than I did sleeping.

I must have dozed off at some point through the night because a hand over my mouth had me screaming awake.

FOUR

My only instinct was survival I jumped up, clawing, and biting at the hand holding me down. "Guard! Guard!"

"Hey, hey, babe, calm down. It's just me come to see you is all."

Greg removed his hand, and I immediately began to call out for help again.

"Shhh." He tried to put his hands back over my mouth, but this time, I sunk my teeth deep into his fingers.

"Ouch." He snatched his hand back and had the nerve to look shocked that I hadn't fallen immediately into his arms. Pompous bastard. What the hell had I ever saw in him?

I kicked him off the bed and sat up. He fell to the floor, splashing water on my face, and hair. I was too angry to care, and simply swiped it away. "What the fuck are you doing in here?"

I thought about the fact that no one had rushed in to save me. "Greg, what did you do to my guard?"

"He's just sleeping." He made a move to sit on the bed again, but I raised my leg, letting him know what would happen if he tried.

He stayed standing, but his voice dropped low and was suddenly filled with honey. "Oh, babe. I just wanted to talk to you for a bit. I miss you. How long has it been since we've been together? I know you have to be missing me too, babe." He smiled, and the only thing I could do was shake my head in disgust. "Do you think we can try again, Delia? Please?"

I laughed in his face. I couldn't help it. He didn't really think he still had a chance, did he? If so, he was more delusional than I'd thought. "Get the fuck out of my room before I rip you apart." I came to my feet, and he flinched back, but still tried to look brave.

He puffed his chest out. "What are you going to do without me to protect you, girl?"

I looked at him with disgust. "When have you ever--" Screams and large crashes came from the other side of the door and kept me from completing that sentence.

"What have you done?" I ran for the door.

He hopped ahead, jumping over my bed, and blocking me from leaving. "You didn't really think I'd just let you go, did you?"

I called out to the water in his body and hurled him across the room. I didn't even have to think about it, I just did it and flew out the door.

My guard lay bleeding on the floor, but there was nothing I could do to help him. I stepped over his body and rushed straight to Leon's room.

He could defend himself, I knew that, but for how long? I skidded around the corner, as two Langunda went flying through his door. He came out, arms outstretched, chest rapidly rising and falling. "Are you alright?" he asked me. "I was just on my way to get you."

"I'm fine. Let's get the hell out of here."

A loud boom sounded from the right, and we charged that way, Leon probably because he was a cop and that's what they did, me because I just needed to know that the twins were okay.

Kyle was on his knees, his sister on his back. Both were shooting light from their eyes and neither seemed to be hit yet. They did a flip, and reversed their positions, but never once stopped fighting.

I felt compelled to help, and without even thinking, jumped right in. Leon followed suit, him using his TK, and me with my water skills.

Klenaya and Kyle came to their feet, and the four of us

stood back to back. "The tacium! We must get to the tacium. It may already be too late." Klenaya ran for the nearest exit, and we followed right behind her.

Bale and Yama met us on the way. Both men wore battle scars, and each were running at a breakneck speed. Bale grabbed both twins by the arm, cradling Klenaya's face in his hands. "Are you hurt? Are you okay?

Klenaya detangled herself. "We're fine, father, but we have to get to the caves!"

Three Langunda rounded the corner and came right at us. Bale picked up one and slammed him so hard that the man's skull shattered and cracked.

Yama crossed his hands, and blue light exploded from them, slicing the remaining Langundas in half. His feet never faltered. "Bale has this. We have to protect the tacium," he yelled.

Instead of Klenaya's cute little boatcar, we loaded up in Yama's much larger black one. He yelled at everyone we passed to follow. "Most know to go, but some will heedlessly try to protect their homes and land. We're taught since birth, no matter what, secure the caves!" Yeah, who cared if you lost everything you'd ever worked for, just protect the tacium. What a messed up way of life.

The car was a lot bigger than it looked from the outside and had enough room to fit about twenty. Leon and I sat side by side, the twins in front of us. Many Kelm residents loaded in, all eager to save what meant the most to them.

I hurriedly buckled my seatbelt, and the car took off with a lurch. We were only in the air for a couple of minutes, before landing in front of the caves, the fight already fully in progress.

All around us, Langunda and Kelm fought hand to hand, power to power. All I could see were blue lights, and bodies being tossed and thrown. The smell penetrated the car, and I put a hand over my mouth as the scent of blood and charred flesh invaded my nose.

My whole body began to shake and my hands went slick. I felt like someone had sucked out all the air and I found myself struggling to breathe.

I couldn't do this. We couldn't do this. I grabbed Leon before he exited the car. "We have no stake in this. We don't have to get out the car."

He nodded as if he agreed, but his expression read differently. "I can't just sit back and watch. Maybe it's the cop in me, but I can't…" He ran for the door and then turned back at the last minute. "You stay in here and keep safe if you have to, but I've got to get out there."

I watched from the window, my soul tormented. My mom and sister would never approve of this, they just wouldn't. They'd want me here in the car, out of the line of fire, and harming no one.

That's what I'd been taught all my life, and the last couple of days I hadn't been living up to that at all.

An explosion rocked my ears and I jumped from the sound. The truth was I didn't owe loyalty to either of these countries.

The Langunda wanted to take what wasn't theirs, and the Kelm wanted to hold on to their monopoly, neither affected me or my life in the slightest.

Water splashed against the window and shook the car. The sound of loud bombs and men and women alike crying out in pain rocked my eardrums, as Langunda and Kelm fought hard in battle.

A shiver ran over me, and I got down on my knees, wrapped my hands around my arms, and begin to rock.

Every part of my body was pulling me out that door, but one flash of my mom's disappointed face kept me rooted to my spot. Another explosion and smoke filled the windows. I needed to get out there, I knew that, and yet I couldn't move.

A screamed, "stop!" and I was on my feet in an instant. I knew that voice. That was Klenaya, and she needed my help.

I didn't take time to think. All I knew was that I had to get to her. Not caring what happened to me, I ran toward the front of the car, blowing the door off its hinges in an effort to get outside.

Four Langunda circled her, and three circled her brother. With the flip of my hand, I tossed them all away and then turned to get back in the car.

Before I could make it, a hard right sent me spiraling. Fire exploded in my jaw, and I looked up to see Amber standing over top of me. I wasn't going to fight her, all I wanted was to get back in the car.

I turned to go, but she kicked me hard in the ribs before I could get away. I fell to the ground, clutching my stomach, and trying desperately to crawl away.

Her voice was like acid as she pulled me to my knees. "All you had to do was help us, but no, you wanted to be a bitch about it. Well, this is what you get." She kicked me again, this time in the mouth, knocking my head back, and causing my mouth to explode with blood.

I hit the ground, my face feeling like it'd been clawed by a bear. Off in the distance, I could see Leon, Kyle, Klenaya, and Yama all engaged in battle.

I wanted to call out to them, get their attention but knew it would be a lost cause. They had their own lions to slay. They couldn't help me now. No one could. She kicked me again, and I instinctively curled in on myself, praying for the pain to stop.

She wasn't letting me off that easy. She rolled me over and kicked me again. "Look at me when I talk to you!" She raised her foot to kick me again, but I turned at the last minute, and she connected with the watery ground instead.

I came up on all fours, blood dripping from my face, turning the water beneath me red. My arms, which were holding me up, begin to tremble and the water under me started a slow, bubbling hiss. More of my blood dripped, and something inside of me started to shatter and crack.

I hadn't wanted to come here in the first place. Hadn't wanted any of this. All I'd done was love a man who could never love me back. I didn't deserve this.

The ground rumbled, and the water began to make small waves. I hadn't wanted to fight. I didn't believe in fighting, but I could feel the rage working its way through my body and knew it wouldn't be long before I lost complete control.

She tried to kick me again, but I snatched her by the hair

and pulled her head back. "Tiis, Grol, Diti!" I head-butted her, making her knees buckle, but I held her up by the hair. "Nst, grul, mui, grol!"

She bled from her nose and mouth, and her eyes showed fear like I'd never seen. "Yia, nst klm, grol, guuo!"

I didn't give her time to answer instead I bared my teeth and then plunged them into the side of her face, ripping her whole cheek out. She screamed loudly, and I spit the disgusting flesh out of my mouth. "Tiis, Grol, Diti!" I clawed at her eyes, pulling them out of her head and squishing them between my fingers. "Tiis, Grol, Diti!"

I knocked her to the side, her bones crushing under my feet as I stepped over top of her. "Dpio."

I walked into the cave. Wasted tacium decorated the walls, and floated in the water. Chaos surrounded me, but I didn't join the fight. I just kept walking.

I found Klenaya and the others up ahead, knew they were trying to talk to me, but I couldn't hear them right now. I had one mission in mind. Greg. I didn't doubt for a minute that he'd be here. This was what he'd been working years for. No way he'd miss out.

I found him and a few other Langunda loading up stacks of tacium on little mobile ships in the next room. "Loveerr booy." I drawled the words, heavily influenced by my mother's native language. "Weeree yoou gooing to leeaave befoore giiviing meee a kiiss?" I rose in the air, my hair standing straight on top of my head. "Give meee a kiiss, loveerr booy." I brought my hand down hard, clawing him across the face.

Leon, Klenaya, and the others had already started taking out the men he was with.

I tore at Greg's face, pulling, tugging, and unleashing my rage. I slammed him to the ground and came down on top of him.

He tried to grab my hands. "Delia! Stop! Please! I love you! All I ever wanted was to make you happy. We can still be together."

He snatched up an overturned package of tacium floating by. "Here, take some, and we can be together forever. We won't ever have to part." He rose to his elbows, with me still on top of him. "You said you wanted a kiss, come here and let me help you remember how it used to be." He reached for me as if to pull me closer.

I recoiled from his touch and everything I knew him to be. He disgusted me, and there was no way he would ever lay hands on me again. I bent his arm back until I heard it crack. "Never again, lover boy." It wouldn't stay broken, but for now, it was enough.

I rose and left him on the ground cradling his arm, shaking and wet. He looked pitiful, and I cursed at my own self. "And this is the man who would do me harm? This is the man who would pass judgment on everything I am?" He tried to talk, but it came out as nonsense and gibberish.

I shook my head. "And this is the man who thought me not worthy." I kicked him to the curb in the corner of the cave. "Goodbye, Greg. Never come near me again."

Leon and the others had disabled the remaining Langunda.

As more Kelm filled the cave, Yama stood up to take charge. He turned to one of the men dressed in the blue and green uniform of Kelm. "See to the arrest of every Langunda you find."

FIVE

Help arrived a few hours after we'd gotten back to the white building. Men and women wearing uniforms the color of their country trampled from room to room getting things in order. Bale was dead smack in the middle, giving orders and directing everything.

He looked weary and dirty, but besides that, just a few cuts and bruises that were rapidly healing. "The jails are full, so now we have to find space to put all these people."

I fell onto a nearby couch. My body ached, and I couldn't stop taking in deep breaths. I didn't think I'd ever been so tired in my life.

Yama sat beside Bale, while Klenaya sat on the arm of their chair. Leon and Kyle sat side by side.

All around us, things were being cleaned up and put back together again. They worked fast and with purpose, probably eager to get back to their normal lives.

So was I. In the fight, I expected that the guards staking out my house and Leon's police station, would have been called back to Langunda to help.

I stayed laying on the couch, too tired to do anything else. "What now?" I asked, hoping he would say we could go home. I'd had just about enough of Langunda and Kelm that I could take.

Yama looked from me to Leon, letting us know that he was talking to us both. "Now you do whatever you like. Stay here, join our military, take a seat on our council. The pay is competitive and the benefits many."

Klenaya, who was now on the floor, dipped her hair in the water, cleaning out the gunk from battle. "Yeah, and if you stay, maybe you can bring some excitement around this boring humdrum place."

Bale exhaled as if all of Kelm rested upon his shoulders. "Who's going to clean that up, Klenaya?" He pointed his finger at her. "You. You're going to clean it up and maybe next time you'll keep your personal grooming to your own chambers."

Kyle laughed, and Klenaya gave him a sour look and then turned back to us. "So what do you say, guys? Will you stay?" she asked.

I shook my head. "Un uh. I want to go home." A lot had happened, and I hadn't had time to process any of it.

There was so much to think about, so many things to put into perspective, and here wasn't the time or place to do any of that. I needed the comfort of my own four walls and the familiarity of my own bed.

Leon cleared his throat. "Tempting as that may be, I think I like the hustle and bustle of my life back home. So yeah, I'll be going back and all."

He took in Klenaya's disappointed face and added. "I reserve the right to come back for visits, though." She beamed brightly then turned to me.

I didn't ever want to come back again, but I found myself agreeing none the less.

"Yay!" She jumped on the couch with me and hugged me around my neck and then went to Leon and did the same. He tried to look annoyed, but I could tell he was at least a little bit touched. "Sure you got this under control?" He asked her father.

"Langunda's rebellion has been squashed," Bale answered.

I sat up, running a hand through my frazzled hair. "How can you be so sure?"

One of the uniformed men whispered something in Yama's ear and then he and Bale conversed quietly. Yama turned to me. "Greg is asking for you. He would like to see you before you leave."

"No." I didn't even have to think about it. That chapter of my life was over, and I had no desire to reopen it.

Bale nodded. "Well, to your other question, Kelm forces, along with three of our neighboring countries have Langunda and its people on complete lockdown."

I thought about that. "What are you going to do with them?" I mean he couldn't kill them, they were immortal, and he couldn't just lock them away forever. At least I didn't think he could.

The look he gave me said I didn't really want to know the answer. "Will you at least stay the night? Get some dinner, and have breakfast in the morning?"

I looked at Leon, and we both shook our head. Good. We were in agreement. It was time to go home.

Bale rubbed a hand over his goatee. "May we call you if we need your help in the future?"

I really wish you wouldn't. "Sure. Just as long as you don't need too much help." They all laughed as if I was joking, except for Leon who caught my eye and winked because he knew exactly what I meant.

"Can I come visit you?" Klenaya asked as we walked toward the room they would send us off in.

"Yeah, me too," Kyle said. "You guys have skateboards there. I only get to skateboard when we go off world."

"We can go shopping." Klenaya piped in.

I hoped they didn't mean tomorrow. "Sure, just give me a couple of weeks to recuperate first, okay?"

She huffed as if I'd ruined the rest of her day. "Okay, if I must."

I laughed and thought maybe it wouldn't be so bad if she and her brother came to visit.

A chain of human-sized containers strolled by, each carrying what I assumed was a Langunda man or woman.

"The ringleaders." Bale let us know. "They won't be seen for a while."

Amber was among them, as was Greg. Amber's eyes were

back, but they weren't healed all the way.

Her face, where I'd torn out a big chuck, was slowly stitching itself back together. She'd be okay soon enough. For now, she looked like something out of a horror movie.

Greg beat repeatedly on his container when he saw me. I stared straight ahead until he passed. The thought of even looking at him sickened me, and I wouldn't give him the satisfaction. Once they were gone, we all stepped into the room that would take me and Leon home.

Bale stood with each of his children at his side. "We want to thank you again. Kelm remembers its friends. Keep that in mind if you ever need anything."

"Yeah," Klenaya piped up. "And I'll be checking on you regularly, so if you do need anything, I'll be sure to let them know."

Yama shook his head looking from me to Leon. "Are you sure you won't stay? We could use people of your caliber around here."

Leon held up a hand. "No. I'm good. Pretty sure the department has already put out an APB. They probably have her," he cocked his thumb my way, "down as my kidnapper. Best get that straightened out as quickly as I can."

I couldn't agree more, because what the hell? Really? Yeah, we needed to get home quick, because I didn't need anything else marring my name.

A few hugs, more promises to keep in touch and finally we were ready. Energy emanated from Yama's hand, and a portal opened in front of us.

Thank you. This was all I'd wanted since the moment we'd arrived. We waved goodbye one more time then simultaneously stepped inside.

Darkness surrounded us again, but this time when we stepped out it was not into a cold watery cell, but to the disarray of my living room.

Someone had tossed the place. Well, it had to have been either the cops or the Langunda. I looked at the broken lamp on the floor and shook my head. For all I knew, it had probably been both.

"I'm going to straighten this out." Leon pulled out his phone and began to punch in numbers, as he took cautious steps down the hall. He was doing what I assumed was a safety check. Which was alright with me.

"All clear," he said, coming back to stand beside me. "I put a call in to the station. Told them I'd explain everything when I got there. Look, I'm going to make sure none of this comes back on you."

I nodded my thanks, and then led him to the door. "Hey, Detective?" I said before he'd gotten too far away.

He turned around, brows raised.

"Don't stop checking on me. I have a feeling I'm going to need someone to keep me in line."

He tilted his head, a slight grin on his face, and then walked on, disappearing after only a few minutes.

I settled in my bed and thought about the last couple of days. I'd found a new side to myself. A side that I wanted to explore more. I knew my mom and sister wouldn't approve, but it was my life, and for once, I was taking control.

PEAR TOWN RUCKUS

ONE

I needed a partner. We'd been playing spades all night and my current one, Aaron, was just wiped out.

He fist bumped with me. "Alright, baby girl. Gotta hit'em in the morning."

"Good game!" I called to his retreating back.

I shuffled the cards, and then scanned the crowd for someone to take his place. The house was packed, but that was nothing new. Three card tables were set up, four pool tables, and every corner held a dice game.

Angry and excited voices sounded throughout the house as people won and lost at their game of choice. The scent of fish, chicken, and alcohol permeated the air, but it was the smoke from the cigarettes and cigars that had me coughing and gagging every couple of minutes.

I needed another win here tonight. If not, I wouldn't be able to pay my rent or utilities. My landlord didn't play around and a five-day grace period was all he was willing to give before he started court proceedings.

Day five was tomorrow. So, If I didn't make the money tonight and hand it over first thing in the morning, I was done for. I'd made enough to pay my electric bill and to eat for the next couple of days, and I would have gladly given all of that to him.

He didn't take half payments, though. With him it was all or nothing, so I needed to make the full amount in order to have somewhere to live after tomorrow.

I'd just about given up hope and was mentally going through a list of shelters when this dude who looked to be in his mid-thirties, just a few years older than myself, with shoulder length black hair, dressed in all black, and about six feet tall, stepped out of the shadows and smiled at me.

I almost choked on my beer at the ridiculousness of it, but caught myself and swallowed at the last minute.

He politely ignored my lack of grace and pointed toward the cards. "How much?"

I took another swig of beer and wiped my mouth with the back of my hand. "Fifteen hundred to sit."

He dropped the cash without even blinking. I sat up a little, a small smile on my face. This was the type of guy I liked to play with. Now we just needed our opponents. Gordon and Rail had called next hand, and those two always had their money straight.

Rail dropped a plate of food in front of me. Rail was tall and skinny, with a beak-like nose and a no-nonsense attitude. His partner, Gordon, was a little shorter and more on the heavy side. "Jinx sent over your fish, Leah," Rail said. "Told her I wasn't your damn servant." He looked to our new friend. "You playing?"

Dude nodded. "Xavier."

My plate held two little cups, one hot sauce, and the other tartar. I poured the hot sauce on my fish and licked my fingers. I had fried taters and onions, but no ketchup. I looked to Rail. "You got jokes. Now give me my damn ketchup."

He held the three packs in his hand. "Call your books out first."

I clicked my tongue at him and then used my telekinesis to float them into my open palm. "Now what were you saying?" I was smug and wanted him to know it.

He gave me a stern look. "No powers at the card table, Leah."

I popped a piece of fish into my mouth. "Sure, Rail." I slid the deck over. "Your deal. We'll bid first."

He winked at me, then cleared his throat. "Well, don't do me any favors."

Rail shuffled the cards a good six times then slid them to Xavier to cut. Around us the sound of gambling and those far into their drinks raged on, at our table it was deathly quiet, as we all looked at our new hands, shuffling and putting things in the order that we wanted.

Xavier looked intently at his cards, he caught my eye, smiled slightly, and nodded. I winked at him to let him know that I got it. At least I thought I'd read him right.

From that little smile and nod, I figured he had a good hand but wanted to give the opposite team a false sense of security. If not, then my next words would mess us up big time. "I can get you two."

"Hmmm." He rubbed a deliberate hand down his chin. "I got four."

I nodded. "Six then."

He made a show of looking over his cards again. "Any possibles?"

"Two, neither strong."

He eyed our competitors cautiously, probably trying to see if they were buying our bullshit. "I got a couple of possibles, but I can't guarantee them. So yeah, six seems safe."

Right on cue, Rail and Gordon began their heckling.

Gordon swallowed down some beer. "Well, Rail, I guess we're in for one boring ass night. Who the hell sits down at a spades game to play it cool?"

Rail pulled out a cigarette and lit it with his fingertip. "Guess we'll have to bid more books just to make it interesting."

I playfully smacked him on the arm. "Hey, no powers at the table. And we're not playing it safe. We're just not being dumb."

Gordon looked at me in disbelief. "And since when is that fun for you?" He took in Xavier's impassive face. "Or are you just trying to impress the new guy? That's not really your style either, baby girl."

I waved his teasing away, not willing to rise to the bait. "You know what? How about this, if we get set, we'll go blind, but you let us look at our hands first." Which would be the dumbest thing any spades opponent could do.

Going blind meant that we didn't get to look at our books before bidding, but whatever we bid was doubled.

Gordon snorted. "That's the opposite of going blind. Bid your hand."

Xavier winked at me, and I smiled, loving this secret game we were playing. "I have somewhere to be later. Give us a ten if it'll move things along," he said.

In any normal circumstances this should have pissed me off, so I pretended that it had. "Thanks, new guy, you probably just got us set."

Getting set was just that, a setback. It meant instead of gaining books we lost them and started the next round with a negative number. A hard place to be in, unless we went blind or set our opponents.

He winked, with a mischievous grin on his face, and I threw out the first card of the game.

We were up eight books when they realized our deception. We wouldn't be the ones being set tonight, not right now anyway. With spades, you went through as many hands as you could until the first team reached the agreed upon score. It wasn't much to lose a hand. We all did that. What mattered was losing the whole game.

Gordon looked at his remaining cards and frowned. "You got us. It won't happen again, but yeah, you got it this time." He took it with ease because that was the nature of the game. Whatever it took to win. That's what I always said.

Twist, one of Jinx's floor workers, brought over another round of beer. Jinx was the owner here. This was also her home. I often wondered how she stood it sometimes, having a house full of gamblers every night. Knowing Jinx, though, she wouldn't have it any other way.

Twist, who looked to be about twenty-five, stood about five feet seven. Skinny as hell, he had piercings up his ears, on his tongue, lip, eyebrow, and chin. He had dark green hair, with red highlights on the tips and black-brown eyes.

I pulled out a few bills and placed them in his hand. "Go ahead and bring another round. I believe these guys be thirsty tonight." I laughed and saw Xavier's lips quirk up in a small smile. I turned back to Twist. "Bring over some pretzels and meat skins. Let's see if we can't amp that thirst up a bit."

Twist nodded but didn't move. Oh, I pulled out a twenty and stuffed it in the waist of his pants. I closed my mouth before I told him to go buy something pretty for himself.

That wouldn't have gone over well I was sure. He left and came back a few minutes later with a bowl of pretzels and a bowl of barbecued meat skins.

He stood again without moving as if he expected me to tip him again. I gave him two dollars. "I can't go broke, Twist. The twenty was good enough." I wasn't sure of success tonight, and if I didn't win, I didn't eat, and I didn't pay my rent, so it mattered that I held on to as much as I could.

He looked like he wanted to argue the point, but in the end, he just gave me a stiff nod and walked away. I turned back to the others. "He already got a twenty out of me. I thought that was being generous."

Gordon waved his hand at Twist's retreating back. "Gave him about thirty dollars myself, tonight. He'll be alright."

We played hard for a while. But when it came down to the last hand it was Xavier and me who were set. I looked over the score. If we went a blind ten and pulled it off, we could win, probably only by a book a two.

Still, a win was a win, and with six thousand dollars up for grabs, I was willing to try anything. I put my hand over my eyes and then flashed both hands at Xavier to indicate what I wanted. He nodded his approval, and I marveled at how well we were getting along so far.

"We're going a blind ten. Go ahead and write that down." I told Gordon, who was the scorekeeper.

His eyes glistened with victory. No doubt he thought we couldn't pull it off. I cracked my knuckles because that just made me want it all the more. He wrote down our bid. "Your game, baby girl."

We were going to lose anyway so why not make a last ditch effort? A blind ten was hard as hell to get, but it could be done.

I'd done so plenty of times before, as had countless others.

We were up eight, with two books still up for grabs. It was very much anybody's game and the mood around the table was tense, as each one of us wanted to leave the table with that six thousand in hand.

I threw out the three of clubs, now just needing my partner to have something to back it up.

Xavier licked his lips, but didn't say anything, only watched the table closely. Gordon threw out the ace of diamonds and my pulse started doing somersaults.

I wiped the sweat from my face and sat up a little more in the chair. We really could win this. It was Xavier's turn now. He already had the card he wanted to play out and face down.

With no preamble he turned it over and tossed it out. Shit. He had the five of hearts. All it took was for Rail to have a higher club, which wasn't hard when all I'd thrown out was a three. Or he could have a spade. Any spade would beat my book and win them the game.

Rail's nostrils flared, and a bit of smoke discharged from his nose. Jaw tight, he threw out the ten of diamonds. It was just what we needed! I tried to hide my excitement, but there was nothing better than a hard-earned win. Even better that we'd actually gone a blind ten and pulled it off.

Since I'd won the last book, it was still my turn. This was it. The card that would determine it all. Either we'd walk away six thousand dollars richer or three thousand poorer. My nerves jumped, making my hands clammy and wet.

I blew out a long breath and then just threw the card out. It skirted over to Xavier who stopped it from hitting the floor and placed it in the middle of the table.

The seven of hearts stared up at me, and my pulse started doing jumping jacks. Now I just needed it to be enough. Gordon wiped a hand across his face and then tossed out the ten of hearts, beating my seven into the ground with a stick.

Not good. I looked at Xavier. He pointedly ignored my panic and threw out the three of spades. Whew, but we still had one more to go. If Rail had any spades higher than a three we were done for.

Twist came to clear our empty bowls away and I stuffed another five in his pocket, to show my appreciation. Rail communicated something to his partner that I couldn't understand, cut his eyes at me, and then tossed the eight of hearts.

It would have won them the game had it not been for my partner's three of spades sitting proudly on the table. Yes! Inside I was singing, but outside I tried to play it cool.

We'd pulled off the near impossible and I sucked in a deep breath, loving the feeling of invincibility that came with that. Xavier's face never changed expressions, so it was hard to know what he felt. I gave him the once over, and heat pooled in my stomach as I wondered if he'd like to celebrate with me later.

His eyes locked with mine, and I raised a brow in silent invitation. He nodded, and I thought we were talking about the same thing, but I couldn't be certain.

Even if we weren't, I'd made more than enough to pay my bills for the next couple of months, and that alone was a reason to celebrate.

Twist came back, and I tossed him another twenty just for the hell of it.

Gordon stood and punched me playfully on the arm. "Good game, baby girl. We'll beat your ass next time. Don't worry about that."

I smiled smugly. "I'm not worried. I got your money in my hand. What's there to worry about?" He shook his head, a small twinkle in his eye.

Rail stood as well. He leaned over and placed a quick kiss on my forehead. "Gonna tell Aaron about this new partner you got here." He crooked a finger at Xavier.

I laughed good-naturedly. "Tell him. Maybe next time he won't be so quick to flip that door knob." He laughed, shaking his head and then he and Gordon headed over to the bar.

That left just me and Xavier. My temperature rose just thinking about the things I would do once I got him home. "You ready?" I asked, anxious to enjoy the rest of my night.

He stood and put his money in his pocket. "A drink first."

A marvelous idea. I motioned Twist back over. "Four whis-key shots and two bottles of beer."

Xavier waited until Twist was out of sight before he raised an eyebrow at me. "You trying to get me drunk, darlin'?"

I opened my mouth and then closed it, because yeah, I was trying to get him drunk, but to be fair, I was trying to get myself drunk as well. "I'm trying to do something," I mumbled.

He still heard me. I could tell from the way his eyes shone, and his lips curled ever so slightly. That look had me breathing hard in anticipation for later.

Twist came back with our drinks. Xavier and I each went for the whiskey first. We knocked our glasses together and then downed them in one gulp.

The liquid was bitter and burned liked hell, sending a warm sensation down my throat. I shimmied a bit, then smacked my lips, letting out an *Ahhh* for good measure.

I picked up the second drink. We knocked them again, then threw those back, before slamming the glasses down.

His eyes held amusement, and I could tell he was enjoying this as much as I was. We picked up the beer bottles. He tilted his my way. "To the game."

I didn't care too much about the game at the moment, but I respected his words. I tilted mine back at him. "To tonight. We can call that a game too." I watched him closely to catch his reaction.

His eyes promised things I hoped his goods could deliver on. "Tonight." He said roughly.

We guzzled our beers and then slammed those bottles as well. It felt good, freeing even, to have someone on the same level as myself. I wondered what he was like in bed. A fire lit in my lower regions; man, I couldn't wait to get him home.

We stood, and I led the way out the door. The cool night air hit us as soon as we stepped outside and I slung my arm around his shoulder in an effort to keep us both warm.

We'd probably walked about six feet when the wind picked up and knocked us both into a brick building.

My arm hit hard, sending ripples of pain from my shoulder

to my fingers. It felt like someone had punctured it with a sharp blade, and I held it tightly to me in an effort to soothe.

Xavier looked a little ruffled but shook it off, his eyes scanning the street for the next attack.

The empty lot across the street had an assortment of rocks, and I called one over to me. I bounced it back and forth, ready to smack whoever upside the head for fucking up my night.

Trash cans were set on curbs up and down the street. Which meant tomorrow was trash day. Xavier held out his hand, and one of the lids rumbled and flew toward him, turning into a baseball bat midway.

I blinked, impressed. Telekinesis along with transmutation made for a powerful combination. I could only imagine the things we could've done in the bedroom. It didn't matter right now. I'd rather have him by my side in a fight than just in my bed for one night.

He looked at my rock. "Want me to make you something pretty, darlin'?"

I threw it in the air, ignoring his condescending remark. "I'd rather you make me something deadly."

He waved his hand, and my rock became a long, curved, shimmering blade. I snatched it up, and swung it back and forward, trying to get a feel for it.

These types of swords were rare and cut with a precision so great they could split a hair follicle down the middle. It was a little heavy, but the more I handled it the lighter it became.

The wind lurched again, knocking our weapons from our hands and flinging them across the street. We immediately shifted so that we were back to back, alert for anything.

Twist stepped out of the shadows and I almost called out to warn him, until he got closer and I noticed the strength of his walk and the determined glint in his eyes. I shook my head as if that would clear the sight of a deranged Twist in front of me. "Twist! What the hell are you doing, man?"

Wind whipped around him blowing his hair back and making his shirt and pant legs flap. "Give me your money." His voice came out hard and flat.

He was an idiot. We were telekineses. It only took a second to call our weapons back. He puckered his lips, probably ready to blow them away again, but I raised my hand and lifted him in the air, I used the other hand to squeeze ever so slightly on his heart, stopping him from any sudden movement.

His eyes popped and his legs kicked, trying in vain to break my hold on him. "Why the fuck do you need my money? I've been tipping your ass all night." I really wanted to know. What did Twist mean by trying to rob me? Someone who knew who he was and where he worked.

He made choking sounds and clutched at his chest frantically. "Why do you need my money, Twist?" I repeated.

Xavier gave me a look that said I should know better. "Let up on his heart, darlin'. He might be able to answer if you do."

Oh. Yeah, there was that. Feeling a little silly at my oversight, I loosened my grip enough for him to speak. "Twist?"

"My... sis... sister," he said, gasping for breath.

I eased off some more. "What about her?" I knew his sister, Laurel. I'd even hung out with her at Jinx's a couple of weeks ago. Come to think of it, I hadn't seen her in a while. I usually ran into her at least two or three times a week, at Jinx's or one of the other places we both frequented.

We weren't really friends, just two people who like the same places. She'd sat down at my card table one night a couple of weeks ago and after the game, we'd gotten together with a few others and decided to hit the town.

She was all right company. Not too bad one way or the other. Still, she was someone I knew and had hung out with recently, so it mattered to me if she was okay or not. "What happened to Laurel?"

"Kidn... kidnapped. She's... been... kidnapped... I need ransom money."

I clicked my tongue. Something didn't add up. Twist was a floor runner. Who in their right mind would assume he had the money to pay off a ransom? I applied more pressure to his heart, making him choke and gasp for air. "Try again."

"Okay.... okay. I'll... tell... I'll tell you... just... just let me down."

I dropped him immediately, not caring about the hard thump his body made when it hit the ground. He came shakily to his feet, holding his chest, and shrinking away from me.

Xavier placed the bat under Twist's chin and lifted his head with it. "Talk." His voice came out low and gravely. Chills popped on my arm because, for the first time tonight, I realized just how dangerous this man could be if pushed. I really wanted to make him release that inner beast but knew now wasn't the time.

Twist deflated like a stuck balloon. "I owe Biles money. He took my sister until I can afford to pay him back."

Xavier and I shared a look. Him questioning, and me pissed. Biles was the lowest of the low. Scum that preyed on the weak and profited off the backs of those less fortunate.

Why the fuck hadn't Twist gone to Jinx for a loan if he needed one? Why borrow from a notorious ball breaker who didn't care who he hurt?

They say great minds think alike and Xavier proved that with his next words. "Twist, Twist, Twist." He sounded like a parent correcting a wayward child. "We both know who you work for, so try again."

Twist hung his head low. "Who do you think I owed the money to? I borrowed from Jinx. Got a few pay advances. She threatened to fire me if I didn't pony up." His voice lowered. "So I went to Biles for the money. Only I couldn't pay him back, not with his two-hundred percent interest rate and all."

I stared hard at him, wondering how he could be so foolish. "Really Twist? Really? Are you on drugs? Why the fuck did you need so much money?"

He didn't answer, and so I guessed I'd hit the nail on the head. "Well, I like to eat and pay my rent and utilities. That's where my money's going. You're not getting it. But I like Laurel enough, so If you want, I'll help you get your sister back."

I gave Xavier a *what are you going to do* look. Because I was pissed that my night with him would be cut short. He wasn't a regular at any of the gaming houses. Which meant I'd probably never see him again. Unless….

"I'll help."

I didn't even try to hide my shock. "You will?"

An easy smile spread across his face, but it didn't quite reach his eyes. "That what you think of me, darlin'? That I could just walk away from a woman in distress?"

He sounded almost offended, but seriously I didn't know him like that. I mean, I was ready to take him home, but that's what's called a no strings, one-night stand.

I licked my lips for what could have been, then straightened. Oh well, the more help, the better, I guessed. Plus, he was a transmutater, which could really come in handy.

I released my hold on Twist, still alert in case he decided to go for broke and try me again. Xavier removed the bat from under his chin and we both waited for him to give us more details.

Twist's eyes glistened and he sniffed and wiped his nose. "I don't know where they're holding her. But I have a couple of clues back home."

Shit, tonight was veering way off course, but sometimes you just had to roll with it. "Fine. Take us to your home. Show us what you've got."

TWO

Twist lived in Liberty View. Liberty View was an apartment community that was often judged as roach and rat infested, rundown trash. Having a few friends who lived there, I knew most of this to be lies.

In fact, the only truth was the roaches. Liberty View did have roaches, but they weren't in every apartment, probably not even in half. As for the other part, I'd never seen a rat in any of the residences I'd visited, and they were far from rundown.

People saw what they wanted to see. Liberty View had two large playgrounds for the kids. It offered multiple after school programs. Its basketball court was built specifically to help the children channel their energy. Also, many volunteers from the community gave up their time and money in an effort to help keep the neighborhood safe and the little ones engaged.

Still, perception was everything. So, the stigma that the people of Liberty View were part animal and not worthy of the most basic of human rights wasn't going away anytime soon.

That's why it wasn't even surprising that the police had swept Laurel's kidnapping under the rug. That's what they did when you came from Liberty View.

A woman was missing, yet I hadn't heard a word about it. No news outlets had covered it. No newspapers had picked it up. No one had been around to question me.

I'd hung out with her not too long ago. I may have had valuable information, but no one had asked. A few well-placed questions and maybe she would have been home by now.

Liberty View housed over sixty, one level buildings, each holding ten two-floor apartments. Twist lived at 212 East Street apartment, six. We walked through the back door, which opened to a small kitchen.

Dishes flowed out of the sink and onto a nearby counter. The trash ran over with empty food containers and crushed beer cans.

I put my hand over my mouth as the smell of rotted food and weeks old garbage made me gag. A small pantry was set off to the right and I didn't even want to know what was in there.

Twist led us into the living room, which was right beside the kitchen. It was a little better in here, the smell was still there, but it was evident that he spent little to no time in here as everything seemed to be in its proper place.

The stairs to the left probably led to a bathroom and a couple of bedrooms. At least that's how most of the apartments were set up.

We took a seat on the couch, which was the only place to sit. No pictures hung on the walls and the only other thing in the room was a small flat screen TV.

Twist stood in front of us, hands shaking at his side. "I got the stuff in my room." He took the steps two at a time and I looked to Xavier to get his reaction.

His eyes were narrowed as he followed Twist's progression up the steps. "What?"

He shook his head, his eyes still on the stairs. "Well, something just doesn't feel right, darlin'. The air around him is shifty. I don't believe a word he says."

I was irritated, and my voice showed it. "I think I've known him a little longer than you, unless you're saying my judgment is off..." I said it like a challenge because that's what it was.

He didn't bite. His eyes took me in briefly, the seriousness in them giving me pause. "I didn't mean it that way, and I think you know that."

"Yeah, well, this isn't exactly the night I'd envisioned, so give me a break."

He chuckled softly, his eyes still focused on the staircase. I couldn't believe he was serious. He acted as if Twist was ready to launch a full-scale assault at any moment.

Twist launched a full-scale assault that next moment. A powerful wind unleashed from upstairs and flew straight toward us.

I dashed to the floor, while Xavier simply turned in his seat. The storm of air missed us at first but then regrouped. This time, it lifted us in the air and kept us suspended there.

To his credit, Xavier never said 'I told you so.' Instead, he kept his focus on the stairwell, which was surely where the next attack would come from.

Twist floated down the stairs, the force of the wind propelling him. Jaw tight, eyes wild and shining, he sneered at me. "Where's my sister, Leah? You were the last to see her alive."

Last to see her alive? Had Twist gone upstairs and puffed on something? Had he actually done drugs while we sat here?

His sister had still been partying when I'd left her a couple of weeks ago. Plus, I thought he said she'd been kidnapped. "Twist, put us down. What the fuck are you talking about?"

He used the wind to pick up a glass figurine and sling it toward my head. I used my TK to aim it toward the wall. The sound of it shattering was enough to distract him and make him loosen his grip on us.

We dropped to the floor, and he whipped around, hand raised, ready to hit us again.

I stood, set to defend myself if need be. "You're acting like a nut case, Twist. I thought you said your sister had been kidnapped."

His face turned to rage, and his whole body shook with it. "She wasn't kidnapped. You killed her. You fucking cunt. Killed her and took all her money."

Oh boy. He really was delusional. What made him think I'd killed his sister and robbed her? Was he serious or just nuts?

Xavier blinked twice, and Twist went from a foaming angry man to a tiny turtle. Transmutation man. I did want to get to know him better. He floated the turtle over and landed him gently on the coffee table in front of us.

He only let him stay that way a few seconds before turning him back.

Returned to his natural form, Twist sat up, eyes wild, nostrils flaring.

He raised his hand as if to strike and Xavier flung him so hard that he put a dent in the wall behind him. "I've just about run out of patience with you, boy. Now tell us what the hell's going on."

Twist got to his feet, hands fumbling in his pocket. "I got this." He pulled out a small jewelry box and threw it across the room, barely missing my face.

I picked it up and turned it over in my hand. What the hell was in here that had Twist convinced I'd killed his sister? With shaky fingers, I lifted the top and then gasped.

I put a hand over my mouth, trying to stifle the scream starting at the back of my throat. This was awful and now I understood Twist's anger a whole lot better. A small tear escaped from my eye, and I wiped it away, still not believing what I'd seen.

Inside lay three long, slim, female fingers, red polish on the nails. I slammed it closed and placed it back on the table. Twist watched me carefully, eyes popping, body trembling. "I didn't do this," I said gently. I was too stunned to say anything else. "Twist, I didn't do this."

I could see the veins popping in his neck and knew he was ready to lose it again. He screamed and spit flew out of his mouth, landing on his face and chin. "They told me it was you!"

"Who?"

He reached into his pocket and threw a sandwich bag full of photos my way. I didn't even have to pull them out of the plastic to see the image of Laurel's lifeless eyes staring up at me.

Bloody black hair flowed around her face, a large wound on the side of her head. I inhaled sharply, I couldn't help it. This was so far beyond what I'd expected to see.

Xavier gently removed the photos from my hands. He shifted through them and then stopped when he came to the last couple. He squinted then raised a brow. "Darlin', I'm sorry, but you need to see this." He handed the pictures back to me.

I bit my bottom lip and tried to prepare myself as I accepted them. Taking a deep breath, I steeled myself for what I was ready to see.

I put a hand over my mouth as I flipped through them. It was me, Laurel, and a few others the night we'd hung out together.

Dozens of photographs, capturing our every move. We'd gone the whole night without realizing we were being stalked. In fact, I hadn't had a clue, and I'm guessing the others hadn't either. But who, and why?

Chills went up my arms and I stood, ready to look out the window. I sat back down, though, not wanting to seem too paranoid. Something hot and heavy settled in the pit of my stomach. How long had they been following me? Were they out there now?

Twist stood stock still, waiting for my reaction. "I don't know what to say, Twist. I really don't. But there are two other girls here." I pointed to the photos. "Why signal me out?"

"Look at the last one."

I stared at him briefly, partly to collect myself, not sure of what I was ready to see, and to make sure he had his emotions in check. Not that I would blame him if he didn't. This was his sister, and these photos were terrible.

I flipped through to the end. It was a picture of me with a red circle around it. This. This was his evidence? Really? "This makes me a murderer. This could mean anything. Come on, Twist, you know better than that."

"They pointed you out. Wanted me to know the truth. Know what you did."

I huffed out a breath, unsure of how to get through to him. "I didn't do this, Twist, but I'll help you find out who did."

That barely contained rage was back full force. "You did it!"

Something wasn't adding up. "I believed you when you said she'd been kidnapped. Why tell me that if you thought I'd killed her?"

He looked at me with disdain, liked I'd disappointed him

greatly and he was finally able to bring me to task. "I gave you a chance! But no, no remorse from you. No guilt." He shook his head as if I was the most disgusting person he'd ever met.

I tried to reason with him. "That's because I'm not guilty of anything. Thank about it. If I'd killed your sister I wouldn't be here now. Think about it, Twist."

"Wanted to see what I knew. Thought you could pick me for information. Thought you could get away with it."

I looked at Xavier, at a loss for what else I could say to get through to him. Twist really thought me capable of this. It was both frustrating and disheartening. The worst part was, I didn't know how to prove to him that I wasn't.

Xavier took us both in. He looked half sympathetic and half like a man who'd thought he was ready to celebrate a big win only to now be caught in a murder mystery that had nothing to do with him. "Let me help you, Twist."

Xavier laced his fingers together. His voice came out warm and persuasive, almost like a lullaby. "I don't know sunshine from rain on this, but I'll do whatever I can to help you bring your sister's killer to justice. I'm offering here. All you have to do is say yes."

Twist gave him a measured look, suspicion in his eyes. "Never saw you around before. Who are you?"

Xavier answered immediately. "Just a card player. Heard Jinx had some of the best games. Thought I'd check it out."

Twist thought about it for a second. A skeptical look on his face, he asked, "And you won't stand in my way if she's guilty."

Xavier looked a little too nonchalant for my liking, but I understood he had to play it that way. "If she killed your sister, then she owes you a blood debt, and I ain't about to get in the way of that."

I thought he was joking. He didn't look like he was, though. Not that I'd killed Twist's sister.

When I'd left Laurel that night, she'd still been partying with Kaylee and Tara. Luckily, they both lived in Liberty View. Kaylee only lived two streets over, so we went there first.

It was four in the morning, but Kaylee looked like she'd just arrived home. She was sitting on her front porch, beer by her side, cigarette in her mouth.

She didn't even look surprised to see us. "What's up Twist, Leah, Dude?" She kept puffing on her smoke and pushing buttons on her phone.

I decided to get straight to the point. "Hey, what did ya'll do after I left that night we hung out at Jim's?"

She looked up from her phone. "What? I don't know, hung out for a bit. Ask Tara, she was a lot more sober than either one of us, remember?" She laughed and ducked the ashes off her cigarette.

My smile was tight. "Yeah, I remember."

She inhaled a little of her smoke. "Why you thinking about that now? Did something happen?"

I wasn't about to get into this with her. "Tell you about it next time." She nodded in a way that said it didn't really matter to her one way or the other, then went back to looking at her phone.

Tara lived two buildings up from Kaylee.

Twist still looked as wild and unstable as ever, so I threw out a few words in an effort to see where his head was. "Believe me now? I wasn't the last one to see her alive."

His hands balled into fists as his strides became more and more exaggerated. "All I heard her say was that she was drunk and doesn't know what happened."

Fair enough. It didn't take us long to reach Tara's. Unlike Kaylee, she wasn't on the porch. I knocked on the door.

The lights were out and the apartment silent. She was probably asleep, but this was too damn important for me not to wake her.

Xavier leaned up against the porch rail, arms folded over his chest. I couldn't get a read on him. Why was he really here? This had nothing to do with him.

Why was he helping? Why not just take his winnings and go home? Before I could ponder it further, footsteps sounded from inside, and an irritated voice asked us what the hell we wanted.

I cleared my throat. "Tara home?"

"No."

"Where she at?"

The voice got even more irritated. "How the fuck do I know? It's four in the morning. Don't come around here no damn more this time of morning or I'ma put the law on your ass."

I didn't blame her. "Sorry," I said, slowly backing away.

Well, that sure as hell hadn't satisfied Twist. He looked more deranged than ever. "Now what?" he asked through gritted teeth.

"She might have gotten lucky, went home with someone. We'll check Jinx's, Jim's, and Top's." Three of our favorite liquor and gambling houses. "See if anyone's seen her tonight."

I turned to Xavier. "You can leave. You don't have to stay for this. It's not your problem."

He looked cavalier as hell when he answered. "Hard to find a good spades partner. You and me, we were in sync in there. Got a big game coming up in a couple weeks. Twenty thousand to sit. Been looking for a good partner. Probably need to keep you alive until then."

I didn't know whether to be insulted or flattered. Probably a little of both. "What makes you think I've got twenty thou? I don't."

He smiled unworriedly. "I'll front you. If we win, I walk away with sixty, you with twenty, that you didn't have before."

An impatient growl from my right reminded me that this was something best saved for later. If I had a later that is. It was becoming increasingly clear to me that Twist was barely keeping it together.

None of the after-hour spots were in Liberty view, not any I wanted to visit anyway. We went back to Jinx's first. Tara wasn't there and we couldn't find anybody who'd seen her.

We hit Jim's and they said she'd just left going to Joy's place. I hadn't thought about Joy's, and by now my feet were starting to ache. Joy lived a few blocks up from Jim's.

Unlike the others, Joy didn't really care if the games spilled out onto her front lawn. A loud dice game went on in one corner of the yard, dominoes in another.

The porch had two card tables on it. One for spades, and one for poker. Tyler, a friend I played with from time to time, pointed at me when I walked up. "You want next?"

I shook my head. "Nah, just looking for Tara. She here?"

He slammed a card down. "Boom!" He looked back at me. "Which Tara?"

"Liberty View Tara."

"She in there." He aimed his head toward the door.

We found her in the back. The smoke was as heavy here as it was in the rest of the house. The smell, not that different than Jinx's place.

All around us was the sound of card games, and other gambling, like dice, and pool. Tara sat on an old yellow couch, a shot of vodka in her hand, a plate of spaghetti in her lap.

I got straight to the point. "When's the last time you seen Laurel? Was it that night we all hung out at Jim's?"

She twirled some noodles around her fork then stuffed them in her mouth. I waited for her to swallow. "You mean when she abandoned me and went off with that dry ass Jeff? Nah, I ain't seen her ass since. Why? She looking for me?" She slurped more spaghetti.

Jeff was Laurel's on again off again boyfriend. Great. Now we had to find his ass too.

We caught up with him in an alleyway two blocks from his house. He had some girl's legs wrapped around his waist, and they were both grunting and moaning.

Oh, boy. This was not good. I could practically feel the rage radiating off Twist. I tried to stop it before it started. "If you kill him, we won't get shit, so…."

His eyes bore holes into Jeff, but he kept his hands at his sides.

I took a step forth. "Yo, Romeo. When's the last time you seen Laurel?"

"What?" Jeff's hips kept moving, brows furrowed, he looked at us as if we'd lost our minds. "I don't know, a couple of weeks. Why?" He picked up the pace and the girl moaned even louder, scraping her nails down his back.

Twist lunged. I grabbed him by the waist and pulled him back, not sure how long he'd let me hold him. "Look, I'm doing everything I can to restrain him, but if you don't start talking soon…"

Jeff's breathing became labored, and he gave a few extra fast pumps, before grunting loudly and letting go. He stuffed himself back in his pants and the woman picked up her purse and took off in the opposite direction. I didn't blame her.

Jeff wiped a sweat-soaked hand across his face. He didn't even have the decency to look ashamed. Hell, knowing him, he probably wasn't. "What you asking me about Laurel for? Go ask that dude she left me for."

Twist narrowed his eyes, and I wasn't sure if he believed Jeff or not. "Some dude caught up to her as we were walking home. Took her back through Almaegrow." Almaegrow was close to Liberty view, only separated by a rail yard.

I shook my head. "And you just let her go?"

"The fuck was I supposed to do? She's a grown ass woman."

"Where in Almaegrow?" I asked before Twist could bring a windstorm down on our heads.

"I don't know. Saw them head over by Pear Town. No way in fuck was I going down there. Fuck it. Fuck her too."

Twist lunged, and I used my TK to hold him in place. I looked back to Jeff urgently. "Run." I didn't have to tell him twice. He took off down the street, skirted around the corner, and disappeared.

I let Twist go. "Believe me now? I didn't hurt your sister."

The look he gave me didn't fill me with much confidence. "Do I believe you could have followed her, waited until she was alone, and then ambushed her? Yeah, I believe that just fine."

Of course. Good grief. Was he never letting this go? I kicked a rock across the street. I couldn't really fault him. This was his sister. She'd been murdered, and the only clue he had was me. Of course, he'd hold on to that for dear life.

I thought back to what Jeff had said. Pear Town. I didn't blame him for not wanting to go down there. I didn't particular want to go down there either.

Pear Town was down under. A city underneath another city. Cops didn't go there. The ones who did never came back. It wasn't just police officers either. Many had gone into Pear Town never to be heard from again.

Pear Town lived by its own rules and they didn't like strangers. It's where those who had no use for law or order had escaped to hundreds of years ago, and they had no plans to come back up top.

A bunch of cops and law enforcement agencies had tried to shut it down once long before I was born.

From what I hear, the death toll had been great on both sides, and since then, Pear was weary of anyone coming in trying to infiltrate their town. So, they did everything they could to keep outsiders out.

Every single time I'd gone down there, I'd had to fight to come back. Not that I went often, but if someone owed me money from a card game, or had stiffed me in some way and thought they could escape to Pear Town and I wouldn't follow, well let's just say they found out quickly how wrong they were.

If Pear had been Laurel's last stop, who knows what really happened to her?

I walked closer to Xavier. "If you go down there, be prepared to fight."

He didn't look bothered in the least. "I know all about Pear Town, darlin'. You don't have to warn me. I've been there my fair share of times."

A feeling of vague uneasiness washed over me. Who was this guy? How did he know about Pear Town? Was he from there?

The questions were endless, but unfortunately, we didn't have the time. I gave him the once over and he stared back, unflinching. I had to ask. "Are you from there?"

"I'm from many places, darlin', but Pear Town ain't one of 'em." He inhaled a big gulp of air. "I get around. Ain't many places I ain't been."

Well, that sounded ominous. We'd talk about it another

time. For now, we had work to do.

THREE

There were many ways into Pear Town, lots of holes in the ground and secret gateways. If Laurel had gone in through Almaegrow, then we would too. I knew a spot.

Through WayWay's house. I pulled out a twenty. You couldn't get into WayWay's house for free. He was used to people traveling to and fro and usually kept two men guarding all exits. I paid my money and so did Xavier and Twist.

We were led down the basement stairs and then down another pair of steps. There was an elevator at the bottom and we paid another twenty just to ride.

I rested my head against the wall and sighed. This was so not how I'd seen my night going. All I'd wanted was to go home and enjoy my new friend. Now here I was, entering Pear Town not even sure if I'd make it out alive.

No streetlights dawned the street. So, with the exception of a few porch lights, we were in total darkness. A few houses sat on either side of the street, a convenience store on the corner.

From the back of the store came two girls and a guy. All three carried baseball bats. Not regular bats. No, that would have been too easy. These were static bats, covered in barbed wire and carrying an electric charge.

From a house across the street came two more guys and another girl. Their eyes blazed and their skin lit up blue and crackled like a live wire.

We were going to have to fight. There was no way around it.

This. This right here was why I hated coming to Pear Town.

There was always a battle. No way to avoid it. Why the hell had Laurel thought it was a good idea to come here? As far as we knew, she could have been killed the moment she'd stepped off the shaft.

Twist pursed his lips and blew out enough wind to lift himself off the ground. He turned in a rapid twisting pattern, whipping up a gust and knocking the three with electric skin off their feet.

Xavier crisscrossed his arms, and the static bats turned to frogs. Stunned, the three Pear residents from the store charged. I quickly tossed them across the street then lifted them in the air and dropped them to the ground hard.

They jumped to their feet and spread out. The female pointed her finger, and a blast of electricity hit me in the chest and knocked me to the ground.

I hit the pavement with a grunt, the asphalt scraping my face and smashing my arm. It felt like I'd bathed in fire for a week, but I didn't have the luxury of indulging it. They were coming for me. All three of them. I had to get up.

Their heavy boots stomped around me. I was in too much pain to move, so I did the only thing I could from my place on the ground. Using my TK, I balled my hand into a fist and cut off their air supply.

They grabbed their throats, choking and gagging. One of the men fell to his knees, his breath coming in short gasps. The other two stumbled but still managed to stay upright.

I had to get them down, but by now my hand was shaking bad, and I knew I wouldn't be able to keep my hold on them for much longer.

I needed help. I looked to Twist, who had the three with electric skin caught up in a whirlwind. Xavier's focus was elsewhere as well. His hands turned in a series of complicated motions, which meant he was ready to transmute the hell out of someone.

I turned my attention back to the two who still hadn't hit the ground. Their knees had buckled, but that was about it. Cutting off their air wasn't working. So this time, I went for the eyes.

The female was the stronger of the two, so I flexed my fingers, and her eyes exploded out of her head. She dropped to the ground, unmoving.

The last guy standing let out a howl like a wolf and then came at me full force. A tree branch by my hand turned into a long silver sword and I worked myself to my knees.

I waited until he was close enough and then stabbed him through the gut. The blade sliced into him, making a swooshing sound as it went. It came out on the other side and I let the handle go, just in time to see him fall.

My hands were covered in blood, and I wiped them across my pants, realizing how disgusting it was. It made me want to choke.

The smell alone was enough to keep me bent over the toilet for weeks. No longer able to stay up, I fell backwards on the street, exhausted. I'd thank Xavier for the sword later. For now, I just needed to rest.

Twist kept his windstorm going and Xavier released his hands, turning the last three into rats. They fell to the ground and then scurried away. They'd turn back in a couple of hours. Transmutation didn't last forever.

Hands on his knees, Twist let out a deep breath. "Shit. I thought they had us for a minute." They'd been six against our three, but we'd worked together as a team, which is probably why we were still standing and they weren't.

Xavier's chest barely moved. He didn't have a hair out of place, and his clothes were still neat and unruffled. He looked like he had just taken a stroll around the block instead of been in a street fight with six to three odds.

I took a moment to get my bearings and then came up to a sitting position. The nerves in my arms felt like they were on fire and my face tingled and burned.

No one else came out of the shadows, which was good because I wasn't sure I'd be able to fend them off if they did.

Xavier and Twist checked our surroundings. Finding nothing, they both came to stand above me.

I could take a hint. Not able to justify sitting any longer, I came to my feet. My legs wobbled and crusted blood stuck to the side of my face. My arm hung at an unnatural angle, and the pain from that had me taking short breaths. The quicker we ended this the better.

Xavier put his arm around my waist, holding me upright as we walked down the street. Any other time I would have rejected the help, but right now I was just glad that he'd offered.

Our eyes scanned our surroundings making sure we were alert for anything. In Pear Town, you had to constantly be on your guard.

The farther we walked, the heavier and more oppressed the air became. The scent of rotted food and animal feces permeated the air, filling our nostrils and making us gag.

It was never a smell I could get used to, but one I knew to expect whenever in Pear Town.

Misshapen buildings and rundown homes greeted us from both sides of the street. Rats and other type rodents scurried about, rustling through the discarded trash that lined the road.

I had a few friends in Pear Town and figured it was best to talk to one of them instead of romping about undirected and getting into more fights.

Sheena owned a beauty shop in downtown Pear. Her customers were mostly strippers from the club next door coming in between sets to get their hair, makeup, and nails touched up.

On the weekend, Sheena took verve pills. Depending on their dosage, verve pills could keep you up for days.

Sheena's shop, *The Wrap Around*, never closed on Friday, Saturday or Sunday and Sheena herself never slept on those days. Servicing one customer after the other, she was almost like a machine in her efficiency and professionalism.

The building in which she housed her business was a small two-story clapboard. The shop took up the first floor. Her living quarters covered the second.

We slipped in through the side door. The place was a little cramped, but she still had six booths set up, a sitting area, a kitchen area, and multiple hair washing sinks. Brown and beige wallpaper decorated the walls, the floor the same color.

Sheena had a worker on either side of her. One doing nails, the other doing hair, and Sheena herself doing a client's makeup.

Blush brush in hand, she looked up when we walked in. "Come to get your eyebrows plucked? They need it."

I waved her insult away. "Hey, you know Laurel, right? Twist's sister. You seen her lately?" The woman in the chair bit her bottom lip, then diverted her gaze to the floor. The air shifted to tense, and I knew right away she knew something.

Sheena shook her head. "Nah, I ain't seen her. Look I got clients lined up out the door. I gotta get back to work. Your papers are in the back room." She dropped the brush and assured her client she'd just be a minute.

She let us through the door that led to her private residence and closed it firmly behind us.

She talked in a hushed whisper, her voice short and frightened. "Look, I saw her go in the club a couple of weeks ago. There's a new player in town. Been taking over all the major money-making businesses.

"This one is smart. There's no strong arming going on. Lots of money's being exchanged. You know how we get down in Pear. Someone coming in and trying to violently take over we'd crush 'em. They went a different route, though, and they're making progress. "

I thought about that. The strategy was smart. "So they're still taking over, just going about it in a way that keeps the people happy and their pockets filled. When all is said and done, though, this person will still own most of Pear Town."

She nodded. "Folks in Pear Town are pretty smart. We know exactly what they're doing. But these people are ruthless. Try not to sell and everything you love mysteriously disappears. It's a bad business, but no one can prove that they're the ones doing it."

She stopped for a minute and turned all her attention to Twist. Her face softened, and her eyes spoke of the heartbreak she might have seen reflected in his. "Leave this alone, Twist. Go home. There's no good that can come from you pushing this."

I gave her a sharp look. Something about her words and her stance put me on guard. Sheena had always been straight with me, so this was more than a little disconcerting. "Sheena?"

She wouldn't even look at me, but her voice was strong when she spoke. "Just get the hell out of here. Go home." She walked out the door without looking back.

That left me stunned. Just what the hell was going on down here? I wondered if they'd approached her about selling yet. She'd carefully managed to keep the discussion away from her own business. I couldn't help but wonder why.

We stayed in the back room, not sure of what our next move should be. I took a seat on the steps that led up to her apartment.

One of Sheena's work girls came in, a basket in her hand. She handed it to me, and then walked back out, never uttering a word. I shook my head, talk about dramatic.

FOUR

Sheena hadn't batted an eye when she'd taken in my rumpled clothes, limp arm, and battered and bruised face. Probably because that's how I always looked when I saw her.

There was always a fight to get into Pear Town. She knew this. So I guess she just had a basket ready for whoever might come stumbling through her door. That, or she'd taken one look at us and decided we were in need of some serious help.

The basket held several bottles of water, three verve pills, a couple of rags, alcohol, and antiseptics. I threw a pill in my mouth and washed it down with some of the water. The rest of the water I poured on one of the rags and used it to wash my face and hands.

The verve would not only pep up our energy, but also escalate the healing process. It didn't take long to take effect, and I could already feel my body tingling as the pill worked its way through my system.

Twist swallowed his pill and then poured the rest of the bottle over his head. He shook his hair from side to side and water splattered on my face and neck.

I wiped it off with my rag and tried not to call him an asshole, as I was sure he'd done it on purpose.

Xavier took his pill dry and put the unopened bottle in his back pocket. "So we go to the strip club then?"

I looked to Twist. "Can we safely agree now that I didn't kill your sister?"

"Why send me her fingers with a picture of you circled, then? What do you have to do with all this? You have to know something."

I wasn't sure if that meant he believed me or not.

Xavier took his water out and downed it in one gulp. He wiped his mouth with the back of his hand and then dropped the empty bottle back into the basket. "I think it's a trap."

I thought about that. I guess it could be a trap. Anyone who knew me knew that I hung out at Jinx's.

Anybody who'd ever been to Jinx's knew that Twist worked there. So it wouldn't have been too hard to get us both together.

The question was why? Also, what did Xavier have to do with all this? Was it a coincidence that he'd just happened to pop up tonight of all nights?

I ran a hand through my hair. "How are we going to play this? Somebody obviously wanted us here. Let's go find out why."

I stood. The verve had taken its full effect by now and it felt like my insides had been hit with a bolt of lightning. That's the thing about verve. You had to do something with that energy, if not, you'd be literally bouncing off the walls.

The club was right next to the shop, so we didn't have far to walk. There was a fifty-dollar cover charge, which we paid at the door.

The smoke hit me as soon as I walked in, but instead of sending me into a coughing fit as it normally did, the verve in my system made it pass through me like a crisp breath of fresh air.

No one danced on stage, but the tables and chairs were full. Which meant they were probably between set takes. We'd only walked about three feet when a clean-shaven man stopped us from going further.

I didn't clock him as a resident of Pear Town, and I wondered if he was a part of the group in the process of trying to take over. "You don't look like you're here for the show."

I didn't try to deny it because he wouldn't have believed me anyway. "We're not. We're looking for a friend. Laurel. Last place she was seen was here."

His face stayed impassive. "Think I know who you're talking about. Follow me." He walked toward the back.

Unease made my steps slow. That was way too simple and everything in me told me it was a trap. He led us to a red door at the end of the hall and opened it.

"Be ready," Xavier whispered under his breath, but loud enough for Twist and myself to hear.

Twist went in first. His sharp intake of breath had me charging into the room, Xavier right behind me.

I stopped short when I saw what was before me. I was sure my eyes looked as if they were ready to pop out of my head. They sure felt like they were.

Twist was on his knees, face buried in the lap of a woman sitting behind a massive desk. That woman was Laurel, and she had all her fingers and looked alive and well. Twist was weeping openly and repeatedly saying that he'd thought she was dead.

Something soured in my stomach as I took in the scene before me. Twist was ready to get his heart broken again, I knew it as sure as I stood there.

The fact that she was the one sitting behind the desk, that she hadn't let him know that she was alive, that she'd appeared at the same time as this new adversary, filled me with cautious hesitation.

Her eyes locked with mine, and I almost flinched from what I saw there. Emptiness. She looked empty and devoid of any feeling.

Had she always been that way? I'd never really paid attention. "Whose fingers did you cut off and why the theatrics?" I asked, because those fingers had been real, which meant that somebody was dead. The photos they could have manipulated, but not the fingers.

She knocked her brother away and stood. "Would you have come if I'd sent you an invitation to a tea party?" She shook her head. "Sorry, dear, I don't do tea parties." She sounded deranged, especially if she thought that shit made sense.

She walked to the front of her desk and sat. "You have to die, Leah." She shrugged as if this was completely out of her control. "Sorry, I don't make the rules."

Beside me, Xavier bristled and I put my hand on his arm to tell him to chill. We needed more information. Right now, I had no clue what we'd walked into.

"Laurel?" Twist came up from his spot on the floor. He wiped his eyes with his shirt sleeve then looked from me to his sister. "What are you doing? Why did you let me think you were dead?"

She didn't even look at him, just raised her hand and blasted him with wind so strong that it had to be hurricane force.

It lifted him in the air and banged him against the wall. He fell to a crumpled mess on the floor and for his sake I needed him to stay there.

He wasn't dead. The verve in his blood stream would protect him, but she hadn't known that. If she was willing to kill her own brother...

I came to my full height. "Whose fingers did you send me?" I growled.

She waved a hand toward the door. "Just one of my hoes."

The verve had me jumping. If she wanted a fight, I'd damn well give her one. "What do you want, Laurel? What's your endgame?"

She snapped her fingers and a door to the side opened, bringing in two men and one woman. They had collars around their necks, and cuffs on their hands and feet.

The man behind them pushed them to their knees, and they went down hard. Their clothes were matted to them, hair dirty and tangled, like a crow's nest.

The sickening crunch their knees made when they hit the floor made my ears pop in despair, as they were already just skin and bone.

Yet, worst of all was the hopeful look in their eyes that said they thought I could save them. I wasn't as sure as they were, and that hurt more than anything.

I swore under my breath. Had I had more verve pills they could have been allies. As it were, they were just three more people we had to try to keep alive.

Laurel stood taller, sparing only a quick glance at her brother's battered form. "Leah? You remember that night we hung out?" She walked to the wall behind her desk and pulled down a blown-up picture of me.

It was the same photo that had been circled in red and I looked at her hoping to finally get some clarity on the issue.

Wind whipped around her as she stared at it, and I wondered if she was about to lose control. What the hell was it about this picture that made her so angry? "We were talking about Pear Town and you were laughing. Bragging about how many of these residents you'd killed. You'd murdered fathers, sons, wives, mothers, and sisters, and you thought it was funny. How long did you think you'd get away with it?"

Get away with it? Was she even serious? "Stop being ridiculous. You know it's a fight to get in here and a fight to get out. Come on, now."

She shook her head. "Not for me it isn't. Twist and I have family here. Spent many holidays and school vacations here. You came down here, killed people's families, and then you sat in a bar and laughed about it." Papers flew off her desk and the chair she'd been sitting in tipped over.

I looked at her incredulously. "Your brother, Twist, who you just assaulted." Talk about irony.

I pointed to where he lay motionless on the floor and tried to tell myself that the verve was still working. "Your brother along with us." I motioned to myself and Xavier. "We were jumped the moment we stepped off the lift. Where were all those friends and family that cared so much about him?"

She didn't even look bothered that I'd told her, her brother had had to fight for his life, considering she'd just tried to kill him, I guessed she wasn't. "Well, he hasn't been down here in a while."

The more she talked, the more I became convinced that she'd truly lost her mind. "Laurel? What is this?"

She pointed to the chained victims on the floor and then to me. "You four are the worst offenders. I targeted you that night. Had someone watching your every move." Ah, so the picture taking had been her idea then. Her trying to learn me so she could find a way to lure me down here.

I shook my head. Who knew it'd be her own brother she'd used.

She looked back to the three on their knees. "They've already been read their rights. Now you will be too."

She snapped her fingers, and the doors on the opposite side of the room opened. A group of Pear Town residents filed in. Some looked and smelled as if they'd bathed in the sewer for a week. Others like they'd just stepped out of Sheena's shop, with varying degrees in between.

She motioned to a man and woman who stood side by side, glowering at me. "You killed their brother. He was on his way home with groceries when he ran into you." She pointed to the next group. "You killed their daughter and son."

The air became tense as the people she signaled out tried to keep their anger in check. This was a lot worse than I'd thought. I'd never doubted my ability to walk away from a fight. Looking at the furious faces of some of these residents, I wasn't so sure I'd be leaving this place alive.

I went for honesty because it was the only thing I had. "Laurel, I never went after anyone that didn't come at me first." I'd never once stepped into Pear Town and not had to defend myself. I wouldn't let her paint me as some crazed person who came down here killing for fun. The whole idea was ludicrous.

If I'd thought my words would help, I couldn't have been more wrong. If anything, they only enraged her more. Wind lifted her off the ground, her eyes wild and unfocused. "So you admit you'd do it again? Did you all hear that? Given the chance, she'd kill your loved ones again."

Jeers sounded throughout the crowd, and a few residents moved in closer. The tension ramped up tenfold, as everyone seemed ready for a fight.

Xavier stood beside me, hands unleashed, teeth bared. At least he was on my side. For now, anyway. Good, because I wasn't going down without a fight. "If challenged I will defend myself," I let them know. It was a warning, and the only one they were getting because I would never apologize for saving my own life.

Laurel strutted in front of me, hands on her hips, the wind keeping her off the ground. "Think you can beat us all?" It was a challenge if I'd ever heard one.

I decided to ignore it. "So you're the new buyer in town?"

She glared at me. "What do you know about it?"

"I know enough."

She shrugged. "Doesn't matter." The wind lifted her even higher. "This is my town now." Her voice turned low and threatening. "Try to stop me." She came at me.

I ducked low and used my TK to slam her against the wall. She hit hard enough to dent it, then crumbled to the floor.

Twist jumped up, bringing a windstorm with him. He spun in the air and sent many residents flying. He landed on his knees and then jumped full force into the fight.

I flexed my hands and the chains on the captives fell away. They looked shocked at first, then scurried to the corner, too weak to do anything else. I wanted to shield them, but I had to get back into the fight.

All around me, residents turned into flies and grasshoppers. So I knew Xavier was doing his thing. I tried not to step on any of them. They'd turn back to themselves later. If luck was on our side, it would be after we were already safely back home.

Laurel bounced to her feet. She looked around for a minute, hair flying, eyes wild. She spotted her brother, holding his own against a man twice his size. The man thrashed and kicked as Twist lifted him off the ground.

Laurel used her wind to knock Twist off the man. He rolled for a minute then came to his feet, whipping around to face his sister. Before she could make another move, Twist called out to her, his voice pleading. "Laurel, stop this! I don't want to fight you!"

Her eyes flashed hard, and her face contorted to something between painful and resigned. "Then join me, Twist. Join me or get out of my way."

His face softened, but his eyes stayed tortured. "They didn't hurt her, Laurel. Not these people. Not Leah. Stop this."

For a minute, she looked like a lost little girl, not sure of her next move. Then her face hardened, her features twisted with disdain. "She was your sister too, Twist, or don't you care at all?"

Tears slipped from his eyes and this time when he spoke it was in a painful whisper. "She wouldn't want this. To see you like this would break her heart."

"Don't you tell me what she would want! They killed her! In the street like a dog! People just like Laurel and these other three."

She pointed to the corner where the newly released victims all huddled together. "They come from up top, murder our love ones, and then go back home to laugh and brag about it. They killed our sister Twist! They killed our sister!"

Rage blurred her eyes, and she shook from the force of her anger. I didn't know either of them well enough to know they'd even had another sister, but a lot of stuff was starting to make sense now.

Two men came at me and I shoved them back, intent on hearing more of the conversation.

"I remember." Twist said, voice low like it hurt to even breathe. "I also remember how I'd found you that night. Blood-ied and broken. Do you know how hard it's been thinking I'd lost another sister? Watching Leah every day, plotting my revenge, thinking she was the one who'd killed you? Do you know how hard that's been?"

Her face said she didn't really care. "Then you should have killed her, Twist. How many of us has she killed already?"

He shook his head. "This is not our home, Laurel. We be-long up there." His finger pointed toward the ceiling.

This only set to enrage her more and she lifted him in the air and tossed him across the room. "Our father was from here. Our sister lived and died here. Traitor! How could you turn your back on your own people?" She talked as if they hadn't just tried to kill him.

Twist came to his feet, but before I could see his reaction, something hard and heavy hit me in the back. I fell forward, but used my telekinesis to stop my fall and then pivoted around.

A woman with red hair and bright purple eyes stood with a large stick raised to hit me again. I snatched it from her, then telekinetically used it to smack her upside the head.

The crack of her bones sickened me, and I turned away, my stomach clenching at the sound. She fell to the ground, blood pouring out of her wound, looking a lot like that fake picture Twist had shown us of Laurel.

That revelation stopped me in my tracks. Was Laurel so wrong in what she'd said? A look around the room saw people fighting for loved ones they'd lost. Didn't they have the right to avenge them? Wouldn't I? At the same time, should I've just laid down my life and let them take me out? Didn't I have a right to fight to live?

I didn't have time to think on it long, as two more residents came at me. I squeezed my hand, cutting off their breath and dropping them to the ground. My mind was in turmoil, and the only thing I wanted was for this night to be over.

The door to the left exploded, and Sheena and eight of her girls rushed into the room. They helped the three who'd been chained to their feet, and one of the girls whisked them away.

Good. At least that'd been taken care of; Now I could focus more on the fight.

Sheena and her girls joined in, ripping and tearing apart everything around them. I was grateful for the help but didn't have time to address it.

The man whose brother I'd killed hit me in the face, his fist hard and solid. I fell back, my right eye stinging. Before I could hit the ground, the sister came at me from the back and busted me upside the head.

The verve helped me shake it off, and I jumped back, ready for more. I didn't have to do anything, though, as Twist lifted them both by the neck and slammed them to the floor.

His eyes locked with mine, and all I saw was sorrow, and maybe a little guilt. We were here because of him. Because he'd been misled. No doubt he thought this was all his fault.

It wasn't. We'd each made our own decision to come here.

Twist loved his sister and had wanted to know what had happened to her.

How could I blame him for that? Especially when any one of us would have done the same for those we loved. That's what this whole thing was about. People fighting for those who could no longer fight for themselves.

That did touch me, but I wouldn't be a victim to it. They'd fought me and I'd protected myself. I'd never meant to kill anyone, but in Pear Town it was always, kill or be killed. So I'd always done what I had to in order to stay alive.

Would I be more careful in the future? I'd sure try. But if it came down to it, I would defend myself. That hadn't changed. I'm not sure it ever would.

The verve in our systems kept us going long after we should have expired. All around us the fight raged on. People turned into birds and snails, wind whipped back and forth, and electricity crackled through the air.

Everyone seemed to be doing their part, but I had no way of knowing if it would be enough.

Finally, the room thinned and the dust cleared. Most of Laurel's people had been taken out or turned into small animals. The few who hadn't were under the control of Sheena and her girls, Laurel included.

Undoubtedly, Sheena and her crew had taken verve before coming here, which put them at an advantage over Laurel and the others. Sheena had them all hog-tied on the floor. A few tried to break free, but wounded and hurt, their powers barely made a spark.

Laurel's eyes promised vengeance, her face hard, and unflinching. This wasn't over. Not for her, it wasn't. I could almost see her plotting her escape. Something hard and heavy settled in the pit of my stomach. She may have been subdued, but something told me we hadn't seen the last of this one.

That was for another day. Right now, I just wanted to go home. "You got any more verve?" I asked Sheena. I could feel the effects of the first pill wearing off, as we'd probably pushed it to its limit. It usually lasted much longer, but the fighting and excessive use of powers had sapped the damn thing dry in a matter of hours.

She shook her head like she couldn't even believe I was asking. "Come on, Leah. I gave you what I could."

I nodded. That was fair enough, but we still had to make it out of Pear Town alive. Sounds from the hallway caught my attention, and a hail of Pear residents flew into the room.

They were with Sheena, as they quickly looked to her for what to do. She turned her attention to me and nodded toward the door. "Get out of here while you still can. We've got this. They'll be no take over as long as I'm alive."

Twist had his hands on his knees, his breath coming in short spurts. Xavier had a small wound on his side. He pressed a hand against it, trying to stop the blood flow. I needed to make sure they were leaving with me, as we had a better chance of making it out of here alive if we stuck together.

Maybe we wouldn't even have to kill anyone to make it home. The thought of doing so left me cold. Probably for the first time in my life, I vowed to take the passive route and not fight unless I absolutely had to.

Xavier and Twist made their way toward me, but Twist stopped when we got to where Sheena had Laurel under foot. "What's going to happen to her?"

Sheena gave it to him straight. "Jail, for her and her cohorts. My crews are throughout the city as we speak, gathering them up."

Which meant this had been planned for a while. I gave her a curious look, trying to figure out how much she'd known, and how much she'd guessed at.

She stared back at me, unflinching. "Been on this since the beginning, Leah. All we needed was a jump off point."

I thought back to what she'd said earlier. The people of Pear Town were smart. I couldn't help but agree, yeah, I guess they were.

FIVE

The streets were full of fighting and vandalism. Buildings burned, causing thick black smoke to pollute the air making us cough and gag. Store windows had been smashed and glass littered the street.

The verve must have still been working a little as Xavier's wound had all but closed.

Bolts of lightning, turbulent wind, and a mix of other powers flew all around us, making our steps rocky and unsure. We walked with purpose, determined to make it to our destination unscathed.

A rock hit me upside the head and though it hurt like hell, I kept going. The last thing I wanted to do was fight if I didn't have to. The only thing I wanted was to make it home, uninjured and with no more loss of life.

This place was in an uproar, and though it looked bad, I felt confident that Sheena and her crew had it under control. It wasn't my business, and I wasn't sticking my nose in it. No more than I had to anyway.

There was a lift on Peach street that would take us back up. It wasn't easy getting there. Loud booms and screams from the battle dogged our every step, and we had to stop more than once to defend ourselves. We didn't kill anyone, at least I tried very hard not to.

What should have taken ten minutes, instead took two hours. Finally, we made it, and I'd never been happier. Once inside the lift, I sagged against the wall, glad to finally be leaving.

We came up in the middle of the woods on the north side of town, more than twenty miles away from home.

There was no way in hell I was walking that far. I didn't think any of us could. I picked up a tree branch and tossed it at Xavier. "Turn this into a car and carry us home."

He didn't even blink. A few complicated hand movements and we were on our way. Twist sat in the back, balled up and breathing hard. I climbed back there with him, aiming to offer what comfort I could.

I reached out to touch his back, then stopped midway, unsure. Telling myself to suck it up, I took a deep breath and put a tentative hand on his shoulder. He tensed immediately but didn't pull away. "I'm so sorry about your sister," I whispered. "We're going to get you home, okay."

"I'm okay," he sniffed, and I decided to leave it at that.

We dropped him off first and watched as he fumbled with his keys. He finally got them working right, then opened his front door and stumbled inside. Xavier waited until Twist flipped a light on then pulled back into traffic.

He drove to the end of the street and then stopped. "Where do you live, darlin'?" Oh, yeah. That's right. I'd forgotten that we'd never actually made it to my house. I gave him directions and then laid back against the headrest.

What a helluva night. Thank goodness it was finally over. The sun began a slow rise in the sky, daybreak just over the horizon. The world would be waking up now. People would be pouring their coffees and getting ready to start their day.

Me? Well, I planned on sleeping for the next week and a half. If I could get away with it, which I probably couldn't. I'd have to hit up another game before long. It just wouldn't be anywhere in the city limits this time.

Xavier pulled up to my house and cut the engine. I didn't know what he had on his mind, but I was quick to set him straight. "No sex. I'm too damn tired, but you can come in and get a little rest before you have to hit the road again."

He patted the wheel. "That's mighty kind of you, darlin'.

Tell you the truth, I'm a little tired myself, wouldn't want you to be disappointed, now would we?" I ignored him as we got out of the car and walked up to my front porch.

I pulled out my keys and turned them in the lock. "How about we just call tonight a draw, how about that?"

He smiled broadly, his eyes lighting up like I'd just issued him a challenge. "I think that's a fine idea, darlin'. After all, there're many more games to be had."

Yes, there were, and I planned on playing as many of them as I could. Starting with the high stakes game he'd told me about earlier. That was a lot of money, and no way was I letting it slip through my fingers.

Neither was he, judging from the fact that he'd stayed and fought with me in Pear Town only because he liked my skills at the card table. At least that's what he wanted me to believe anyway. I had my doubts, but that was something to be discussed at a later date.

My house opened into a living room, and I flipped the lights on so that he could better see where he was going.

Xavier took a curious glance around. "You want me on the couch?"

Whether he meant it as a double entendre or not, I chose to ignore it. Walking right past him, I dragged myself toward my bedroom. At the last minute, I turned and motioned for him to follow.

I fell onto my bed fully clothed, pulling him down with me. "Sleep," I mumbled, before closing my eyes and doing just that. His big arm wrapped around me and I leaned into his embrace, grateful for the comfort after such a long and tiring day.

Tomorrow would bring its own set of problems, but for now, Pear Town was safe, and Twist at least knew where his sister was. There was a lot of healing to be done there, and I wasn't sure Twist would ever get his sister back. Not the way he wanted her anyway.

As for Pear Town? Well, I didn't plan on going down there for a very long time.

BELLE OF THE BALL

ONE

Feet hit pavement as I ran as fast as my legs would carry me. The cold sliced through me, chilling me to my bones and making me shiver with every step I took.

Man, what I wouldn't give for a good thick, winter coat. Hell, even a warm sweater would be better than the rags that hung from me now.

Still, I trudged forward, knowing if I didn't make it to the shelter in time, I'd be locked out for the night. Not only would I be forced to sleep in the cold, I'd also go to bed on an empty stomach again. The last thing I'd eaten had come out of the dumpster beside the library. I didn't want to have to go there again.

I arrived gasping for breath, taking in the large building that housed the shelter. Jones, the night guy, looked at me sadly and shook his head. "Sorry, Kerry, just let the last one in." I felt like crying. It took everything in me not to fall to my knees and beg.

Squaring my shoulders, I gave him the best smile I could muster and walked away. Begging would do no good, I should know, I'd tried it many times before.

It hadn't always been this way. Once I'd had a good job as a weaver, with good benefits, and in my mind, I was an upcoming star. Well, maybe that was exaggerating it a bit, but before the old mill had closed, it'd employed over half of my city at one time or another. With a population of just over fifty thousand, I thought that was saying something.

It wasn't very hard to meet someone, who, if they themselves hadn't worked there, they at least had family, friends, or even acquaintances who had.

In my small city, "the mill" had at least six different buildings set up at one time. Large industrial places, each employing workers in the thousands.

I'd gone there straight out of high school, as had many others. Three months later and I'd put down the payment for my first car. Three months after that, I had my own place, leaving my parents' house for the freedom of my own.

They were gone now, my parents. They'd both worked at the mill until they'd retired. Hell, they'd met there, so I guess it was fitting.

The short end of it was, it closed, and left many of us hanging by a nail. Some regrouped and scooped up openings at one of the many other factories in town. Some went back to school. Me? I sunk deeper and deeper into a depression so great that it ate me from the inside out.

I never tried, not really. By that time both my parents were gone, I had no other family, and I just didn't feel as if I had a reason to go on. I stood by in unmovable indifference as my house, car, and everything else I owned were taken away from me. I didn't care.

At first, sleeping on the street was a cold comfort to where I thought I should be. That was two years ago when I'd been twenty-four. Now, a little older, well, now I was just cold.

Stomach aching from the lack of food, I headed to one of the benches in front of the library. I'd try to be up before daybreak. I didn't want to be here when the staff arrived. In fact, I took great care to avoid them. The look of pity in their eyes was just too much for me to bear sometimes.

I'd probably been shivering in and out of sleep for a good fifteen minutes when a hand on my shoulder jerked me awake.

Damn it! Did I oversleep again? I could swear I'd just lay down. "Okay, I'm going. I'm going." I came to a sitting position, body cold and head swimming. I had to make it to the shelter today. No way could I withstand this weather for another night.

Once I got my bearings and could to stand, I realized two things: One, it was still too dark to be morning, and two, the clock on the Sears building said it was only three a.m. Before I could ponder that further, I heard laughter coming from my left.

"Not need to rush off, Kerry. I just wanted to talk to you for a bit."

It took a second for the face and voice to make its way through my sluggish brain. When it did, I squinted my eyes so that I could get a better look. "Ed?" I said, finally recognizing the gray-haired, long-bearded man in front of me. Like me, he was a street dweller, someone I'd talked to from time to time throughout the last couple of years.

I sat back down, and wrapped my arms around myself, trying to stave off the cold. "Haven't seen you in a while, Ed. What's been going on?"

"This." He flipped open a small, oval shaped device and pointed it at me. Something that looked like a portal opened, swirling blackness that kept getting closer and closer.

Heart in my throat, I jumped up, trying desperately to get away. Ed stood in front of me, blocking my escape. "I just want to help you, Kerry. Now you have to go." He pushed me inside and suddenly I was twisting and turning through a large, empty space. Rigid with fear, I closed my eyes, thinking maybe this would be the end of me.

With nothing to hold onto, I was basically in a free-fall until my body landed on a hard, solid surface.

I sat up immediately, eyes searching, looking for anything familiar. All I saw was a brightly lit room, housing a TV, couch, loveseat, and recliner.

"Well come on, sweetie, get off the floor, we can't get anything done with you down there, now can we?"

I looked up to see a medium height, medium built woman dressed in red staring down at me. Brown hair, tinted with hints of gray covered her head. She had on red and gold earrings and a big smile on her face.

I had no idea who she was, but she didn't appear hostile, so I decided to try my hand. Maybe she could even help me get out of here. "Where am I?" I stood up, hoping to put us on more equal footing.

She held her nose and stepped back a few steps. "Have you smelled yourself lately? My God, a trash sewer smells better than you."

"Well, it's not like there's an abundance of baths and showers out on the street," I deadpanned.

She nodded, her features softening just a bit. "Yes, yes, Ed told me all about you. We'll talk about that when you're done. First things first. Let's get you cleaned up."

Ed, the man who'd brought me here? I'd forgotten about him. "Look, lady, I don't know what's going on but--"

"Come now, Kerry. You're not giving my wife a hard time, are you?" Ed came into the room and stood beside the woman in red, whom I assumed was his wife.

I gave him the once over. There was something different about him... Ah, it took me a minute to realize what it was. He was clean, the beard was gone, and he didn't stink.

I'd been played. I knew that as well as I knew my own name. Anger turned my hands into fists, and I took a couple of steps forward, not able to stop myself. "What the hell did you do? What gave you the right? And how the hell did you get so clean!"

Ed looked at me with disappointment. "Now, now, Kerry, we've been friends too long for all of this." He stared at me with those same kind eyes that had first drawn me in. "How about a nice bath? Hmmm? Doesn't that sound good?" He sounded placating as hell and I wasn't buying it.

He went on as if he hadn't noticed the enraged look on my face. "A hot bath and even hotter food in your belly. We'll talk after that, okay?"

No. Not okay. I didn't even know where I was. I didn't know who they were. My stomach growled, and I realized that the promise of a hot meal wasn't such a bad idea.

Ed and his wife had been nothing but kind so far. But common sense told me they'd kidnapped me for a reason. I had no plans of sticking around to find out what that reason was. Just the thought of it made my skin crawl.

So I'd play their game for now, but as soon as I got the chance, I was out of there.

"I could take a bath, and it's been awhile since I've had a hot meal," I said, in a calm voice that in no way conveyed my plans for later.

Ed's wife smiled kindly and then motioned for me to follow her down the hallway. We walked into a large bathroom, with brown walls and brown floor tile to match.

In the middle of the floor sat the biggest bathtub I'd ever seen. It looked like a mini pool, except for the clawed feet. It wasn't hooked to any plumbing that I could see, which led me to believe that the water came from underneath.

The bathroom itself smelled fruity and clean. My clothes itched on my skin and I couldn't wait for her to leave so I could get inside that tub.

"My name's Renee, by the way. In case you wondered." She pointed to a shelf beside the sink. "All your toiletries are in there. Anything you could possibly need."

"Thank you." I looked down at my dirty rags and wondered if I could find something else to put on after having such a clean bath. If I could, then maybe I could convince someone outside of this house that I was a decent citizen and persuade them to help me get back home.

Renee must have noticed the look on my face. "Oh, no, sweetie, don't worry about your dressing. We have plenty fresh clothes and undies for you to choose from in your room. You go head now and bathe."

I waited until I heard her steps fade away, before locking the door and stripping off my clothes. Did she say my room? What the hell made her think I'd be staying that long?

TWO

After my bath, Renee led me to a large room, with a bed, desk, dresser, and TV. The bed looked to be a queen, and the dressers matched the blue and yellow of the headboard. Everything was spotless, no dust in sight, which told me it was cleaned often.

"You'll find clothes and other such things in the closet, some in the dresser." She waved her hand around like a Realtor would when showing a new apartment. "I hope you like it, Kerry. Your own space. Bet you haven't had that in a while, have you?"

I didn't answer, just took another look at my surroundings. It was a nice room, and it was warm and smelled like the fruity soap in the bathroom. Everything looked fresh and brand-new. Which led me to wonder just how long they'd been planning this.

She kept right on talking as if I was still paying attention. "Once you finish in here, come on into the kitchen. I fixed oxtails with rice and beans for dinner."

It sounded heavenly, and she seemed nice, but still, all of this was more than a little wonky.

I had so many questions, and I figured the only way to get answers was to play their game. For the meantime, anyway.

I blow-dried my hair and then changed into a pair of blue jeans and a red T-shirt. The smells from the kitchen called out to me, and I followed my nose toward the delicious scent.

Renee beamed when she saw me. "Just in time. Oh, sweetie, you look so lovely. Who knew what a pretty face you had hiding behind all that dirt?"

I took a seat. The table held one large bowl filled with ox-tails and three bottles of water. Renee encouraged me to fix my own plate, and I heaped it high, not ashamed of my hunger. Still, I waited until they'd each eaten from the same bowl before sticking any in my mouth.

"Why am I here?" I asked them after I'd had my second helping of food.

Renee patted my hand in a, "there, there" motion. "We need your help, sweetie."

They both looked at me expectantly. "With what?" I asked, sure I wouldn't like the answer.

Renee smiled as she got up to clear the table. "Best we talk about that in the morning, dear." She and Ed shared a brief look and then he began to load the dishes up, taking them to the kitchen.

I thought I saw silver sparks fly from Ed's hands, but I couldn't be sure. Still, it had looked like he'd lifted a plate with no hands and guided it into the cabinet.

I continued to watch them both, a cold feeling settling in the pit of my stomach. They were planning something, plotting. I just didn't know what. "When can I go home? I appreciate the bath and nice meal, but now I think it's time for me to go."

Renee had her back turned, but it stiffened when I asked that question. "We'll talk about it tomorrow, dear. For now, let's just get a good night's sleep." It was pitch black outside, and I had no idea where I was, or what danger lay beyond this house, so I decided to stay for the night, and then at daybreak, I'd run as fast as my legs could carry me.

I tried to stay up. I even sat with my back up against the wall, but somewhere in the middle of the night I must have fallen asleep, because the next thing I knew, a knock sounded at my bedroom door and I was told to get dressed, it was time to go.

I sat on the side of the bed, trying to figure out my next move. That we were leaving the house could be played to my advantage. If I could get a good look around, maybe meet a few people, it could go a long way toward helping me escape when the time came.

I looked over the clothes in my closet and picked out a pair of blue jeans and a blue and yellow blouse. It would take more than one day to form a relationship with someone, much less learn the lay of the land. So I'd give it a couple of days, maybe a couple of weeks. Until then I'd play the part of the perfect guest.

I made my way to the bathroom, snatching up my tooth-paste and toothbrush as I went. What I didn't understand was why they'd kidnapped me in the first place? Why hadn't Ed just asked me to come?

He'd sent me through a wormhole of some sort. I chuckled and shook my head. A wormhole. I'd never believed in such things, but I didn't know how else to explain it. If that was true, did that mean I was in a different universe?

The bathtub had a panel with a myriad of buttons on it. I pushed the one for hot. Water erupted from multiple holes, filling the tub in seconds. I stepped inside and sighed. This really was nice; I'd long since forgotten what it was like to be clean every day.

Once we'd dressed and eaten breakfast, Renee announced it was time to go. We stepped outside to a nice humid morning. Back home it was still winter, here it was clear that summer was in full effect. Trees blossomed with blue and red leaves, flowers lined the walkway, and the air smelled fresh as a spring day.

No pollution stained the air, and one look around told me why. I didn't see one vehicle. Not in the driveways, not riding up and down the street.

People floated by on little white metal disks, the same color and material as the street. I'd never seen anything like it and I tried not to let the awe show on my face, but my mouth did hang open just a bit.

We stepped on the street and onto one of the little white things. I thought I'd feel unsteady, but my feet sunk into the disc, almost as if I was glued to it. A panel came up in front of us, and Renee typed in our destination.

We took off flying through the sky, with no seat belt, yet steady as a car ride. The wind blew my hair back and danced play-fully across my face. I loved it! This feeling I got from being up in the air. Adrenaline spiked through my veins, and I found myself looking forward to doing this again. Living on the streets taught you to always look for that silver lining, and I guessed this was one.

We ended up in a large room with a stage, and below it was a large group of men and women. "You go over there with them." Renee pointed to the people on the floor. "Me and Ed will take our places on stage. Go on, now. We'll catch up with you later."

I watched them climb a large platform with multiple chairs and take a seat beside the other couples already up there. I looked around trying to gain some insight as to what was going on.

The people beside me on the floor milled about with blank faces and confused eyes, almost like sheep on their way to the slaughter. At least that's what it felt like anyway.

Renee and Ed talked to others around them, pointing me out and nodding their heads agreeably. The pleased look on all their faces left something cold and hard in the pit of my stomach. Just what the hell did they have planned for us?

My breath caught in my throat, and I realized in that moment, just how scared I really was. More so than I'd ever been living out on the streets.

These people meant us harm. I could feel it in my bones. I took a few steps back but ended up stumbling sideways.

Just before I hit the floor, strong arms wrapped around me and hauled me upright. "Don't let 'em see your fear. They get off on that. No matter how nice they may first appear to be. Once a guy tried to oppose them, and with the wave of a finger they set him on fire in front of all of us. A good way to make sure we didn't get out of hand, I guess." An unfamiliar voice whispered in my ear.

I stilled, not knowing what to do, or who was talking to me. "Watch and learn from everything you see. That's the only way to survive around here." A different voice spoke, but the accent stayed the same. Two males speaking in the same baritone made me wonder if they were related.

"Wha- what do they want from us?" I hated the way my

voice broke, but there was nothing I could do about it.

"Hold your head high," the first one said. "Don't give them what they can't have."

I looked up to see who was doing all the talking. Two men stood in front of me. One about six feet tall, with a bald head and brownish blue eyebrows. The other had a small patch of blue brown hair right above his forehead. The rest of his hair was shaved close to his head.

Though one was lighter than the other, the resemblance was unmistakable. "You two brothers?" I asked.

The taller one nodded. "I'm Andrew, and this is my brother Lincoln." The first voice belonged to him.

I'd wanted to meet people who could help me. I didn't know if they could, but I saw no harm in giving them my name. "Kerry."

Andrew pointed across the room to a man in a white shirt with short curly black hair. He was deep in conversation with a woman, about my height with short pink hair. "That's our friend Gerell. One of the first people we met when we got here."

Not knowing what else to say, I simply nodded.

Andrew watched me closely. "Do you want to be here, Kerry?" Something about the way he said it, told me he'd asked for a very specific reason. I didn't know why, but I decided to be honest with my answer anyway.

"No." I turned an angry glare toward the stage. Ed and Renee talked and laughed with those around them as if they didn't have a care in the world.

My fist balled at my side, but I remembered what Andrew had just said, and so I took a deep breath and tried to control my emotions. The last thing I wanted was to be set on fire like the guy he'd told me about.

The thing that made it difficult was that someone I'd trusted had tricked me. Life on the street was hard and the number one rule was to trust no one. Still, Ed had endeared himself to me in such a way that I'd let my guard down. I said as much to them, not about the homeless part, just that I'd been tricked into coming here.

Andrew's nostrils flared, but he kept his cool. "That's how they got a lot of us."

Lincoln's eyes turned fierce as he looked over at Gerell. "Yeah, and some they just snatched right off the street. Taking them from their homes and everything that they loved."

Andrew followed his brother's line of sight. "We were coming from a party when they picked us up. No reason." He nodded at Gerell. "That one? On his way home from work."

We chatted for a while longer, until one of the men on stage stood. A plump fellow of average height, he picked up a silver microphone and cleared his throat. "Now, I know some of you are wondering what you're doing here." I was sure all of us wanted to know the answer to that question.

He pushed his glasses up. "You've been so patient and I want to thank you for that." I narrowed my eyes in disgust. He acted like we actually had a choice in the matter. "Today we start at the beginning." The fact that he was so happy about that one statement sent cold chills racing down my spine.

Andrew swore under his breath. "The more they talk, the less I understand. They have a special way of putting you off your guard around here." I nodded because I couldn't agree more.

The man on stage kept talking, "I'm Max, by the way, and now Andre will take it away."

Andre stood and began separating us into groups of six. My eyes searched frantically around the room. I didn't know what I was looking for, but it seemed better than just standing there doing nothing.

Andrew, seeing my distress, placed a comforting hand on my shoulder. "Be cool, Kerry. Don't let them see your fear. Pay attention and try to remember everything you see and hear." I nodded and then stood with the group I'd been assigned to.

They divided us into twos. I recognized the woman who'd been talking with Gerell earlier. The pink in her hair matched that of her brows and eyes. She introduced herself as Lia, and apparently, we'd be partners from this point forward.

We walked into another room, a large gym, where we were weighed and measured. "Why do they need to know what we weigh?" Lia asked me once I stepped off the scale.

I took a deep breath and looked around the room at all the exercise equipment. "Whatever it is, it's not good. I heard they once set a guy on fire for failing to comply."

She nodded. "Yeah, it was awful. I can still hear his screams sometimes." She shook her head and quickly changed the subject. "Let's keep a list of everything they make us do. Put it together and see what we come up with."

"I could do that," I said, deciding to put the ever-present threat of burning to death behind me for now.

We followed Andre toward the women's locker room. "Good. We'll compare notes as we go."

After we'd changed into workout clothes, we were told to get on the treadmill. We ran for twenty minutes and then switched to the bicycle. After that, we lifted weights, did stretches, and then worked on stomach crunches and legs.

I thought I'd be tired after going so long without exercising, but life on the street meant a lot of walking, so I guess I wasn't as out of shape as I'd thought.

My breath came hard, and my body ached, but it was in a good way, and I could see myself getting into a workout routine once I got back home.

We were allowed to take showers, and sitting on the bench afterward, Lia asked the question I'd been wondering about. "Why do they need us in shape? Did they steal us to make us compete in some type of strong man competition or something?"

I slipped my shoes back on. "Who knows, but that's one more thing to add to the list."

Ed and Renee came to get me after that. I shared a lasting look with Lia before following them out the door. They asked me how my day had gone and seemed especially interested in knowing if I'd been comfortable and had had everything that I'd needed.

Renee fixed a nice dinner and made sure that I ate my fill. The same silver sparks I'd seen on Ed seemed to dance around her hands as well. It made me curious, and I vowed to watch them more closely in the future.

I slipped into bed after supper, mentally compiling all the things I'd learned today. The fact that they could set people on fire with the flip of a hand weighed heavily on my mind and scared me more than anything, because my only thought was who was next. Me? Andrew? Lia? It hurt to even think about.

I awoke later that night, my bladder begging for release. On my way back from the bathroom, low, hushed voices drew me toward the kitchen. Not wanting to be discovered, I hovered just outside the door, making sure I couldn't be seen.

Ed's voice boomed with pride. "Picked a good one this time, didn't I?"

Renee let off a soft affectionate chuckle. "Gonna get a pretty good rep for her, no doubt."

That feeling of dread settled over me once again. What did these people want from me? What did they want from all of us? There was some ugly shit going on here, and I just hoped when the time came, we'd be informed enough to fight back.

THREE

The next day we once again gathered in the room with the stage. Andrew stood in a huddle with his brother and Gerell, talking animatedly and using a lot of hand gestures. He smiled when he saw me and walked over.

"Get a chance to stretch your legs yesterday?"

I laughed, because boy was that an understatement. "Got a better work out then I've had in years. Be good if I knew what it was for."

He looked toward the stage. "Something only they can benefit from. Whatever it is, it's not for us."

I nodded and then surveyed the room. Multiple people met in small groups, talking in hushed tones, and continuously glancing around as if scared to be overheard.

A thread of tension ran through the air, touching down on every one of us. I didn't even try to keep the hopelessness out of my voice. It was a feeling I'd come to know well over the years. "What are we going to do?"

Andrew seemed unfazed. "We got some things in motion."

"Who? You, Lincoln, and Gerell?"

"And a few others."

I let that sink in, but still wondered if it would be enough.

Max was back, smiling brightly as he cleared his throat and reached for the microphone. "Today you start your beauty regimen. That means hair, nails, and skin." He held up a finger.

"Everything must be accounted for. After that, we start dance lessons."

He sounded so damn happy for us, and it chilled me to my bones. Why did they need us in shape and beautiful? If I could figure that out, it could give me a clue to what was going on here.

Andrew locked eyes with his brother and they nodded at each other.

I thought about what I'd overheard the night before between Ed and Renee, and told Andrew about it.

He listened attentively and then repeated what he'd said before. "Listen. Remember. Compile."

I nodded like my life depended on it because it probably did. "Sure. I can do that. I can do that, no problem."

They separated the men from the women again. I searched out Lia and smiled with relief when I saw her already walking my way. "Yesterday they exercised us to within an inch of our lives. Today they paint our toenails. What gives?"

"They need us pretty and fit?" I deadpanned.

"Sounds like an infomercial," she said drily.

I laughed, glad to release some of the tension out of my shoulders. Andre came and told us to follow him.

We stepped upon the white disc, which I'd found out were called soarers. Lia and I stood side by side. We landed on the second floor in front of a door labeled SPA.

Lights hung from the ceiling and lit up the floor. Pools of water, both big and small, covered the entirety of the room. A lady with brown hair introduced herself as Tina and asked me to follow her through one of the side doors. I looked to Lia, who nodded and followed behind a different lady.

The room held a single table and multiple stones. "We have a lot to do, so let's start with your massage first."

I pulled my clothes tighter around my person. "Why do I need a massage?"

She looked at a small device in her hand, reading and nodding along. "You've been through a lot, Kerry. Living on the street for years. That was no good for you, was it? Let me loosen some of those tense muscles. I promise it'd make you feel better."

She smiled and sounded pleasant enough, but something in my gut told me if I refused, that calm demeanor would vanish in an instant. My mind immediately went to the guy who'd been set on fire and I vowed to have a different fate.

I allowed her to give me a massage, but I couldn't really relax. I was too worried about what came next.

From that room, we moved to another and then another. My hair was curled and then wrapped and brushed down. It looked good and the style really fit my face.

My eyebrows were plucked, my eyelashes thickened, and my legs and all other body parts shaved.

My fingernails and toes were painted gold and yellow respectively. Measurements were taken, and the dress they gave me was a shimmering gold that matched my nails perfectly. They also gave me a pair of open-toed high heels in the same color.

With all the pampering, I should have felt like a princess. Instead I felt like a guinea pig headed for slaughter.

Tina beamed like a proud parent. "This is not for the ball. For that, you'll have something much more spectacular."

"Ball?"

She smiled and then winked at me. "You're going to be the most beautiful one there."

I swallowed hard. "And when will this ball take place?"

She waved her hand as if swatting a fly. "Oh, don't worry about that. We're going to keep you exercising and keep you eating healthy food to bring back that special glow to your face. You'll be the belle of the ball, just you wait and see."

She didn't answer my question, and I realized that she wasn't going to. Still, I had another piece of information to file away, so I rated that as a win.

Finished with the spa treatment, we all gathered in the stage room again. Lia too was dressed in gold, her short hair spiked and shining.

"I feel like a science experiment," she said with a small frown on her face.

I chose to ignore that, even if I knew exactly what she meant. "Heard something about a ball. Don't know when they're planning it for, yet."

She nodded. "Yeah, I heard some rumblings. I'm going to work the crowd. See what else I can find out."

One thing I'd already picked up on was that all the women wore yellow and gold, while the men sported white tuxedos with yellow ties and gold bowties.

My pulse sped up as the creepiness of the whole thing hit me dead in the chest. I tried to breathe, but my breath caught in my throat. Fear crawled up my spine and around my neck, choking me and rendering me helpless to do anything but stand there.

One man, whose face read agitated, ripped off his tie and threw it to the ground. "Who do you think--" He didn't get to finish the sentence before he exploded into flames. I gasped and jumped back, as the man's charred remains hit the floor. A hush fell over the crowd and no one dared to breathe a word.

A tall slim man snapped his fingers and three men dressed in uniforms appeared. "Clean this up and get it out of here." The men did as they were told and slowly the room became abuzz again.

I stood frozen to my spot, not sure of what to do.

Andrew walked over and tried to comfort me. "Don't, Kerry. Don't give them your fear. When the time comes, give them your anger. That's the only thing people like this understand."

I nodded and decided to focus on him instead. He looked really nice in his white suit. "You clean up well," I said, wanting to change the subject, if just for the moment. There was nothing I could do for the man who'd been killed, but I knew he'd haunt my dreams for a long time to come.

Andrew's eyes said he knew exactly what I was doing, but he let it go anyway. "And you were just as beautiful before your makeover."

It wasn't true, but I appreciated him saying it. "Thank you," I said quietly, not feeling worthy of the praise.

He squeezed my hand. "Kerry, look at me." I raised my head. He smiled slightly, his eyes holding promises I wasn't sure he could keep. "We're going to be okay. You have to believe that."

I didn't. Not really, but I nodded my agreement anyway.

As before, Max stepped on stage and grabbed the microphone. "Good evening ladies and gentlemen. You all look very nice. Just beautiful. Now, grab a partner and prepare to learn the fine art of ballroom dancing!"

I placed my hand in Andrew's, the thought of dancing with anyone else frightened me greatly. He smiled and led me to the middle of the floor.

A slow ballad started, and the men were told to put their right hands on the small of the women's back, then to use their left hands to guide us around the floor.

Andre picked up the mic and began to call out instructions. We were told when to step left, right, and twirl. Dancing over the spot where the man had been burned alive sicken me, but being scared that the same thing would happen to me, I kept dancing.

This went on for about two hours nonstop. By the time it ended, we had the steps down pat and didn't need his voice to guide us. I tried to keep up, but in truth, my feet ached, and my arms felt like jelly, after keeping the same position for so long.

Once the music stopped, Andre and Max ushered us into the next room and told us to take a seat at a table, with candlelight atop white and yellow tablecloths. In front of each chair, sat multiple dishes and a yellow napkin with a small red pill on it.

My hand trembled uncontrollably and I looked at Andrew to get his reaction.

With furrowed brows, his eyes never left the contents of the table. "They could be planning anything," he whispered. "Just be ready to fight if we have to."

"I'm not taking that pill," I said with conviction. Who knew what they'd do to us once we were incapacitated.

Behind each seat was a man or woman dressed in black pants and fancy white shirts. They pulled out the chairs for us, a smile on their faces the whole time. Everyone took a seat, nervous glances all around.

Max stood in front, watching us closely. "Now ladies, tell

the person who pulled out your chair, thank you. Blink once and slightly bow your head." I along with the other women did as we were told. I could feel the burning behind my eyes, but I was determined not to give in to it.

Max seemed pleased. He beamed at us, something akin to pride on his face. He turned to the men. "Fellows, nod thanks to the person who pulled out your chair. Reach into your coat pocket and pretend to hand them a small tip. Once done, smooth out any ruffles you may have made to your jacket and turn back around. Put a look on your face that says you are now prepared to receive your meal."

Andrew's nostrils flared, but he, as well as the other men, did as Max instructed. I watched in silent horror, my eyes stinging a little more at the indignity of it all.

I needed to breathe and get a better handle on my feelings. Crying would help no one. I should know, I'd been crying for years.

The servers disappeared and then came back, each with a different sized dish in their hand. They began placing food in front of us and loading it onto our plates.

Different aromas and spices competed for dominance, yet the one rising above all others was fear. I was scared shitless, and my stomach turned in on itself, making it impossible for me to eat anything.

One bowl held a clear white broth with parsley and lemon wedges floating inside. On one plate was a small salad. On the other plate, we had baked chicken breast, mashed sweet potatoes, and what looked like creamed corn. Baskets of rolls, biscuits, and cornbread sat the length of the table with dishes of butter beside each one.

To drink we had coffee, tea, and water. The servers stepped back, and Max raised his eyebrow as if prompting us to remember our manners. With trepidation, and a subduedness more akin to a funeral than a fancy dinner, we went through the assigned nod and blink from before.

Max waited until we finished, a critical eye on each of us. He then smiled and announced it was time to eat.

165

The air hung heavy, fraught with tension and despair. No one moved a muscle and Max's eyes looked knowingly as if he'd been through this many times before. He walked behind us, looking from plate to plate. "I'm going to assume you all know how to pick up a spoon and fork to eat. If you don't, then raise your hand, and I'll be happy to help you. If you do, then eat. You know how. Pick up your utensils, wipe the crumbs from your face, and enjoy your meal. You've earned it."

A nervousness settled around the table, as no one wanted to be turned into flames. I swallowed hard and picked up my fork. My server placed a napkin in my lap and I picked up some of the salad and placed it in my mouth. It sunk like lead in my stomach, and I wondered if the rest of the meal would be as bad.

The sound of scraping spoons and forks were the only noises throughout the hall, as none of us dared utter a word.

Servers cleared the dishes away and filled all empty glasses. After that, they stood behind our chairs, hands at their side, waiting.

Max stood in front of the room again. "No doubt you've noticed the little red pill to your right. Don't be alarmed. It's not anything that will hurt you. We wouldn't want that, now would we? Not after bringing you this far."

He straightened his shirt tail. "It's just a little something to help you get on better while you're here." He looked around the room, making sure all eyes were on him. "Nothing to worry about. Take the pill, drink it down with a little water, and then we'll complete our evening with dessert."

My eyes immediately snapped to Andrew. He turned my way, but we couldn't talk, as the servers behind each of us came closer. I fumbled with the pill in my hand. Max said it was nothing to hurt us, but why would I believe him? He hadn't told us what it was, and something "to help us get on better" could mean anything. I set the pill down and saw a lot of others do the same. Good. They couldn't force us to take the damn things.

The tension tightened as the servers moved in even closer. There was one way out of this. When I was a kid and didn't want to take my medicine, I would hide it under my tongue, hoping my mom or dad wouldn't find it.

I placed the pill in my mouth and immediately shifted it underneath. The server was on me before I could even blink. A raised brow and harsh look and I deflated completely.

I flipped the pill back over and held it on my tongue. The server pointed to the water, eyes dead on me. A small tear escaped from my eye, the server right there staring holes into me. Tears fell as I swallowed the pill and chased it with the water.

All around the table scuffles broke out, as no one wanted to take the medicine. Max blew a whistle and more people dressed in serving uniforms entered the room.

They doubled teamed us. Two and three on one. Heads were slammed onto the table, mouths pried open, and pills forced inside. That and the ever-hanging threat of being caught on fire ensured that every pill was taken as they wanted.

Andrew was one of those people, as were Lincoln, Gerell, and Lia. I'd been the only one mindless enough to take the pill without at least putting up somewhat of a fight. My stomach tightened, and the glass in my hand shook so bad that I could hardly place it on the table.

Andrew put his palm over mine and guided it down without incident. The tears wouldn't stop coming, and the only thing I wanted was to go home. Back to my bench in front of the public library, where I at least felt safe and secure.

Under the table, Andrew rubbed soothing patterns into the back of my hand. That helped some, as I noticed my breathing became just a little more controlled. I smiled a thank you at him, but dared not do more in case someone was watching.

Max stood guard until every pill had been taken. He then nodded to the extra servers, who quickly disappeared back into the shadows. The mood around the table was somber, as we all tried to process what had just happened.

Max smiled brightly, continuing to keep up the facade. "I think it's best to forego dessert this one time. You did good tonight and we'll practice more later. For now, you're free to go home with your sponsors."

Ed and Renee walked toward me, big grins on their faces,

giving me a thumbs up as if they were my parents and I'd just completed some difficult task. I bared my teeth. These people disgusted me. Just who did they think they were? And what did Max mean by "your sponsor"? What exactly were they sponsoring us for?

The closer they got to me, the harder I gripped Andrew's hand. At that moment, he was the only thing that made me feel at least a little secure and I just didn't want to let him go.

His eyes said he knew my panic and he squeezed my hand even harder to let me know he understood.

"Well, didn't you just have a great day?" Renee ran her fingers through my hair, smiling brightly. She acted as if this was my first day of kindergarten or something.

Ed nodded his agreement. "You look beautiful, Kerry." He looked around the room. "You all do."

Renee rested her hand on my shoulder, and the only thing I wanted was to knock it off. She'd touched me without permission, and left behind a few silver sparks in the process.

I'd never hated two people more in my life and just wondered how much longer I'd have to stay here. "Well, we'll finish your lessons at home." She said it like this was something I'd been compliant with, and we were all just having a great day. I didn't want to go home with them, but I really had nowhere else to go.

Andrew eased his hand out of mine, giving it a small pat at the last minute. I stood, head down, worried what the rest of the night held in store for me.

Once home, I was allowed a quick shower and told it was okay to change into my night clothes.

I walked into the kitchen afterwards, my palms wet with sweat, chest pounding. I still didn't know what effect the pill would have on me, and that along with everything else kept me in a perpetual state of unease.

Sitting at the kitchen table, Ed and Renee presented me with a set of goggles. They had a pair of headphones attached to them and I wondered if this was a part of my lessons as well.

Renee fitted them to my face, silver sparks seeping from her hand. She adjusted the earphones and made sure the goggles were secure.

They fit tight, and for now the only thing I could see out of them was Renee's smiling face looking back at me. "Now don't take these off all night. There's a lot of information being downloaded. You'll need to know these things. Makes it a lot easier in the final tallying, let me tell you."

I didn't know what she was talking about and I didn't care. I wasn't staying here forever, no matter what her and her husband thought. Tomorrow I'd talk with the others because there had to be some way out of here, we just hadn't found it yet.

I nodded and then made my way back to my room. It wasn't until my head hit the pillow that the goggles and headphones came to life.

An image of a woman appeared, telling me that I would now learn the history of their world and many others, as well as be given an extensive lesson in science, arithmetic, languages, and a host of other subjects. The first thing she explained was two plus two.

I awoke the next morning with a bunch of newfound knowledge skirting the perimeter of my brain. It was there. I knew it was there, but unless I focused on it, I couldn't readily pull it through.

At the breakfast table, Renee and Ed questioned me extensively. Each answer pushed through the moment it was asked and I had no clue where some of it came from. But I knew it, somehow, I knew it, and it did nothing but make them both beam proud smiles my way.

Ed poured himself another cup of coffee, silver sparks flying from his hand and dissipating in the air. "She's going to be number one, Renee, just you watch," he said.

Renee patted my hand. "No argument from me, Ed. I'd say we really picked ourselves a winner this time."

I bit off a piece of bacon and tried hard to fight that old sick feeling that had been with me since I'd first arrived. They talked about me like I wasn't there because they didn't care that I was.

I was an object to them. A thing to be used and tossed aside whenever the mood struck. I shook my head. I'd never met two more despicable people in my life, and I couldn't wait to be free of them.

FOUR

We ended up in a large gym this time. Red and blue mats lined the floor, and I wondered if we were expected to do push-ups or something. My eyes sorted through it all and found Andrew. He was talking to his brother and their friend Gerell. I made my way over to them. "Were you guys given an overload of information last night?"

Andrew nodded. "They're gearing us up for something big. Been trying to put the pieces together but nothing fits." The frustration showed clearly on his face, a feeling I think we all shared.

Lincoln took in the empty mats around the room. "I think they're going to make us fight. Probably more of their nonstop training." He looked to Gerell. "Are you okay with that? Do you think you'll be able to keep from hurting someone?"

Gerell closed in on us so that we formed a small circle around him. His right hand shook uncontrollably, and a spark of silver light erupted from it, hitting the ground, and then fizzling out.

My eyes widened when I saw it. It was the same silver sparks I'd seen from Ed and Renee, and I told them as much.

Gerell nodded. "I haven't had much control of it since taking that red pill last night at the dinner. I don't know what I'll do if I have to fight someone." His voice sounded strained, his breathing labored.

Lincoln ran a hand up his arm, face full of concern. "Just stay near me. I'll shield you as much as I can."

Gerell rested his forehead against Lincoln's. "I don't want to hurt you," he whispered.

Lincoln's voice came out low, tone soft. "Better me than anyone else, Ger."

Both men spoke with pain in their voice and agony on their face. Their need to comfort each other was palpable and almost made me feel like a peeper for watching. I turned away, not wanting to intrude on a private moment. Andrew tapped me on the shoulder as a door to the side opened.

Max and a woman with short, brown, curly hair came to stand in front of the room. He cleared his throat and called our attention. Once everything quieted down, and all eyes were on him, he began to speak. "Today we learn how to protect this world and the people on it. This is something that will be expected from each of you."

Confused glances throughout our group. These people were insane. Did they really believe we'd be on their side if an invasion occurred? Were they really going to teach us to fight? I looked to Gerell. He moved in even closer to Lincoln, his hand tight on the other man's arm.

Max stepped back a bit and then he and the woman turned to face each other. I took a deep breath and prepared myself for the next set of lessons. Maybe they didn't really expect us to fight each other. Maybe.

Max turned to us for a second, making sure we were watching, then raised his fist, and brought it down hard toward the woman's face. She used an arm to block him and then dipped to the floor and kicked his feet out from under him. Instead of falling, he hovered in the air and then came back to his feet, as if it was the most natural thing in the world.

My breath hitched, and I looked around the room to make sure I wasn't the only one to see it. Andrew whispered something undeterminable under his breath, while Gerell and Lincoln both stared on, eyes big with fear.

Max went for the lady again. This time, the same silver light that I'd seen light up Ed, Renee, and Gerell's hands, lit up hers. She aimed for his face, but he dropped low and the silver spark hit the wall behind them, causing a small fire in the process. Servants wasted no time putting it out before it had a chance to grow out of control.

Mouth dry, I stared at the smoke left from the flames. Could all the people who lived here do that? Could Ed and Renee? Is that what all those silver sparks had been about? Could Gerell now do that? I looked at Andrew and Lincoln and we all gathered around Gerell in an effort to hide his new gift from the others.

The fighting stopped, and Max turned to us, one finger raised in the air. "No one wants someone in their home who can't defend themselves. This is one of your most important lessons to date. You must be able to fight and defend those around you. Especially if those people can't defend themselves."

I scoffed and then put my hand over my mouth, hoping I wouldn't be signaled out. This guy was seriously saying he expected us to die for them. The words *I felt like I was in an alternate universe* had never been more relevant. Except I suspected we really were in an alternate universe, which made this even more ironic.

He watched us closely, taking in our facial expressions before he spoke again. "Some of you have probably noticed the same silver energy coming out of your own hands. Those who haven't, will. That's what today is all about. Learning how to handle that energy and fight with it."

Andrew, Gerell, Lincoln, and I shared a stunned look. How stupid were these people to arm us with the means to defeat them? Or were they so conceited that they didn't even believe we'd try?

Max must have read my mind because his next words crushed any hope I had that we could somehow fight our way out of this. "Please don't think you have even a fraction of the power that we do. If any one of you tries to attack me or any other member of this world, we will execute the entire lot of you. So, think about that before you dare."

He gave us a moment to let that sink in. "No. Your powers are a lesser version of ours and at the discretion of those who sponsor you. You'll do as you're told. There is no room for argument on that point."

My fist clenched, as hurricanes of emotions slammed through me. We were nothing more than property to these people. Property to be thrown away or killed at their whim. They held our lives in their hands and felt they could do with them as they pleased.

Max snapped his fingers. "Now, find a partner and line up."

Andrew and I stood opposite each other, as did Lincoln and Gerell. Max walked around the room, coaching us along. We were told to hold our right and left hands loosely apart and focus all our attention on the area in the middle.

We did as instructed. Nothing at first, but then a small tingle started in my palm and spread to the rest of my fingers. Gasping out loud, I almost dropped my hands from the shock of it. I hurriedly put them back together before anyone could notice. This time, the tingle turned into a silver ball of energy. There was no feeling or texture to it, but I could clearly see that it was there.

My eyes snapped to Andrew. He held a little ball of energy in his hand as well. His mouth hung open a bit, as he bounced it from hand to hand, making it appear and disappear at will.

It was amazing, and I immediately started to plot a way to turn this to our advantage. There had to be something we could do to make this work for us.

Max walked through the crowd, checking that we were all on the same page, and doing the same thing. Once assured of that, he went back to the front of the room.

"Now try to take down the person in front of you. Don't worry about hurting them. You can't. You're not strong enough."

Andrew smiled reassuringly and I smiled back, not really concerned that he'd try to do me any harm. I didn't want to hurt him either, so I thought I'd do a test run first.

Aiming toward the floor, I let the power shoot out of my hand. It sparked for a second, then fizzled out, not making much of an impact at all. Nothing like the fire the woman with Max had caused.

Andrew tried it and had the same results as me. Jaw clenched, he shook his head. "I'm not willing to be some strong-arm bodyguard for them."

I didn't have an answer, only to say that I felt the same. I nodded my agreement, and then we lined up again.

Max stood with his hands behind his back. "Just so you know," he started, voice raised a couple of octaves, making sure he was clearly heard. "The only time you are to use these powers is here in this training room or in defense of your sponsors. Caught using it any other time and you will be killed. On the spot. No questions asked. Don't even use it when you're alone. Not even in the privacy of your own room. Get caught calling forth this energy without permission or reason, and your life will be ended."

A fire boiled in my veins, running through my whole body. Silver energy exploded from my hands and hit the floor with a bang. Not the big fire that Max's partner had caused, but the most I'd done so far.

Stunned, my mind immediately went back to when I was six years old and learning how to ride a bike for the first time. All the big boys and girls were doing it, and I wanted to be just like them.

They made it look so easy, and I just couldn't understand why I was the only one still sitting on the sidewalk. Yet, every day that summer there I was, getting on my bike and trying to stay upright.

It took weeks, but I worked hard at it, never gave up, and soon I was riding just as easily as the older kids.

That incident helped set the tone for the next few years of my life. I wanted to join the volleyball team in junior high, so I worked hard, stayed after school, and got my game up to a competitive level.

When I'd first started at the mill, my job was one of production. Which meant I got paid a hefty base rate as long as I showed up and worked. But, if I surpassed my production rate, then I could bring home an extra five or six hundred dollars on an already nice paycheck.

I didn't know how to do the job when the mill first employed me, but I stayed past my shift, worked twelve to sixteen hour days, and soon I was bringing home an extra six and sometimes seven hundred dollars every week. Hard work, putting forth an effort, and training every day, had always netted me the results that I wanted.

I tilted my head to the side as the thought fully formed in my mind. Why should this be any different? Max and the others didn't want us using these powers unless they told us to. There had to be a reason for that.

Maybe the more we used them, the more powerful we got. Maybe if we practiced and learned how to better control it, we'd be able to defend ourselves against even them.

I flipped Andrew over my shoulder while we waited for Max to tell us what to do next. I bent his arm behind his back and whispered in his ear. "Get Lincoln and Gerell and meet me by the dance hall, three hours after bedtime."

Renee cooked steak, with baked potatoes and tossed salad for dinner. I ate my fill knowing that I would need the extra energy for later. Renee and Ed seemed pleased when I asked for seconds and happily piled more onto my plate.

I brushed my teeth, took my bath, and then retired to my room like always. I didn't have a lock, so I turned on my side, away from the door. I closed my eyes and focused my energy. The silver ball appeared, and I made it disappear immediately, only to bring it back again, trying to be faster each time.

Many years on the streets had taught me how to move with stealth and slip in and out of places completely undetected. I waited until I was sure Renee and Ed were asleep and then crept out into the cool night air.

I didn't take one of the little white soarers, as I was sure a record of my activities would be recorded and sent to my sponsors. I went on foot instead, keeping to the shadows and hiding and ducking whenever necessary.

When I finally arrived, the place was empty, and I had a single moment of panic thinking they'd stood me up. A sound to the right caught my attention, and I started to duck away, then Lincoln peeked from behind a tree and waved. Relieved it was them, I made my way over.

The city was different this time of night. It was almost eerie how quiet it was. The only sound that could be heard was the scurrying of small animals hunting for food and chasing down prey.

Gerell's hand fidgeted at his side. "What are we doing here?"

I moved in closer. "We need to talk, but not out here like this."

Lincoln and Gerell shared an unreadable look, and then the former nodded. "There's a spot we go to sometimes." Voice low, he kept his eyes on Gerell the whole time. "When we can get away that is."

Andrew and I followed as they led us through the back of the dance hall and down a tree lined street. Careful to avoid discovery, we walked at a crouch and spread out as much as we could.

Finally, we came to the entrance of a small forest. It brought back painful memories of playing in the woods as a child, and I cleared my throat and tried to change the subject, knowing that line of thinking would do me no good right now. "How did you all find this place?" I asked Andrew.

He shook his head and pointed to his brother and Gerell. "Not my gig."

So this was something private to the two of them. I'd thought as much.

We walked on, following a well-used path that made me wonder just how often the two were able to come here.

We went on for about ten more minutes before coming to a small clearing. Large rocks lined the bank, and a river of water flowed downstream, clearer than any water in the middle of a forest had the right to be.

Throwing rocks and watching them splash and bounce around in the water used to be a favorite of mine. Hell, even being able to dip my toe in would have been nice, but those were activities best left for a different night.

Knowing that our sponsors could discover us at any time, I got straight to the point. "I don't believe Max when he says that we can't be as powerful as them. Renee and Ed's power leaks out in silver sparks sometimes, but I've never seen them be violent with it. What about you guys? Notice anything about your sponsors?"

Andrew nodded. "Sometimes, but they probably only really use it when it's time to fight. Might take too much out of them otherwise."

I took a seat on one of the rocks and stretched my legs out. A slight breeze blew through the air ruffling my hair and sending a feeling of peace all through me.

This was such a lovely place, and any other time I would have enjoyed it greatly, but right now the seriousness of the situation kept me from fully embracing it. "We may not be as strong as them now, but if we keep practicing, using it whenever we get the chance, who knows what can happen," I shrugged.

Andrew sat beside me. "It's a good idea, but the four of us can't take on a whole city. It's just not possible. We need help."

I wouldn't be deterred. "So, we talk to some of the others, get the word out, surely they want to be free of this place just as much as we do." I knew Lia did, and she couldn't be the only one. She just couldn't be.

Gerell picked up a rock and tossed it in the water. "Some maybe, but a few may believe they actually have it better here."

At my dumbfounded look, Lincoln decided to explain. "A lot of people were living in poverty on their home worlds. Many even slept on the streets. Here, they get food, and a safe clean place to lay their head, I'm not so sure they'd want to go back to how it was before."

It used to be when the subject of homelessness came up I would bow my head in shame. I refused to do that now, refused to be cowered anymore. Not ever again.

I held my head high and made sure my voice was strong and self-assured. "Well, speaking as one of those people who was homeless when they snatched me, I'm here to say that I'd do anything to go back home. Even if I do have to sleep on a park bench in the dead of winter."

A surprised look or two, but no one said a word, so I kept talking. "This whole thing gives me the creeps. Why are we here? They've got something planned and we better be ready for it. I mean, anything's better than living with the constant fear of being set on fire if we get out of line. Isn't it?"

Gerell nodded and then looked around as if he expected our sponsors to emerge from the trees and set us aflame that very moment.

I thought about something else that'd been bothering me since Ed had first kidnapped me. "You know, I don't have to lift a finger back at Ed and Renee's. They cook for me, keep my clothes clean, make sure I've got a comfortable place to sleep. I could almost understand their motives if they'd brought us here to serve them, but it's the opposite, they're the ones serving us. Why?"

Andrew steepled his fingers together, a contemplative look on his face. "They're getting the geese fat for dinner day."

A bunch of different threads tied together, and the story of Hansel and Gretel popped into the forefront of my mind.

I inhaled sharply as I realized he was right. "Why did it matter if we knew how to ballroom dance or the correct answer to an algebraic equation?" I ran a frustrated hand through my hair, I felt like pulling it out, but that wouldn't help anything.

Lincoln tossed a rock from one hand to the other. "We can talk to a few people, try to get a feel for allies, but it's a gamble. It's hard to know who to trust around here."

"And we need as many people fighting with us as we can get," Gerell finished for him.

"We need somewhere to gather with them too." Lincoln picked right back up. "They can't come here. I'm not willing to give this place up."

He and Gerell shared a soft look, and I decided to let it go. I almost wished I'd found this place first. I would love to be able to sneak out here sometimes when it all got to be too much, but horning in on someone else's private time wasn't my style. It never had been.

Andrew stood and wiped down his pants. "I think we should only try to meet once or twice a week, more than that is just too risky."

I stood as well. "It's all risky, but I see your point. First, we find a spot, and then we bring in others, a little at a time."

Gerell nodded. "We get as strong as we can."

Lincoln put a hand on the small of Gerell's back. "We learn how to fight together."

Andrew's eyes went hard, a determined look on his face. "We get them before they get us."

I snuck back into Ed and Renee's without incident, giddy that I was finally doing something to take control of my own fate.

FIVE

For the next couple of weeks, we kept our heads down and did as we were told. Nightfall was our time, and we took full advantage of it. We only met about twice a week, and mostly we focused on using our powers and working together.

We did learn a few fighting moves too, from one of the guys who'd been taught back on his home world.

Lia had joined with us. I should have asked her in the beginning and wasn't sure why I hadn't. She had new information tonight and I couldn't wait to get to the meeting place to see what she'd found out.

In the last couple of weeks, I'd learned to carefully check the house over before opening the front door and easing out.

I'd only made it about three feet up the sidewalk when Renee's sharp voice stopped me dead in my tracks. "Kerry, dear. Just where are you going this time of night?" Shit.

I closed my eyes slowly, trying to calm myself. She knew. She had to. Why else would she be out here in the middle of the night? "Couldn't sleep," I said, turning around, a faux smile on my face. She and Ed stood side by side, watching me. "I figured a walk around the block might help."

Renee threw a hand around my shoulder. "Now, Kerry, I think you need to come on back inside, right, Ed?"

He nodded. "Been hearing a lot of talk about some usurps. They'll soon find out that they should have just left well enough alone, I believe."

Renee opened the door and ushered me back in. "Got patrols out now rounding them up." My breath hitched at the thought of Andrew and the others being captured. Especially since I had absolutely no way of warning them.

Renee walked me to my bedroom door. "Now you don't want them mistaking you for one of those people, do you, Kerry?"

Ed led me to my bed and sat me down on it. "No, Renee, she don't want that. Not with her big day coming up tomorrow."

That gave me pause. "My big day?" I asked, voice weary.

Ed and Renee smiled at each other, and then Renee wiped a small tear from her eye. "Oh, Kerry, I'm going to miss you so much. It's been such a joy having you here. You've brought such light to these old halls."

I balled my covers in my hand, then stopped when I realized what I was doing. Was I going somewhere? Were they sending me back home? I chuckled at my own stupidity. Of course, they weren't. But what then?

I thought back to the look of desperation on Lia's face when she'd asked to meet tonight and cursed under my breath. Perhaps she'd figured out a way to get us home or discovered what was really going on here.

I hissed through my teeth. Why did they have to pick tonight of all nights to bust me, and who had snitched? I guess we'd find out tomorrow.

Ed drew his wife close. "You say that every time, dear."

She slapped his arm playfully. "Oh, I know, but even you have to admit that this one here is special."

Ed smiled at me. "It's been a pleasure knowing you, Kerry. I wish you well in your new life."

They closed my door after that, leaving me stunned on my bed, fearful of what the sunlight would bring.

I lay there about an hour longer, sleep evading me. The thought of Andrew, Lia, and the others being captured just wouldn't leave me alone. Jumping up to a sitting position on the side of the bed, I decided I had to warn them.

The house was quiet, so I decided to pretend to go to the bathroom just to get a feel for things. I heard Ed and Renee's laughter the moment I opened the door. They sat at the kitchen table, drinking coffee and eating the muffins from earlier. Frustrated, I closed the door and went back to bed.

A couple of hours later I tried again. They were still up, in the living room with two other couples. I did go to the bathroom this time, just to get a feel for what was going on.

If they saw me, they didn't say anything, so I listened at the door for a second, hoping to hear something useful.

Renee talked about a woman name Thala, who she'd been courting for the last year and a half. Scared of being caught, I crept back to my room, flipping this insight over in my head.

So it wasn't just Ed who kidnapped people, his wife participated in this activity as well. I guess every couple here did, judging by how many of us were being held against our will. A cold shiver ran through me as I thought of what tomorrow would bring.

I sat down hard on my bed. Ed and Renee would be up all night, making sure I stayed in my room. So why not get a little practice in? I held out my hands and focused on bringing that silver energy forward.

Our little group had been practicing so hard trying to get a handle on these new powers. We weren't perfect, but we could cause explosions now, which at least meant something.

The next morning, I had breakfast waiting for me when I got up. Ed and Renee were already dressed and eating. I sat down and picked up the cup of coffee that was placed before me.

Renee patted my hand. "You have appointments all day, dear."

I sat my cup down. "I do?"

She ticked off a list on her finger. "Hair salon, makeup, nail shop, dress fitter, and that's just to start. You're going to be the belle of the ball. Just you wait and see."

My eggs felt cold in my stomach as I realized that today was the day of reckoning and after this, everything would change.

Right after dinner, Renee led me to the spa and dropped me

off with a lady named Linna.

Dressed in a black smock, she smiled at me and told me to take a seat. I did as she asked, already plotting how to get out of this mess. She wrapped a towel around me and flexed her hands.

She started off by shaving my eyebrows and making my eyelashes stronger and fuller with the help of mascara. Blush was applied to my cheeks, foundation to my whole face. Three lipsticks were tried until she found one she thought to be perfect. Black eyeliner traced my eyes and blue eye shadow was applied to my lids.

I'd never been so pampered in my life. I went on to have a massage, along with a pedi and manicure. My legs were soaked in lukewarm oils and shined so much they glistened. My hair held a mountain of curls, some falling over and slipping into my face.

The dress I was to wear was floor length, light blue and sleeveless with an A-line neckline. It tied around the neck and from the feel of it, was made of pure satin.

Tiny silver beads covered the entire dress, my earrings, and bracelet, in the same style. It was beautiful. I was beautiful, but not knowing what the day held, or where I'd end up after this, only left me empty and cold.

I slipped on blue shoes, with small silver beads covering them, same as my dress. My gloves sparked with the same jewels and matched the dress and shoes perfectly. They went up to my elbows and were fingerless, fitting perfectly on my hands. After all was done, Linna gave me a small silver satin purse to complete the effect.

All around me, other women got the same beauty treatment as myself. Lia was one of them. She looked absolutely stunning in a pink satin gown that hung low to the floor and matched the pink in her eyes.

I waited until no one was looking and pulled her aside. "They had patrols out last night. I'm glad you didn't get caught."

She waved her hand as if it was nothing. "Nah, we saw them and decided to call it off. Never even made it to the meeting place."

A woman walked by and raised her eyebrow. We waited until she passed and then lowered our voices even more. "Who told?" I asked, anxious to find out who the traitor was.

She looked thoughtful for a moment. "Someone we asked who didn't want to join? It wasn't one of our group, if it were, then the patrols would have found our meeting place and as far as I know they haven't, so…"

"What was so important?" I asked.

She looked around then answered in a hushed whisper. "This. I'd heard they were planning this for today."

I nodded and then wandered off, not wanting the same lady to come back and catch us talking again.

We entered the ballroom later that night, the lights low and silver and gold balloons flying. The smell of chicken and beef filled my nostrils, making me want to gag.

I didn't want to eat, just the thought of it had my stomach clenching in disgust. I was terrified, and no pretty lights and fancy music were going to make me feel better.

They'd pulled out everything they could to relax us, to give us a fake sense of security. Too bad it felt like we were going to the slaughter instead of a beautiful dance. Sweat dripped from my brow as I stepped down the stairs and into the crowd.

My eyes sought out Andrew and found him immediately. He stood out in a navy-blue suit and silver tie. He looked amazing, and I think my jaw may have hung open a bit as I stared at him. His eyes caught mine, and he took a step back and blanched. Trying to hide my small smile, I tucked a lock of hair behind my ear, hoping that meant he thought I looked okay.

Gerell and Lincoln stood beside him. Gerell in a white suit and Lincoln wearing a charcoal gray one. They looked great together, and I thought it was cute how they kept giving each other quick glances and then hastily turning away. Both fidgeted with their hands and ties, trying hard not to look at the other but failing miserably.

I smiled despite myself, wishing this was a different place and a different type of dance. I turned to go toward the juice table and smacked dead into Ed and Renee. "Sorry," I said, patting my hair down, determined to look anywhere but at the two of them.

Renee shushed me and then pulled me into a hug. I stayed stiff in her embrace, but either she didn't notice or just didn't care.

She stepped back and then pinned two tags to my chest. I ran my hand over them, then looked down to read what they said. One had my name written on it, and the other said, sponsored by Ed and Renee Caviler.

Heated anger ran through me at the indignity of it all. It was like she was marking me, and my hands itched to tear the damn things off. I didn't dare, though, who knew what would happen if I even tried.

I looked back to Andrew and the others. They looked as nervous as I felt, but kept the conversation flowing between the three. From my talks with them, I knew that Andrew and Lincoln were from a completely different world than myself and Gerell. Not that Gerell and I were from the same place either. A quick look around the room told me that some of these people had to be from a different land altogether.

A man with a beak, and a pair of wings held a crystal glass in his hand, smiling and talking to a woman who had fur covering her face, hands, and legs. She also had a tail that wagged back and forth whenever she talked excitedly.

One man was so tall that he had to stoop in order not to hit the ceiling. Another so short that he barely stood at the knees.

I'd never seen anything like it in my life and wondered if they'd been invited here specifically for the ball. If so, why? What did they have to do with all of this? Before I could ponder it further, Max called the room to attention.

Ed and Renee pointed me toward the stage, and I saw Lia, Andrew, and the others being directed that way as well.

Andre greeted us with a smile and then lined us up one by

one behind the podium. So this was it. The moment that would decide our fate. My mouth went dry, and I swallowed hard, trying to keep the fear off my face. A small tear escaped from my eye, and I angrily wiped it away, not even sure what I was crying for.

Max picked up the microphone and turned toward the floor. "Ladies and gentlemen, Siana would like to invite you all to the annual Sponsorship Ball." His voice rose slightly at the end, and the crowd was quick to clap their approval. "This year's specimens are some of the best we've seen in a very long time."

He spared a quick glance our way and then turned back around. "A little something about them. These men and women, every single one of them behind me, put in fourteen to sixteen hours every day. And let me tell you something else, folks. They never complained once." The crowd clapped again. "They've worked hard to get here today and most certainly deserve your respect and admiration." Another round of applause.

I stole a glance at Andrew, but he looked as confused as I felt. How was Max up here singing our praises, knowing that he and his people had kidnapped us against our will?

A thought entered my mind and I wondered if the people in the crowd knew that little detail. If not, maybe they'd be willing to help us. I decided to put that on my list of things to find out before the evening was over. This could be what we'd been waiting for and could spell freedom for us all.

Max turned his attention our way, and I decided to focus on that later and listen to what he had to say. "Siana has been good to you, and you've been good to Siana," he started. "We've loved having you here, and are sad to see you go." My hand gave a slight tremble as the meaning of his words really began to sink in. "You all have been chosen. The men and women here are from a host of different worlds. Tonight, they get to choose one of you to go home with them." A nervous murmur buzzed among us. The more he talked, the worse it got "One of these men and women will pick you for a spouse or concubine."

A tremble started in my hand and went through my whole body. I felt like every decision I'd ever made had led me to this moment and the only thing I wanted to do was flee. I wasn't going home with any of these people. If I had my way, none of us would.

Max was still talking, and so I tried to pay attention. Information was my friend and probably the only thing that could get us out of here. "Now I know that you all are new to this, so let me explain how it works. You are to mingle with the men and women on the floor. Some will take a liking to you, others won't. After enough time has passed, you'll be brought out on stage one by one."

I let out a deep breath of air as the meaning of what he said started to seep in. He kept talking. "All those who like you will give a price. The one with the highest number wins you as a spouse." He said it as if it was the most natural thing in the world.

He finished talking to us and turned back to the crowd. "Remember, that all monies must be paid to the sponsors before we sit down to eat. Once that's taken care of dinner will be served. After that, we'll have the last dance of the night. Then, of course, you're free to take your purchases home. Now we expect the price to match the purchase.

"All here have been anointed with that unique Siana power, meaning that they can defend you, fight for you. As always, we chose them because their bodies can handle such a power, where yours cannot."

He stopped for a moment and smiled at the crowd. "Which is what makes these balls so special. You get a companion and a protector all rolled into one. Folks, how can you beat that? Who will challenge you now, when you have power and beauty right at your fingertips. Siana will always bring you the best. Remember that, before the next ball."

The more he talked, the more I could feel that foreign energy coursing through my veins. I wanted to hurt something, someone, them, every one of them who would mean us harm.

The audacity! The privilege it took to tell yourself that kidnapping and selling another human being was okay. Also, the level of delusion that we would go along with this.

Or maybe they didn't give a fuck how we felt. That was

probably closer to the truth. To them we were little more than doomed cattle, moving along with the rest of the herd to slaughter day.

A somber mood dogged our steps as we made our way off the stage and onto the floor. I looked for Andrew, but he was lost among the many swirling bodies. I hadn't been on the floor three seconds when a tall slim man tapped me on the shoulder and asked if I wanted to dance.

He smiled as if we were on equal footing and were simply attending our annual New Year's ball. I didn't feel as if I had a choice, so I placed my hand in his and let him sweep me around the dance floor. I felt sick and swallowed hard so I wouldn't end up throwing up on him.

He didn't seem to notice, and engaged me on a number of topics, almost as if interviewing me for a new job position. I answered as well as I could, but couldn't really put my heart into it. I guessed this was where the lessons we had had with the goggles and the headphones came into play.

Once the song ended, he thanked me for the dance and moved on. The next man to take my hand had four eyes, which all seemed to move independently of one another.

He too talked about a number of subjects, seeking out detailed answers and taking several seconds to process each one. I waited patiently and nodded politely when he finally let me go.

I scanned the dance floor and caught sight of Andrew dancing with a woman dressed in red. Lincoln was being chatted up by a woman in a floor-length black dress. While Gerell was stuck in a corner with a woman who seemed to be showing him her nail pattern. The eyes on all three of them were empty and devoid. I imagined my own eyes looked somewhat the same.

After a while, the faces and voices began to merge together, and the only thing I wanted was to go home and be free of it all.

One man, tall and regal, with black shoulder length hair, of muscular build, with a clean shave, and orange-blue eyes, wore a coat with many different medals on it. He touched my hand and Renee, who was nearby, gave a quick inhale of breath and called Ed over to watch.

He introduced himself as Charles and told me how beautiful I looked. He asked me where I was from and when I told him he said that he'd never met a woman from my world before.

He whisked me by Ed and Renee, both so giddy I thought they would burst. When the dance was over, he delivered me to their hands as if we were a couple of teenagers and he was just bringing me home from a date. I felt more drained after my dance with him, than with anyone else and I wondered why. Maybe I was just tired of it all, I reasoned

Ed and Renee waited until he walked away before they really begin to gush. Renee pulled me into a hug. "He is one of the wealthier men here. He's famous for coming to these things, dancing with three women the whole night, and picking only one to be his wife." She hugged me again. "Just think of the money we'll receive and how happy you'll be."

Ed looked at me as if I'd just made him the proudest father in the world. "I knew there was something special about you that first time I saw you. Oh, Kerry, you have no idea how lucky you are. How proud you've made us."

Renee wiped a tear from her eye. "Just think of the luxury you'll live in now. So much better than those mean streets you came from."

I bit my lower lip. "I'm going to get something to drink," I said, pointing to the punch bowl. I poured red liquid into my cup, downed it, and then poured another.

"You look flustered." Lia had a glass of orange punch in her hand.

"Yeah, well, where I'm from, at a party like this, these things carry alcohol. I could really use some of that right now."

She pointed to a table that held many flutes of champagne and wine. "But we need you clear headed. I've heard murmurs. That man you just danced with, he's a big player here. He may not stick around to the last dance. He may try to take his purchase home before that."

A curious glance around the room found him sitting off to the side, legs crossed, looking dead at me. He looked more inquisitive than anything else, but he still gave me the chills. I shuddered and turned my attention back to Lia. "I don't know if I can do this. I feel like I'm ready to pass out. Feel my hands. They're ice cold."

She drank her juice and sat her glass on the table. "What choice do we have, Kerry? It's either them or us." A man came up and asked for her hand. She gave me one last meaningful look, before she accepted his request, and stepped back onto the dance floor.

As the night wound down, it came time to do the bidding. Renee and Ed assured me they'd been offered top dollars for me and had refused several times as they believed Charles to be true in his affections.

They said it like they expected me to celebrate with them or something. Like we were all in this together and I wasn't forced to be here against my will. I didn't even answer. My fists curled at my sides as I walked to the back with the rest of the group.

They gathered us in a small room behind the stage, each of us waiting until it was our turn to be called up and auctioned off.

Andrew found me in the corner, literally wringing my hands together. "Steady, Kerry. It won't be much longer now."

I grabbed hold of his coat sleeve. "I'm scared," I whispered. Sweat dripped down my face mingling with the tears falling from my eyes. "I just want to go home," I choked.

He rubbed small circles into my back. "None of us know how to open a portal or whatever they used to transport us here."

I let out a big breath. "I've lived on the streets before. I survived. I'll survive being homeless here too."

He smiled and squeezed my hand. "Long as I'm around you will."

I gave him a watery smile back, and then Max began to speak.

"Ladies and gentlemen, the moment you've been waiting for all night is finally here. Get your money out and your taps ready. Here is Limey Slinks. I know you love him, so here he is, ready with our first participant."

All chatter died between us, as those words slammed back home the reality of our situation. From our spot in the back, we had a clear view of the stage and some of the audience.

Renee and Ed sat up front, holding hands and smiling. I growled low in my throat and turned my head.

They made me sick and their insistence that they were doing this for my own good, and not to line their greedy pockets, was insulting to the point of being dehumanizing.

Another man, probably this Limey Slinks, gave Max a friendly pat on the back as he took the mic from him. His high-pitched nasal voice was like tiny burn marks on my soul. He called the first name up and I felt my knees buckle.

This was true. It was really happening, and there wasn't a damn thing we could do about it.

Andrew put a comforting hand on my shoulder. "Don't tap out on me now, Kerry. We're almost at the finish line."

The woman whose name had been called turned toward us, panic in her eyes. She grabbed the person beside her, crying and begging them to never let her go.

The other woman, whom I assumed was a friend, also began to cry, but told her that at least they'd have a home now. That only made her cry harder, and the whole backstage lit up with silver light, as anger flowed through us all.

One of the workers took her by the arm and pushed her on-to the stage. She stumbled for a second and then walked head held high, tears flowing as she awaited her sentence.

The lady she'd been holding onto let out a cry so filled with hurt and anguish that it doubled her over. She put her hands around her waist and cried out the hurt that each and every one of us felt.

A woman beside her, tears running down her own face, grabbed her up in a tight hug. Another man, standing off to the side, his eyes also wet, joined. Then another and another. I grabbed Andrew's hand, and we too joined in until every single one of us were crying and holding on to each other.

The gavel banged down and the words "sold" echoed through the building and into the veins of every one of us. Such a small word, but my, what power it held.

Silver energy swirled around us, and I could feel it. I could feel the power in this one spot, could feel the desperation peeking through.

We wouldn't go down without a fight, no way in hell were we going down without a fight.

The next name was called, and I froze for a full three seconds as it was my own. My feet moved slowly toward the stage.

I received many pats on the back as I went, along with a few words of encouragement, and a hug from Andrew so tight that I wondered how my ribs weren't broken.

He wiped my eyes and kissed me on the forehead. "I won't let them take you. Keep that in mind. You're not going anywhere and neither is anyone else here."

I nodded stiffly, gave Lia, Gerell, and Lincoln a sad smile and then squared my shoulders, held my head high, and walked out on stage.

The light hit me square in the face and I had to squint to make it less painful. The energy in the crowd was like that of a feeding frenzy, and I felt disgusted just being associated with it.

The silver energy in me sped up, and I didn't know how much longer I'd be able to contain it. I could all but see Ed, Renee, and the others counting their money, and it pissed me off to the point that I could barely stand still.

The man beside me, this Limey, began to talk in that same triple fast, rhythmic, hypnotic cadence that so many auctioneers from my home world used. I couldn't follow. I did hear the taps, though. Charles and a few others were tapping their hearts out.

Tap. Tap. I felt my spirit break. Tap. Tap. I shook my head because no, not here, and not today. Tap. Tap. I felt the rage inside me rising. Tap. Tap. I held my hands up and let the light shine through.

Silver energy exploded through the crowd. Shouts rang out, and tables and chairs were overturned as people scrambled to get out of the way. Ed grabbed ahold of Renee and covered her body with his own.

Ed who'd brought me here. Ed, who'd pretended to be my friend for two years just so he could kidnap me and sell me to the highest bidder. All to make himself and his wife all the richer.

Renee, who already had another woman in her sights. A lady she'd pretended to be friends with for the last year and a half.

I released a hail of furious energy their way, screaming out my hurt and pain in the process. It hit Ed square in the back, knocking him to the ground. He groaned, and blood leaked out his back as he tried desperately to crawl away.

Renee threw her palm out and knocked me back with the force of her power. It hit me in the shoulder and pain exploded through my whole arm. "Ugh." I put a hand on it to stop the blood when someone from a different direction hit me in the side. "Shit." I fell to my knees. Fire exploded through my body, making it hard to move or think.

My breath came in hard gasps, and I took a minute to work through the pain, before coming back to my feet ready to fight again.

I opened my mouth and energy flew out in a wave, completely taking out the people in the front row. Alarms sounded and more people in the crowd joined the fight. They tried to rush the stage, but my comrades from the back burst through and then everything turned to chaos.

Hurt and bleeding, from my side and arm, I continued to fight on.

Stunned for a moment, I watched as Lia snatched up energy directed at her, mixed it with her own and sent it back out twice as powerful. Where had she learned to do that? I had no idea and didn't have time to think about it, as someone grabbed my leg and tried to pull me off the stage.

I twisted and turned, trying to get loose, but the person had an ironclad grip on me, and no matter what I did, I couldn't shake them off. Lia jumped the four feet on stage, and damn, I didn't know she could do that either.

She cut their hand off, got me to my feet, and then jumped back into the fight. I stood open-mouthed, trying hard not to think about the sound my head would have made, had it smacked up against that floor.

Lincoln and Gerell were fighting together, moving as one and taking out every single person in their path. Andrew stood at a crutch. Turning in a circle, he was going for the legs and feet, stopping the Sianas in their tracks, making sure they'd never walk again.

I hopped from the stage and started shooting every enemy I saw. I opened my mouth and held out my hands. The force of the energy lifted me in the air, and I shot down every single member of this freak show that I could find.

After a couple of minutes, my head started to swim and my eyes became unfocused. I swayed in the air and didn't trust myself to land without getting hurt.

Andrew popped up below me. He held out his arms and I floated down to them. He had a gash over his right eye and a welt across his chest. He placed me gently on the floor and snatched up a tablecloth. "I'm going to stop the bleeding." I'd almost forgotten I'd been hurt. At this moment, the only thing I felt was woozy and tired.

Andrew used his energy to rip the tablecloth in half and then tied it over my arm and around my waist. "I think we're getting the upper hand. That Lia is a firecracker. Who knew?" I nodded as best I could. Who knew indeed.

I took a minute to collect myself, then got to my feet. Andrew and I fought back to back. We moved at a steady pace and took out anybody that challenged us.

Once we met up with Gerell and Lincoln it was all four backs together, fighting anyone who came our way.

I turned to the left, taking out the Siana woman who'd fitted me for my dress. Back to the right I saw Max's prone body on the floor, unmoving. To the left again and this time I stopped cold.

I took in the sight of the two women who'd held onto each other, sisters I think. Now that I had a better look, I noticed the striking resemblance they bore to one another.

They lay side by side, eyes fixed, blood leaking out of their heads and throats. To die in an unfamiliar place, surrounded by people they didn't know just seemed like one of life's cruel jokes, and damned unfair.

I scanned the crowd trying to catch sight of Ed and Renee. They were nowhere to be found, but Lia burst through.

Her dress was completely gone now. Her white petticoat was well past her knees, and she had on a tee strap that hid her upper parts. Her face was bruised and swollen and her chest rose and fell rapidly. "We have them down for the moment. I'm going to call in my people now and put an end to this."

Her people? Did I miss something? She held out her hand and blue light came from it. It twisted and turned and then a small wormhole slowly opened.

Men and women dressed in blue and red suits burst through, blowing whistles, and taking some of the ones left down to the ground.

Not knowing what to think, I turned to Lia, hoping for some type of explanation. "Who are you?"

She wiped a trail of blood from her face and then held out her hand for us to shake. I didn't, and neither did the others.

The resigned look in her eyes said she'd expected as much. "Look, I'm sorry, okay. My name is Lia. I'm with the coalition of interplanetary crimes, and we've been watching Siana for a while. I wanted to tell you, but I didn't know who I could trust and I just couldn't take the risk."

All around us the Sianas and their auctioneer friends were being lined up and brought to a halt.

I'd try to process it all later. Right now, the only thing getting through was that Lia knew how to open a portal. "What happens now? Will you let us go home?" I asked, trying not to get my hopes up too much.

She nodded. "If you want, but I think I may have a better offer for you. Follow me."

She opened another wormhole. I took one last look at the place that had been my home for the last couple of months. So much pain and hurt had gone on here. What these people did wasn't right and I was so glad it was finally coming to an end. I'd lost my soul here, hopefully with where I was going, I'd finally get it back.

SIX

Lia brought us to her world. Bright lights blinded me, as we entered a large facility. The sign on the wall read, decontamination center.

Everything around us looked white and sterile. Medics stood off to the side and scooped us up as we came through.

They tended to our wounds and made sure we had a hot bath, food, and a clean change of clothes. The same things I'd had when I'd first entered Ed and Renee's.

I closed my eyes and tried to breathe, taking a moment to collect myself. Could I have jumped out of the frying-pan and into the fire? I'd have to wait and see.

Once everyone was cleaned up and stable, we were called into a large room, with a conference table. I sat beside Andrew with Gerell on the other side and Lincoln on his right. I spared a quick glance their way, but I think we were all a little too nervous to talk. We'd been here before. Every one of us. So I understood the reluctance. I felt it too.

Lia stood in the front of the room. She'd changed to a black jumpsuit and had her hair smoothed down instead of spiked. "For some of you, you just want to go home and that's fine. We'll open a portal and send you straight through. I know some of you were out of work and some were even living on the streets. We'll help you with that too. What you've done today, fighting, and taking back your right to live freely, is amazing and us here at the coalition are willing to help you anyway that we can."

A peaceful coolness floated over me. That's all I wanted. To go home.

"But," she said, holding up a finger. "There are many other worlds out there like Siana or worst. No. Not all deal in human trafficking. We just stopped a world a few weeks ago, that would invite other cultures over, only to poison them, effectively taking out their competition. Another world got rich by holding business partners from other worlds hostage, only letting them go once they'd signed over the entirety of their bank accounts. So, while they got richer, every world surrounding them got poorer."

She dropped the file she held in her hand to the table. "If you're willing to go through the training, we could use some help. Here we teach you how to ask the right questions. What signs to look for that something is not as it seems. We teach you how to fight and how to defend yourself. We go over problem solving skills, so hopefully it doesn't always lead to a fight. We teach you how to collect information. Everything I learned about being a coalition agent, you'll learn. There's also some psychological testing involved as well, to better fit you to the right position."

One woman sitting up toward the front raised her hand. "Will we be paid?"

Lia nodded. "We offer a competitive salary that we'd put up against any other coalition organization around. We'll also assist you with housing and anything else you need when starting life in a new world."

The lady up front shook her head. "I don't want to fight."

Lia waved her concern away. "There's a number of testing and a lot of training. Some of you may be better at data and collecting information. Some of you will do better at sorting that information.

"We offer a range of different jobs, and yes, some of you will be going to other worlds just like I do. Sometimes you'll go in an official capacity, and other times you'll be undercover. But we deal with each operation on a case by case basis." I listened carefully, soaking it all in and weighing my options.

The only thing I'd wanted since this whole thing started was to go home. Now I wasn't so sure. What did I really have to go home to? Nothing really, nothing that I couldn't recreate some- where else anyway.

I thought about maybe being able to get a job once I re- turned. Then I thought about the people of Siana, and how there were others like them, out there hurting innocent people like my- self.

I felt a fire in my belly and my fist curled at my side. I want- ed to stop them. Every one of them. I couldn't just stand by and let others suffer the same way that I had. I wouldn't. "I'm in," I blurted out. "I want to train. I want to learn how to stop them."

Lia nodded at me and smiled.

Andrew, Lincoln, and Gerell were caught up in a rapid con- versation until they apparently came to an agreement, raised their hands, and announced that they were in as well.

I was happy for that. I'd grown rather fond of all three men and was glad this wouldn't be the last I'd see of them.

Andrew leaned toward me, his voice loud enough for only myself to hear. "What do you think they'll have us doing first?"

As long as they kept their word and helped us as they prom- ised, it really didn't matter. Anything was better than being back on Siana. "Let me get a good night's sleep and a hearty breakfast, and I'm game for anything."

I lay in bed later that night thinking about my journey so far. Lia had set me up in a nice two-bedroom apartment, and I'd been able to get credit from my first paycheck to get the things I need- ed for it.

Andrew, Gerell, and Lincoln lived across the street from me and had decided to stay together in a three-bedroom, two-bath duplex. We were some of the few that had remained, as most people just wanted to go back home.

My story was probably no different from many others and that's what made it so upsetting. Renee and Ed had to be two of the most disgusting people I'd ever met and I cursed out loud at the thought that I didn't even know if they were dead or alive.

It didn't really matter. Lia's crew had that whole city on lock down and with the help of a few other coalitions were slowly making their way through that entire world.

I sunk deeper into the covers, happy to finally be on my own after living in somebody else's home for so long. This was a new beginning for me, and one I planned on embracing with everything I had.

Two years ago, I could have never seen myself here. I'd been through a lot, been challenged in ways I'd never dreamed, but I'd made it.

When I thought about it, I guessed that's all that mattered. No matter what life threw at me, no matter how far I sunk, there was still a light shining at the end of the tunnel.

I didn't always fight for it, half the time I didn't even know it was there. Yet, every day I stayed breathing, was a day I had a chance to make a difference in my life and the lives of others.

So, yeah, I'd take this second chance. I'd take it, and do everything I could to help others who couldn't help themselves.

They'd been me once, and I, them. That I'd lived on the streets the last couple of years, then been kidnapped, and almost sold, but still came out on the other side, meant that others could as well.

My resolve strengthened, and I vowed to never turn a blind eye to those in need, as many hadn't turned a blind eye to me.

A GATHERING OF SUCCUBI

ONE

The only light in the club came from the blue and silver strobes illuminating the stage. I ordered a beer from the bar and sat down to enjoy the show, glad to finally have a night off work.

The smell of spiced beef and whiskey permeated the air and I inhaled deeply, loving the scent. It wasn't often that I got to come here, but when I did, I made sure to enjoy myself to the fullest.

The incubus on stage shook his hips and sashayed back and forth, doing everything he could to earn those hard-earned bills lying dormant at his feet.

I pulled out a stack of ones, about twenty or so, and placed them on the table. That was all I was willing to spend on a night out. Now I just needed to get my ground game going.

I whistled and tossed out a couple of dollars, thinking I needed to save some for that private lap dance I hoped to get later.

Guyess, who was currently humping the floor, stood about six feet tall, his dark skin tattooed with the mark of the clan Glecics. That meant he was a descended of one of the First Families.

There were five First Families living in Dupoint. I'd lived here all my life and had no plans of moving.

I was descended from one of the First Families as well. I didn't put much stock in it, though. Hell, I figured we were all interconnected in some way or another.

Yet, to some, just the prestige of having the mark of a First Family meant everything. It did come with a certain amount of respect and maybe a freebie here and there, but that was about it.

The First Families were those whose iron fist had ruled since man had walked on all fours. Each country had them, and all laws that governed the magical community went through them.

With the flip of the hand or the wink of an eye, they could seal your future in death and despair or prosperity and prestige. Their word was final, and no one dared challenge it, not even those of us descended from them.

Guyess lost his shirt, and the crowd erupted in screams. I laughed, enjoying the show, and tossed a few more bills his way. He rocked to the floor, came back up with a spin, unleashing his claws and baring his razor-sharp teeth.

My drink arrived, and I downed half of it, never taking my eyes off the stage. Guyess's tongue, which reached well past his chest, flicked out and a hush fell over the crowd. My, what a talented one he was.

Heat flooded me, and I squirmed in my seat, wishing I could get in on the action tonight. I wanted it, wanted him, but my body wasn't ready to receive love at such a high voltage level.

I called for another drink and hiked one of my legs up on the seat in front of me. I'd have to find a lesser lover for tonight because I'd already reached my threshold for the month.

Guyess dropped again, this time taking his pants off, and throwing them into the crowd. The other succubi around me rushed the stage, and I braced myself because this was the moment I'd been waiting all night for.

The sooner he finished his routine, the sooner someone would come out that I could take home for the evening.

Underpants now gone, Guyess threw himself into the crowd. Horny succubi snatched him up and carried him to one of the private rooms in the back. At least that's what I think they did with him anyway.

I exhaled deeply, because hopefully, the next dancer wouldn't be an incubus, which meant it would be safe for me to have sex with him.

The strobes changed from blue and silver to black and red, indicating the next performer was ready to take the stage. I licked my lips, eager for the action, so of course, that was the moment my damn phone decided to ring. I pulled it out and scowled before answering. It was my boss, which meant my evening was now canceled anyway.

"Time to suit up, Kia. Got an illegal draining over in Morse town." I rolled my eyes as I stuffed the phone back into my pocket and called for another drink. That meant either a succubus or an incubus had drained a human of its life, and now it was up to me and my partner to go clean it up and find out who'd done it.

The crowd cheered as a tall hunkering figure came out, barely clothed and skin glistening. Disgusted to be missing it, I said fuck the second drink and walked into the night air of a hot Virginia summer.

I headed for Klemn, the name of the house I lived in and the last place I'd seen my partner. It was a home shared by many mystical creatures like myself. All who lived there were in law enforcement, but with different skill sets and agendas.

My partner, Boya, was a dranghum, and I knew I'd probably be sharing a room with him tonight. Dranghums were descended from dragons.

They existed in human form but had many characteristics of their late ancestors. Some believed them to be more powerful than succubi and incubi, but that wasn't a line of thought that I encouraged.

I'd wanted to give him a break from me and my sexual needs. Not that he wanted one. I just didn't like draining him too much, too fast. He could take it. I just didn't want to wear him out, as I knew I'd need him again sooner or later.

Walking up the front steps, the first person I saw was Lin. With light brown skin and a close shave his was simply breathtaking. His broad chest and clearly defined muscles were a testament to his weekly work-out schedule and careful eating habits.

He sat, shoulders hunched, eyes drawn together, staring at an empty spot in the yard. My heart softened at the sight of him, and a small smile tugged at my lips, as it often did when we were together.

Lin was my go to incubus for, well, anything. If I wanted mind-blowing, out of this century sex, I went to Lin. If I needed a shoulder to cry on or someone to help me rip the world apart, I called Lin. But like with many good things, it had its drawbacks.

Sex between succubi and incubi could only happen once a month. It was just too destabilizing to do it more than that. Our bodies couldn't take it. Two high voltage entities coming together often canceled each other out, such was the case with us.

The thing about incubi and dranghums was that their bodies stayed hot, while succubi, like myself, constantly ran cold. Which is what made Lin and Boya such excellent lovers for me. We completed each other. Their heat warmed my core, while my ice tampered their fire. Which was a satisfying deal for all involved.

Then there were those nights that Boya and Lin spent together. Nights I wasn't a part of… but that was a whole other story altogether.

Lin still hadn't looked up yet. I walked up the last few steps and took a seat beside him on the porch. "What's wrong?" I rubbed my fingers on the back of his hand, electricity shooting through us both from the brief contact.

He laced his fingers with mine and brought them to his lips for a small kiss. That was all we dared while our bodies were still recovering from our last sexual encounter.

"Got a call from Misha's roommate. Misha's in a bad way. Roommate said she needs help or she's not sure what might happen. Thinks she might have some kind of powers now." His voice came out low and sad.

I gave his hand a quick squeeze. Misha and Mitch were twenty-year-old twins, and for two years, Lin had dated their father. He loved those kids and I knew he'd do whatever he had to just to make sure they were okay.

He'd broken up with their father three years ago, but he'd never been able to fully detangle himself from the twins.

I ran my fingers through his hair, trying to offer what comfort I could. "What are you going to do?" I asked quietly. He wanted me to help. That much I could sense, but I had this case the chief had just given me, and I had to get on that before it grew too cold.

"I know," he said, reading my mind. A feeling of warmness spread through me at his easy acceptance, and I couldn't help leaning over and placing a small kiss on his cheek.

Energy sparked between us, and I pulled back before it got too out of control. "Be careful."

I left him on the porch and walked into the house. The smell of garlic and onions filled the air and I knew that somebody was hard at work in the kitchen.

Still, with twenty-something agents in residence, that could be just about anyone. A series of whoops and groans led me to the den.

Boya sat at our card table, playing a game of spades with Steva, of panther descent, Iscca, another dranghum, and Ninia, a succubus. Boya and Steva were teammates and sat across from each other. As did Iscca and Ninia.

Boya slammed down his last card, and jumped in the air, pumping his fist. "When ya'll gonna learn not to fuck with the awesome combination of that dragon and panther magic." His brown hair stuck to his forehead with sweat, a nice contrast to his tanned skin. Most of his hair reached just below his chin, and was curly enough, without being too curly, but still thick and full.

Steva, who was about the same complexion as myself with jet black hair and emerald green eyes, drowned his beer and stood. He was a tall man and loomed over my five-foot-six frame by about three inches, as did Boya. "Gotta get on the beat. Come on Ninia, we got a case."

Ninia's skin was a little darker than mine. Where I was a shade beyond walnut, she was a more beautiful, smooth ebony. She stood about five-foot-seven and her short spiked red hair perfectly complimented the red in her eyes. "Hey, Kia. You find something for later?" Succubi, we needed sex every night, couldn't function or think properly without it.

"Not yet, you?"

She downed the rest of her beer and went to stand beside

her partner. "Got a bear lined up for later."

Oh, good one. Those descended from bear DNA had an excellent sense of smell and often knew your favorite sexual position without being told. They made spectacular lovers and it was something for me to keep in mind for later.

"You got the deets?" Boya asked. Because, of course, he'd been too busy playing cards to answer when the chief had called. No doubt he'd looked at his phone and taken it for granted that I'd have the information when I got here.

I gave him a hard stare. Boya was a top-notch investigator, but his competitive spirit just couldn't allow him to fold on a game, no matter how high the stakes.

"We're going to Morse town."

Boya slid the cards across the table to Iscca. "Next time you and Ninia deal."

Iscca waved a hand over his head. His hair was black but cut so close that you could hardly tell. He also had an earring in his nose that sparkled and shined from the overhead light. His skin was paler than Boya's, but not by much.

He decided not to ignore Boya's taunting and blew a small line of fire toward the other man's head. Boya bent down, caught the fire in his mouth, and shook himself all over. "Thanks for the energizer, bro. We gotta go."

Lin was no longer on the porch, but I hadn't noticed him come inside, which meant he probably went to check on the twins. To be honest, I expected nothing less of him.

Boya came out behind me, still throwing jabs at Iscca. I shook my head at his foolishness. "Why tease him like that?"

He laughed and then jumped in the car. I got in on the driver's side, and he waited until I was seated before answering. "That's how you play. Shit talking is the name of the game. You know that."

Yeah, I did know that, but Boya always seemed to take it a step too far. "You have to be able to take it if you give it," I scolded him.

He ignored that and asked, "What's happening in Morse Town?"

I'd almost forgotten that that's where we were headed. I gripped the wheel tight. "Another succubus draining."

He nodded, but didn't look happy, which was about right. None of us really liked going into Morse Town. It was just too easy to get in trouble there.

Dupoint was split into four parts. The human part, which was Morse Town. The humans who lived there had no clue that a bunch of magical and mystical creatures existed among them.

Then there was Spray town, which is where said mystical and magical creatures lived, well most of us anyway. Next was Winn town, which is where both humans and magical creatures lived, many who'd married and started families together.

Most of Winn's human residences were Samg, human families who'd aided and supported the supernatural community for thousands of years, and were paid handsomely for their help.

Each otherworldly family had at least three Samg families on call at all times. Other human residences of Winn consisted of those who had somehow found out that the creatures from their childhoods were real. They were the lucky ones.

Some of my kind killed humans on the spot once they realized they'd been discovered. It was illegal, and if found out, the perpetrator would be held accountable. Still, that didn't stop some from striking out and getting rid of anyone who would threaten our way of life.

I turned right, going into the wealthier part of Morse. I'd known from the address that this was going to be a big case.

Large brick houses loomed around us. Every single one sported manicured lawns, perfectly placed porch furniture, decorative mailboxes, and cars that cost more than my whole year's salary. This is what you got on the Northside of Morse town.

The last part of Dupoint was Riverwalk. That's where the First Families lived. Riverwalk made Morse town look like an upscale junkyard.

Numerous wards protected Riverwalk, alerting the residents and guards anytime anyone got close.

This also helped to ensure that the only people who got into Riverwalk were those who'd been specifically invited.

Magical creatures like myself and Boya would have a heavy price to pay if we were caught trying to sneak in there. Nobody got into Riverwalk unless the residents wanted you in Riverwalk.

The First Families had handed down many ill-taken decisions over the years and were probably scared that if left open and unguarded they'd be ambushed and wiped out completely.

They may have been right, but just one member of the original First Families held more power than myself and three of my kind combined, so it wasn't an easy feat any way you looked at it.

Boya breathed a small amount of fire into his hand and began to play with it, tossing it back and forth like a ball. "Been getting a lot of these succubus killings lately. Something bad is going on."

I agreed. The amount of illegal succubus drainings had almost tripled in the last couple of days. Boya shoved the ball back into his mouth and swallowed with a smoking burp.

"Do you have to do that?" I asked, waving smoke out of my face, and trying not to cough. I refused to give him the satisfaction.

That sly grin spread across his face, the one he sometimes got when he knew he'd done something wrong. "Now don't be like that, K." His eyes lit up, happy and pleased with his own mischief. "I thought you liked it when my smoke curled around you."

"Only when we're fucking, which we're not right now, so…"

He chuckled loudly, and I smiled. One thing I loved about Boya was his ability to turn anything into a joke. His offbeat sense of humor often lightened up my most rugged days.

I parked the car, and we got out. The yard looked like someone had taken a hairbrush and patted down each blade of grass until they were all the exact same length. The house sat a good length from the road, and was red brick, with blue shutters.

Somebody had obviously worked hard at making it into a home. They'd probably thought they'd spend lazy Sunday evenings sitting on the front porch sipping lemonade and watching their grandkids play.

It wasn't fair that their lives had been cut short and my jaw tightened at the thought of someone snatching it all away for their own sick pleasure.

"Figured we'd see you two," Detective Rosen said. Detective Rosen was a tall black woman who was a member of a Samg family. Her partner, Detective Mason was a tall white man, also Samg.

Unfortunately, neither worked for my family or Boya's and as such, they held no loyalties to either of us.

Boya smiled. "Thought we'd show you two how it's really done. What do we have?"

Rosen lowered her voice so that the other officers around, the ones who only knew us as special investigators, couldn't hear what she had to say.

"Definitely a succubus." She dropped to a hushed whisper. "Look, I'm going to clear the room. Give you guys a chance to do your thing."

I did like when they cooperated. It made things easier for all of us.

I appreciated it too, because she knew like I did, that if we didn't solve this quickly, the First Families would hold all succubi and incubi accountable. Until they found the culprit they'd probably gather us up, lock us away, and maybe even torture us until they got to the truth.

They'd done it before with other creatures. Once a black panther was out of control and ripping the throats out of humans and magical beings alike. They'd taken Steva that time, and he'd come back an empty shell of himself. It'd taken months of Ninia and Iscca being patient and working with him to restore him to his former self.

The same had happened with Boya when an enraged dragon kept setting half the city on fire. Boya had only been gone three days, until the guilty dragon (who'd counted a wife and three children among those being tortured for answers and clues) confessed, but it was three days that had marked a part of him that neither myself or Lin could reach.

I didn't want that to happen again. I needed to solve this to ensure the safety of myself and all other succubi and incubi around me, Lin and Ninia included.

TWO

The bedroom was on the top floor. Pictures of a smiling middle-aged couple lined the stairwell. A young man appeared in some of them, and I wondered if he was their son. If so, we needed to get in contact with him ASAP.

The sight that greeted us upon entering the murder room was one of disarray. Clothes had been pulled out of the draws and tossed about. The flat screen lay cracked on the floor. The woman's purse had been emptied, its contents piled in the corner.

Boya studied the curtains that now hung loosely on a cracked rod. "What about you, K? You really think a succubus did all this? What the hell for? Seems like overkill to me and that's not really ya'lls style, now is it?"

He was right. I looked at the two figures on the bed. Hollow. That's the first word that came to mind.

You could see their bones peeking out through the skin. Their eyeballs were now sunken, and the hair on their heads looked like wigs, fitted after their deaths. Chris and Alley Hemsworth, husband and wife, and latest victims of a succubus gone wild.

That was the working theory anyway, but the destruction of the room made me wonder why a succubus would bother. It seemed like too much of a hassle unless they were looking for something specific. The only question was what?

Boya checked over the bodies. "I can't find a mark."

"We'll let the chief know. The agency may need to take possession until they're found." I didn't even want to think of the chief's face when we delivered that news. It wouldn't be pretty.

Each succubus and incubus family carried a distinct marking often left behind after a killing. The problem was when two members of different families got together and created an offspring, who would of course, have a different marking. Then, if two people with changed marks had a child, well you got the picture.

We'd figure it out eventually, but it would take a while. The best thing for us to do now was collect any clues we could find and dissect them.

We needed to start with why a succubus would target Chris and Alley Hemsworth in the first place. Or was this just a random act brought on by a starving succubus who'd had no choice but to feed or die?

Then why mess up the room? I stepped over a cracked picture of the couple and picked it up. The two stood together in their front yard, beaming, a sold sign behind them.

It was cases like these that I tended to take personally. Two people who'd had their whole life ahead of them had been snuffed out because one of my kind couldn't control themselves.

The good news was that someone had had sex in here recently, and so it was easy for me to pick up a scent. I closed my eyes and tried to get a feel for the last few minutes of these people's lives.

A flash of sharp teeth flittered across my mind's eye, and then the Hemsworth's horror-riddled faces, right before they were drained of life. After that, nothing. "Shit." I shook my head, frustrated with myself.

I couldn't tell who was doing the attacking, or confirm them to be a succubus or maybe even an incubus.

Boya, who had been on his hands and knees looking under the bed, popped back up after hearing me cuss. "Anything?" He looked like he already knew the answer. His eyes were sympathetic, probably because he knew the fear of having the First Families pressing down on you.

"No," I said dejectedly. At this point, we had more questions than answers, and that was never a good way to start an investigation.

He gave me an, "it happens" look, before going back to his own search. Boya had a special talent for sensing things out that didn't fit with the other objects around it.

If the symmetry was off, if something was there that shouldn't be, he'd find it. He always did. Especially if it was in the first forty-eight hours. After that things tended to get muddled.

Finally, he came out from under the bed with a hand full of frog spit. Yuk. Frog spit was long, thick, yellow, and white. There was no way to mistake it, as nothing else looked like that. He'd been wearing a glove and he slipped it off and placed it in a plastic evidence bag to be analyzed later.

Using this new information, I closed my eyes again, determined that something would really click this time. An image gradually came to shape, black hair, long nails, and an overpowering desire to kill. My eyes popped open. There was a purpose behind this. I could feel it. I just didn't know what it was yet.

I told my partner what I'd seen.

He nodded and collected our supplies. "Guess we're going to Spray town then."

I let Boya drive when we got back in the car. He had a few frog informants, and so I figured I'd just sit back and let him do his thing.

He looked at my disappointed face and said something that he probably thought would make it better. "Got a clue this time. That's something."

I thought back to the feelings I'd had while in that room. "This was done deliberately. There was no loss of control. I'm almost sure of it."

He nodded, not doubting me at all. Which is one of the reasons we worked so well as partners. He always trusted my readings and never tried to contradict me or tell me I was wrong. Hey, it made for a harmonious working relationship if nothing else. "We can hit Gull up. See what he knows."

Gull was one of Boya's informants. Of frog descent, he had

his hand in many illegal elements. If he didn't know what was going on, he knew someone who did.

Gull lived in a nice, four-bedroom brick house, in Forest Hills. One of the more affluent communities in Spray Town. He ran numbers and did a host of other things that we'd never been able to make stick. Luckily for us, Gull hated competition and so he'd rat out his fellow criminals wherever the mood struck.

Gull had two teenage daughters. One opened the door and let us in. Tall with pale skin and black hair reaching just past her shoulders, she was used to seeing us by now and seemed more bored with our presence than anything else. "He's in the study," she said, then went back to the glowing screen on her iPhone.

Gull's house was nice and well kept. The furniture looked like it hadn't been sat on, ever. Rigid and firm, every piece still had the plastic on it. Pictures of him and his family lined the walls of the living room and either side of the hall. A small silver stand sat in the hallway, right beside the bathroom, with a golden antique phone on top of it. The phone actually worked, as I'd seen him and his wife use it on multiple occasions.

We had to go through the kitchen to get to the study. It too was immaculate. The scent of apples and cinnamon floated from the stove, infusing the whole air with the sweet smell.

t was warm and inviting, and my stomach growled as I realized that I hadn't had dinner.

Gull's study was a typical man cave. A large sunken recliner rested in one corner, a big screen TV right in front of it. His desk was in the center of the room and off to the right was a long brown sofa, with a chocolate-colored carpet covering the whole floor.

Everything smelled knew and looked a lot more expensive than I could afford, which told me that maybe crime paid well after all.

Gull was lying back on the couch, arms behind his head, bare feet crossed, remote on his stomach. He was a large man, skin slightly tinted green and eyes so big they bucked.

He sat up when he saw us, sweat breaking out on his forehead.

I cocked a brow at my partner. This was new. Gull was never nervous and the fact that he was now was more than a little disturbing.

The tilt of Boya's head told me he'd caught it too. He pulled the chair from behind Gull's desk and took a seat, rolling it across the floor and coming to a stop in front of the couch.

Usually cocky and self-assured, Gull squirmed in his seat, determined to look anywhere but at us.

Boya snatched the remote off Gull's belly and then cut the TV off, which was playing a new episode of a popular froggy crime drama, that I myself watched from time to time. "What did you do?" he asked the other man.

Gull stood, rubbing his hands on his jeans and looking as if he'd rather be anywhere else than locked in a room with the two of us. He grabbed another chair, sat it behind his desk, and made a show of shuffling some papers around. "It's late."

Boya shook his head. "I gotta say, Gull, you're making me wonder. Perhaps I should search your office, see what I can come up with." Boya tapped a finger to his chin. "I'm sure I'll find something." He made a show of looking through a few shelves and opening a couple of drawers.

Gull swallowed hard, teeth biting into his thumb until he realized and tucked his hands away.

Boya sat back on the edge of the desk. He leered toward Gull. "What are you hiding? I'm going to find out. You know I will. Best to tell me now, and maybe we can make it go away."

Gull's eyes darted from the floor, to the ceiling, to the bar. He seemed determined not to look our way. The only question was why.

A glass of liquor sat beside a folder on his desk. He tried to pick it up, but his hands shook so bad that he ended up dropping it to the floor. Brown liquid spilled out, immediately disappearing into the dark of the carpet. He stared at it for a second, then bolted from his seat, making a run for the patio doors.

Boya gave chase immediately, me following right behind. "Damnit Gull!"

Gull was gone. Jumping and leaping, he was halfway down

the street by the time we made it outside.

Smoke flared from Boya's nose and ears. "I'm going to take to the sky."

I nodded. "I'll follow on foot."

I felt for Gull when Boya finally did catch him. There was nothing he hated more than when a suspect made him run, or in this case fly.

Gull wasn't a man that scared easily, so for him to behave this way meant we were dealing with some bad shit.

I'd probably ran about three blocks when a force like a windstorm knocked me off my feet and into the brick wall behind me. I hit with a whoosh, the hard surface sending tiny sharp sparks up and down my back. A minor discomfort, but not enough to keep me down.

I sprung back up, hands out, energy flowing, ready to take on whatever creature dared challenge me.

Another hit and this one lifted me in the air and dropped me to the ground. Pain exploded behind my eyes and ricocheted around my face.

A pounding started in my ears and I sucked in a breath, trying to ease myself through the pain. "Fuuuck." I rolled on my side, hands massaging my face and neck.

I had to get up. If I stayed on the ground, they'd surely have me. This had to be about the Hemsworth's murder, no way would someone just attack an agent of the law without cause. Not unless they had a death wish anyway, which wasn't often the case.

I shakily came to one knee, sweat dripping from my face and down my back. Who the fuck? I tried to stand, but another hit sent me sprawling. Blood flew from my nose and I heard the bone when it cracked. I put a palm to it, trying to stop the bleeding.

A frog didn't have this kind of power. This wasn't Gull, besides he would never. "Stop being a coward and show yourself!" I tried to sound hard, but it came out garbled and disjointed, about how I felt at the moment.

I'd almost made it to my feet when something long and sharp plunged into my stomach. It felt like a thousand tiny pins ripping my insides apart. "Ugh." I fell to the ground, blood pouring from my abdominal wall.

My breath came hard now, my whole body sleek with sweat. I placed my hand on the wound, trying to slow down the leakage.

My eyes clouded over, and I blinked repeatedly, trying to clear them. It didn't work, but I couldn't dwell on that. Holding my hand out, I fired off a few weak energy blasts, hoping to stall whoever was after me.

My vision blurred again, and I knew from experience that I'd soon lose consciousness.

From far away, I heard a voice calling out to me. "Kia, what the fuck?" Boya. He sure sounded scared. I had no idea why, all I felt was cold. If I could just sleep a little while longer, then everything would be okay. I closed my eyes.

"Kia!" This guy again. Why was he so loud, and why did he sound so damn scared? Someone should tell him to chill. Not me, though, the only thing I wanted was a nap.

He dropped to the ground beside me and shook my shoulders. Interrupting me again. What was this dude's problem? As soon as I woke up we were going to have a long talk about boundaries.

He placed his mouth over mine and really, now wasn't the time for that. We really needed to talk, because-- "Take my energy so you can heal yourself."

Heal myself? Heal myself... Oh shit! I'd been stabbed, and was probably bleeding out.

I opened my mouth and drew his life force into me. The pain lessened to an ache, but I still needed more. Sex. I needed sex. Nothing healed a succubus or incubus better. I fumbled with his pants, trying to get the zipper down. "Please, Boya, I need..."

He kissed my forehead, moving a few strands of hair out of my face. "I know, baby. I've got you. Don't worry. I've got you." He removed his pants, and kissed me again, giving me more and more of his life force.

I tried to take my own pants off, but my hands were too sweaty and kept slipping. "Boya!" He snatched them away with one fluid motion, and then eased himself between my legs.

Trembling with anticipation, I wrapped my arms around his neck and pulled him closer. "Don't hold back," I whispered in his ear. "I want to feel every part of this." My back firm against the ground, I closed my eyes and allowed myself to heal.

By the time we finished, my wounds had started to close, and the pain was at least bearable. I picked up my pants, which Boya had ripped to shreds. Wondering what the hell I was going to wear home, I balled them up and threw them at him. "Good job, asshole."

He laughed and slung them down the alley. "Come on, baby. Now you know I'm going to fly you home."

I glared at him. "You're enjoying this, aren't you?"

He held out his arms and I limped into them. He lifted me up and I wrapped myself around his neck. "Finding you bleeding to death in an alley? Nah, K. Nothing enjoyable about that at all."

I closed my eyes and willed the burning behind them to go away. I hadn't thought of it from his perspective. How scared he must have been to walk up and find me bloody and unmoving.

I ran a hand through his hair, just to let him know that I was okay. He smiled slightly, which I took to mean he was grateful for the effort.

"Who did this to you?" he asked softly.

I shook my head and buried my face in his neck. "Didn't get a good look at them. Take me home."

He nodded. "Finally caught up with Gull about six blocks away. All he said was he'd rather go to jail than talk." Boya seemed resigned. "I'll leave him alone for now, might need his help on another case soon. Don't want to rattle him too much, right?"

I let him know that I agreed with his decision and we took off through the sky.

If we didn't find anything, we could always come back to Gull. If he knew something, we'd just have to find a way to get him to talk, because I wasn't willing to face the wrath of the First Families just because he'd chosen to stay silent.

Boya flew me into my bedroom window and deposited me on the bed. He made a move to get up, but I pulled him down beside me.

He raised an eyebrow.

I pointed to my half-closed stomach wound. "I'm not fully healed yet so…"

He gently stroked my face, his expression tender and loving. "I got you, babe," he mumbled against my skin. His lips were like a gentle caress, and I smiled in pleasure, always wanting more of him.

Flipping him over, I straddled his hips. "Seem like I've got you this time, babe."

He laughed and rubbed his rough hands up and down my bare arms. My eyes fluttered closed. Sometimes it was so easy to lose myself in his touch. "Everything's a competition with you, girl."

I kissed him again, sucking more of his life force in. "Only when you make it that way, boy."

Boya ended up healing me throughout the night and by the next morning I felt a lot more like myself.

The threat of the First Families still hung over me, though, and that made the whole night more bittersweet than anything else.

THREE

I walked into the kitchen that next morning completely healed and with nothing but food on my mind. Lin sat at the table writing something in a notepad. He had a plate of food in front of him, a cup of coffee and juice to the side.

Steva, who was doing the cooking, piled my plate high and handed it to me. "Didn't hear you come in last night."

I accepted it and took a seat beside Lin, nibbling on a piece of bacon. "Didn't know you were waiting up."

Ninia poured herself a cup of coffee. "He was just waiting for everyone to go to bed so he could sneak that siren chick upstairs."

Steva tore off a small piece of toast and threw it at his partner. "Why you gotta put me on blast like that, though."

Ninia batted the toast away and laughed. "Hey, you're the one who told everybody about my toenail fetish. I'm just returning the favor." She seemed pleased with herself, sipping her coffee with a sly grin on her face.

I laughed and scooped up a fork full of eggs.

Lin stood, and put his pad in his back pocket. "Going to talk to Misha. Come with?"

I dropped the eggs back on my plate and stood. My stomach growled its displeasure, and I patted it, promising to fill it up later. Lin wouldn't have asked unless he really wanted me there, so food could wait. "You owe me for this," I let him know, looking longingly at my abandoned breakfast.

He downed the rest of his coffee and pulled me close. "I'll let you give me a blowjob when we're done."

I squinted, and pushed him away. "Good way to get your dick bitten off, but you know, if that's one of your fetishes who am I to judge? Maybe you and Ninia could compare notes."

Ninia choked on her coffee. "Hey, don't put me in it, that's your mess."

She threw an apple at me, and I caught it with one hand. "Thanks." I took a large bite. "But your partner's the one that put you on blast, not me."

She playfully shooed me away, and I took another bite as Lin and I walked out the door.

Coming from a Samg family, the twins, Mitch and Misha, both resided in Winn Town. Lin took a deep breath, his hands flexing at his sides. This wasn't going to be easy, and if they were in trouble, it would be even worse.

I rubbed his back. "You good?"

His eyes stayed on the door. "Depends." He went ahead and knocked.

"Whataya want?" a small voice asked.

Lin put his hand on the door and leaned in. "It's Lin, Misha, open up."

"Come back. I'm busy now."

Lin looked at me, eyes intent. I raised a brow, letting him know that I was down for whatever he wanted to do.

He fired up. Energy flowing all around him, his hands pulsating with a power that would get him through that door whether she wanted him in there or not. "You going to make me do this?" He was hesitant.

I understood the reluctance. He didn't want to overstep his bounds. Like it or not, it was her right to hide behind the door and not open it if she didn't want to.

This was different, though. He was concerned for her safety. If he walked away and something happened to her, he'd never forgive himself. I just couldn't let that happen.

I powered up, ready to go in, but he looked at me and shook his head. "Don't do that. Let me talk her around."

I stepped aside, willing to do this his way. He knocked again. "Just need a minute, Misha. Open up."

The door creaked about an inch wide, and a small dark head peeked out, eyes cast toward the floor. Misha, just like her brother, had olive colored skin with short black hair.

Lin got straight to the point. "Heard you got powers now. How?"

She lifted her head, and her eyes flashed a wolfish yellow-orange. Whoa. I took a stepped back, not sure what we were dealing with, but ready to fight if I had to.

Lin put his hand on my arm to stay me, and then turned his attention back to Misha. "This what you want? You do this or was it done to you?"

Misha's eyes flashed bright and she growled low in her throat. "Gonna do the Riverwalk." With that she closed the door, leaving us stunned on the front porch.

I think I may have blinked three times before I could say anything. Because what the hell was she talking about? "Lin?"

He furrowed his brows, his gaze darting between the door and the living room window. "Come on." I hoped he wasn't thinking about breaking in. I was sure that wouldn't end well.

It wasn't until we were back in the car that he let me know what was on his mind. "Got to set up surveillance on her and her brother, see what's going on." Not sure they'd take too kindly to the intrusion, but I'd let him figure that out on his own.

I took out my phone, looking over my messages. "I need to meet up with Boya, anyway. I'll call you later to see what you've found out."

Boya was coming down the steps when I arrived back at the house. "Got a lead, come on."

His lead ended up being a cemetery in Winn town. A white-haired, milky skinned banshee sat on a bench, wiping her eyes and softly keening. Oh boy. "Helena, hey. What's the word?" Boya asked.

Her voice alone sounded like that of three, its musical quality only making it that more eerie. "Something is coming. The First Families are in danger. The balance is set. It is not final." She never looked at us and faded into thin air before we could question her further.

Boya ran a frustrated hand down his face. "Now what the hell does that mean?"

I stared at the spot she'd just vacated. "It means we're going to Riverwalk." My phone rang, and I whipped it out, already knowing who was on the other end. "Lin? Find something?" That was fast.

"Yup. Need you."

I said goodbye to Boya and then made my way to where Lin had asked me to meet him. He was parked on a side street three blocks from Misha's apartment. I scooted inside. "What are we doing?"

"Went to see Mitch. Thought he might have information about his sister. Got the same reaction."

I threw my hand over the headrest. "So his eyes are glowing too?"

Lin tapped his thumbs on the wheel, a clear sign that he was frustrated. "Think we're dealing with an absorber. Don't know who they're working for, though."

I sighed, because depending on who held the strings, this could be a big problem. Absorbers were rare. Highly sought out, these magical creatures could transfer powers from one being to another for short lengths of time. "They could stay that way for months," I said incredulously.

His jaw tightened, and I knew he was doing everything he

could to keep his anger in check. "To what end? Why power up a bunch of Samgs?"

"You think it's more than those two?"

His tapping intensified. "Couple of things Mitch said. Made me think there's at least a dozen of them."

Well, that wasn't good, but it was more than we'd known before, which was a start. "Seems like you got more out of him than his sister."

He shook his head. "Not much. We need to talk to Kevin."

I thought about the twin's father and how he and Lin had parted ways. I scrunched up my nose. "I'm pretty sure he hates you."

He chuckled, but it had no humor in it. He ran a slow hand across my face, his features going soft as he stared at me. "Yeah, well." He leaned over and placed a soft kiss on my lips.

I greedily took him in, as we exchanged energy and fed off each other. I slipped my fingers around his neck and he wrapped his arm around my waist and pulled me onto his lap.

Hmmm. It felt so good to be with him like this again. I placed my hands on either side of his face and guided his lips to mine. We exchanged more energy and then I started to feel myself go weak.

It was too soon. We still had a whole month to go before we could have sex again. Trying to force it before our bodies were ready would leave us both vulnerable.

My breath rugged, I tried to tamper down my desire. "We have to stop, baby. We can't do this."

He rested his head in the crook of my neck, trying to regulate his own breathing. "So easy to get caught up in you." He sat back in his seat and I hopped back over to mine.

"You want me to go with you? To talk to Kevin," I asked.

"Yup."

Lin started the car and I patted down my hair and wiped a hand across my face, trying to tell myself there were only a few weeks left before we could be together again.

We didn't really talk on the way, as Lin's attention seemed focused elsewhere. Probably on what he was going to say once we got there.

We'd only driven about ten minutes before the familiar house came into view.

Kevin lived in a one-story yellow clapboard. Lin pulled to the side and cut the engine. We got out and Lin knocked on the door a couple of times, while I stood off to the side waiting.

The unforgiving southern sun bore down hard, causing us both to constantly wipe sweat from our brows and face.

Kevin was tall, bald-headed, and had a set of eyebrows that needed their own personal barber. There was no mistaking his look of displeasure when he finally opened the door and saw it was us.

This was his usual greeting, and I found myself bracing for his icy response. "Didn't think I'd ever see you two again." It was said like a question.

Lin cleared his throat, his voice rough and scratchy. "You been good?"

Kevin's face stayed hard as stone.

Lin didn't let that stop him. "Mitch and Misha are in trouble. Let us in."

That gave him pause, and he stepped aside, granting us entrance. The house was very clean, but cluttered beyond belief.

The living room was small but was still expected to host two couches, a love seat, three armchairs, a coffee table, an entertainment stand with multiple objects on it, an open cooler with several bottles of beer sticking out, and a bunch of rectangular and square shaped odds and ends placed throughout the room.

The furniture looked to be about ten years old, but still sturdy and in good shape. The whole place smelled like sweet spiced cherry. The type left behind after someone had long ago put out a cigar, yet the smell refused to go away.

Kevin sat in one of the armchairs and crossed one leg atop the other, placing his clasped hands on his knees. He gave us a pointed look, disdain evident in his every move. "I could tell something was wrong when I talked to Misha the other day, but what I'm not sure of, is how that involves you, or you." He looked from me to Lin.

Lin's gaze never left Kevin. "Got a phone call. Checked it out. They have powers, Kevin. Eyes glowing orange and yellow. What have they been up to lately?"

Kevin swallowed hard. "I don't keep up with their day to day activities. They're adults now, out of the home. I'm very proud of them both." It sounded almost like a challenge.

I licked my lips. The air was charged, lots of intense emotions floating about.

Kevin sat back in his chair and picked up his coffee cup. "Good thing you didn't need anything, Kia. We may not have ever discovered what was going on with the twins."

This was an old argument and I refused to rise to the bait. Kevin had always resented my relationship with Lin, and insinuating that Lin would put my needs over the twins was nothing but insulting.

Lin and I were together before him and Kevin. We stayed together after him and Kevin. It's how we worked and anyone trying to get close to either of us already knew that. We never hid anything.

Like me, Lin ignored the comment completely. "Know anything that'll help?"

Kevin's lips tightened and his scowl intensified. It didn't faze me in the least. He was probably just pissed that we wouldn't give him the argument he so clearly wanted. "They've been hanging out a lot on Front street. I don't know what goes on there."

Lin stood, probably coming to the decision that there was nothing more to get out of him. "You'll know when we know."

Kevin walked us to the door. Hand on the handle, he looked at me. "Let's hope you don't have any unforeseen emergencies before then. I hate to think what will happen to my children if you do."

He gave a fake smile, then slammed the door in our faces. Like daughter, like father, I guessed.

Lin stared at the closed door for a second, and then started down the steps. "Need to check out Front street."

I nodded. "Well, I'm going to find my partner."

The chief called before I made it to Boya. I closed my eyes and answered my phone with a sigh, already sure of what he was ready to say.

"You got twenty-four hours to find this killer, Kia, before the First Families take all succubi and incubi off the street." He sounded both regretful and helpless. "You know how they are. Doesn't matter how many of you are innocent, as long as they have the guilty one in custody, and no more murders are taking place."

"Okay," I mumbled and hung up the phone.

I could almost feel the hands of the First Families starting to reach down and strangle me, and I rubbed a tensed hand around my neck, even though I knew nothing was there.

Once they turned their eyes our way, there'd be nothing that could stop them.

If these killings had been contained to magical creatures only, they wouldn't be so bothered, but humans had been killed.

The First Families focused so much on keeping the universe balanced and all things in its place that I wondered if something had happened before, that made them value human life above all others.

Either way, it meant that a resident of Morse town didn't get killed by one of my kind often. Now that they had, though, it was up to me and Boya to find out who'd done it. If not, then all other succubi and incubi would be in danger.

Four

Boya called while I was en route, and told me to meet him in an alley on Lee street. Apparently one of his sources had given him some useful information.

I shook my head in awe of his skills. No one knew how to work a contact the way Boya did. I didn't tell him about the time limit the First Families had imposed, figuring I'd focus that energy on the case and maybe have a breakthrough before my time was up.

The alley was in Winn town and I was starting to sense a pattern. Remembering what had happened the last time I'd walked unguarded into such a place. I powered up immediately, alert for anything out of the ordinary.

I walked down the alley Boya had specified and immediately saw him leaning up against a building, a black cowboy hat covering half his face.

"Is this you being incognito?" I asked.

Still leaning up against the wall, he slowly turned my way. "I wanted to look all dark and mysterious for you."

I chuckled slightly. "Really?"

He nodded. "Really."

I ignored that with the wave of a hand. "What we got here?"

He pointed to a small white house on the left side of the street. From what I could see, it looked decent, but a little rundown. "Word has it that they know something."

Okay. "Did you want to knock? Or…"

He shook his head and then pancaked himself against the wall, pulling me along with him. "According to my contact. There's a big meeting tonight." He hooked a thumb over his shoulder toward the house. "These people are supposed to be going." He looked at the time on his phone. "Right about now."

A couple of minutes later a door opened and two figures walked out. One male and one female. The guy appeared to be in his mid-twenties, while the woman looked to be pushing thirty. They were both dressed in black, heads down, they walked at a super-fast pace.

Boya called out before they could get too far. "Hey," he said, walking up to the pair. "Saw this gruesome double murder the other day over in Morse town. Wanna hear all about it?"

Two heads snapped up, teeth bared, eyes shining orange and yellow. "See you on the other side of the Riverwalk," the guy sneered.

I took a closer look at him and blanched. The pictures on the Hemsworth's wall… His hair was black now instead of brown and his nails were long and curled.

Though officers had notified him, Boya and I hadn't had the chance to talk to him yet. "Daryl Hemsworth?" I asked, mouth hung open a little in disbelief. "Did you kill your parents? Why?"

His eyes flashed again. "They saw something they weren't supposed to."

I powered up, knowing that trying to arrest him would most likely lead to a fight.

Boya's fingertips lit up, flames dancing across his hand. I blew energy out of my mouth, forming it into a ball, ready for one of them to make a move.

Boya took a step forth. "So, they saw you like this and you killed them?"

Daryl didn't look one bit sympathetic. "Never really liked 'em anyway," he smirked. "Besides, Rome wouldn't like that. Them knowing what they shouldn't."

I didn't know who this Rome was, but figured he was the one controlling them.

I bounced the energy from one hand to the other. "Or you didn't want them to get in the way of your 'Riverwalk'?"

The woman narrowed her eyes and pulled on Daryl's shirt. "Come on, Daryl. Rome wouldn't like this."

"Did Rome order you to kill your parents because they became a threat to your Riverwalk?"

A slight flinch. Slight, but still there and so I kept pushing. "Maybe he'll have you murder your grandmother next."

He jumped at me, much like Gull had when he'd escaped from us the day before, and that explained the frog spit that had been left behind at the murder scene.

Chris, didn't have frog DNA, though, so this had to be the absorbers doing. Why though? I didn't have time to ponder it farther as I needed to protect myself from his attack. I threw a powerful ball of energy, knocking him against the wall so hard that a few bricks crumbled behind him.

That would have killed a normal man, but Daryl apparently was no longer a normal man. It did stun him, though, but then he was up and lunging again.

The woman looked on, wringing her hands and mumbling "Rome won't like this." Repeatedly.

Boya pointed one of his fingers and fire leaped from his nail and wrapped itself around Daryl's neck. The other man fell to his knees choking and gagging, trying hard to remove the flame.

"Rome says to kill anybody that gets in the way." The girl's eye's flashed, and before I knew it, I was on the ground looking up at the stars. This bitch! I recognized her energy as the one who'd blasted me in the alleyway the day before.

No way was she going to get me again. I'd made a mistake the last time in trying to search out where she was coming from. This time, I simply laid still and focused.

It only took a second, and I knew she was coming up behind me. I raised my hand and knocked her back with a power blast before she could advance any further.

Knowing how fast she could move, I hurriedly jumped onto her prone body. She'd been stunned, but her eyes flashed the minute I touched her.

Not wasting time, I opened her mouth and proceeded to suck out enough of her life force to subdue her.

I licked my lips when I finished, feeling a powerful sensation that flowed through my veins and over my whole body.

Hmmm. I hadn't expected this much of a boost. I'd never known a human to have this much power. I wasn't even sure how her body could contain it, but that spoke to the skill and knowledge of the absorber involved.

That was something to think about later. For now, I cuffed her and turned to check on my partner.

Boya stood above Daryl, who had an impressive rope burn on his neck and whose eyes were fixed and staring.

I gasped at Boya. "Did you. .?"

Boya pulled a card and a few other items out of the man's pocket. "Come on, K. What kind of dragon do you think I am? I didn't kill the boy. I just stunned his ass."

Realizing how tired I was, I rested my back against the wall and pulled out my phone. "I'm going to call in a cleanup crew. Me and you, we have to get to Lin."

He paused in his searching. "Why?"

I punched in the number to our chief. "Cause we are all working the same case."

He looked at one of the cards he'd pulled out of Daryl's pocket. "This is marked with today's date, but the only thing it says is 'Riverwalk'."

I advised the chief of the situation and assured him we'd wait until help arrived. "No address?" I asked Boya after I'd hung up the phone.

He playfully tsked at me. "Come on now, babe. You didn't expect them to do all the work for us, did you? Where's your sense of adventure?"

I still hadn't caught my breath yet, so he could keep his adventure. "I think I've had enough for one day," I said dryly.

We needed to talk to the First Families. Riverwalk was where they lived and there had to be a reason that Daryl, Misha, and the others kept mentioning it.

We met up with Lin on Clay street, which was the closest we

could get to Riverwalk, without causing the underlings and body-guards of the First Families to blast us.

I wrapped my arms around myself, a small shiver passing through me. It gave me the creeps being here. I came from a First Family, and even I couldn't just walk into Riverwalk whenever the mood struck. "How do you want to do this?" I asked Boya and Lin.

Boya looked to Lin and I shook my head, not understanding their dynamic at all. Any other time Boya would have jumped right in with some outlandish plan.

With Lin, it was almost like he was scared of disappointing the other man. I briefly wondered how they were in bed together when I wasn't around. I could've just intruded on their thoughts, their sexual thoughts that is, but I tried not to pry into other people's minds unless I absolutely had to.

I shook my head trying to clear it. Now wasn't the time, and no way did I need to know the things they did when I wasn't around.

Lin turned his attention to the sign that stated where Spray ended and Riverwalk began. "Misha still reads as human. What about the two in the alley?"

I thought about it and realized that'd probably been the reason they'd been able to sneak up on me. "They read human too."

Lin looked toward the sign again. "We can't get closer. They can."

Yeah, they could. Something about this resonated with me. I thought about it for a second, turning the pieces over in my mind. They'd all mentioned Riverwalk, there had to be a reason why.

We all knew that humans could drive straight up to the entrance. They'd be politely turned away, but they were never phys-ically harmed, and those who guarded Riverwalk would never use magic if the person read human.

Boya shook his head in disbelief. "So this Rome character figures he'll get into Riverwalk using these super powered hu-mans? For what? To make a move on the First Families?" He pulled out his phone and walked a few steps back. "I'm going to call the chief." Which is exactly where my thoughts were going. Of course, they were going after the First Families. The only question was why.

Lin seemed preoccupied with the glowing screen in his hand. "How do you want to play this?" I asked him.

He held up the gadget he'd been staring at. "Put a tracking device on Mitch's car. It's stopped between Craighead and Industrial Avenue."

I shuddered just thinking about it. Craighead was filled with warehouses. The things that went on in some of them was probably better left in the shadows. There'd be hundreds of energy signals there too, too many for myself and Lin to handle alone.

I picked up my phone and begin to punch in numbers. "I'll call Ninia and Steva and tell them to meet us there." I only had to talk for a minute for them to understand and agree to help.

Boya hung up his phone. "Chief said not to engage until backup is available."

I thought that was a good idea. Especially since we didn't know how many assailants we were dealing with. "Ninia and Steva are on the way. We need to meet them there. Try to at least find where Rome and his crew are. Maybe get some kind of count."

I opened the car door, ready to get back in, when a powerful signal stopped me cold. I whipped around, powering up, Boya and Lin doing the same.

A man stepped out of the shadows. He was dressed in plain black slacks and a brown shirt, but his eyes were drawn tightly together, his face mean and hard. "You've been here over ten minutes. Why?" His voice was brittle and his stance like that of a brick house.

Lin was the first to answer. "Got word of a threat against the First Families. Came here to warn them."

The man didn't even flinch. "Leave."

Boya stood up straighter. "We're not at the mouth of Riverwalk. What's the problem?"

The muscle man's hands turned to claws. "Leave." He said it just a little more forcibly this time and I took a step back without even realizing.

I tried to reason with him. "Look, just a heads up, there are some humans running around, infused with a whole lot of power. If you let them get close enough they could do some real damage."

He didn't look impressed and I didn't know what else to say to make him understand. I had one last thing I needed him to know. "You can tell the First Families that it wasn't a succubus or incubus doing the killings. It was just made to look that way. The super powered humans work for a guy named Rome. He's the one who orchestrated this whole thing. No Cubus hands got dirty this time."

I knew that probably wasn't enough to save us from them, not if we didn't have proof, but at least it was a start. I slipped into the passenger side of the car, my eyes on the muscle man the whole time.

His face gave nothing away, but I had felt a slight spike in his energy signal when I'd mentioned the name Rome.

Whether they knew about this new danger or not, the name Rome wasn't foreign to them. I raised a brow at Boya and Lin, letting them know that I had something.

Boya hopped into the driver's seat then changed his mind and sat backwards out of the rolled down car window. He placed his hands on the hood. "Well, I guess we'll go do your job for you then." He scooted back in his seat and I shook my head at him.

"You just can't help yourself, can you?"

"It's why you love me, dear." He ran his hand through the back of my hair and pulled me in for a soft kiss. "Come on, let's go kick this Rome guy's ass."

FIVE

Ninia, Steva, and Iscca were already there searching when we arrived. Ninia held her hands out in front of her, focusing her energy. "There's a lot of weird shit going on here, but we haven't found any yellow-eyed humans yet."

Steva's claws twitched at his sides. "Saw an orgy over there." He pointed to another warehouse. "A wedding ceremony in there." He hooked a thumb. "Dude has an office set up in that one."

I reeled at the enormity of it all, but we weren't vice agents. That was somebody else's ground to cover. Tonight, my only concern was keeping my kind save from the unfair roundup and persecution of the First Families.

Ninia walked toward the right. "I feel humans."

I laced hands with her and together we used our powers to reach out and search for the signal that humans gave off. The thing that helped us was that regular humans never really entered Spray, and so if we found any, it had to be the super-powered ones.

Boya walked forward. "Chief said to wait for back up. I'd say you three are back up." He pointed to Ninia, Steva, and Iscca. "Lin?"

Lin powered up. "Mitch's there. Probably Misha too. I say let's go."

Boya looked at him like he'd just gifted him the moon, the

sun, and the stars. Lin's faced softened under the scrutiny, and without warning, he pulled Boya in for a quick kiss. Their foreheads touched for a moment before Lin pushed him away, both breathing hard and licking their lips.

I watched with interest. These two together were a mystery to me. Boya melted like a stick of butter whenever Lin was around, and even I didn't have that effect on him.

At least I didn't think I did. I cleared my throat. "If you boys are finished, I'd like to get this over with."

We fanned out in six different directions. I'd probably searched for about ten minutes when I came across a large brown warehouse set off in the back, sandwiched between a small tin one and another brown one. The energy signal was huge, a lot of them humans. *I think I found it.* I communicated to Ninia.

On my way.

Boya crept up beside me, and I nodded toward the building I suspected. He powered up, and I reached out to Lin to let him know where we were.

Ninia made contact. *Got Steva and Iscca with me. We're going in from the back.*

Ok, we'll cover the front.

Lin joined us in mere seconds. I thought about how we could handle this. "Ninia and the others are around back. Lin, you go to the right. Boya you hit'em from the left." I cracked my knuckles, trying to psych myself up for the battle I knew was coming. "I'm going to knock on the front door."

I called out to Ninia. *Count of three?*

Gotcha. She replied.

One, I powered up. Two, I raised my hands in the air and walked closer to the door. On the count of three I called out to Ninia, and we damn near tore the whole warehouse apart. The doors made a loud booming sound and then exploded from both ends.

Twenty human men and women were lined up side by side. Eyes glazed over, they stared at the alluring figure in front of them. I found it strange that none of them had reacted to the blown off doors. As I got closer I began to understand why.

This man, this Rome, he was an absorber all right, but it was more than that. He stood tall, with short cropped brown hair and a long nose that said aristocrat.

His skin was a few shades lighter than Boya's, but not quite as pale as Iscca's. Sweat trickled down my back as the power in him called out to me.

I took a deep breath and tried to regain my emotions. I'd never felt anything like this. The pull alone was enough to draw you in, to make you want to stay. It was… hypnotizing, this vibe he gave off. At the same time, it felt so damn familiar that I knew I'd felt it before.

Ninia named it before I could. *He has incubus blood. Be careful.* Of course, that's what it was. I was in contact with enough incubus daily, that I should have known.

Still, he was an absorber too. Those two things mixed together made for a very powerful combination. An incubus absorber, I'd never met one before, but I knew we had to proceed with caution.

I threw that thought out to Lin and then looked at the two beings beside Rome. One was the Banshee, Helena, from the cemetery and the other was a Pantue. Pantues were descended from pig DNA. Very smart, with above average intelligence, they were often used as business advisers and personal counsels.

Helena looked at me from under her eyelids. Her smile crooked and victorious as if they'd already won. "Perhaps it was *your* deaths, I foresaw." She sang. All twenty humans turned our way after that.

The attack was swift, but I was ready. I had three come at me, but I waited until they got close before I blew them back with my energy.

They fell to the ground hard, but were back up in a second as if I'd simply knocked a fly off their shoulder, no harm done at all.

Vicious grins on their faces, they circled around me, as if trying to figure the best way to take me down.

Ninia also had three circling. Boya had three. Lin five. Steva three. Iscca three. We'd walked into a trap. I could feel it down to my bones. They'd been waiting for us.

Misha circled around Ninia, while Mitch was one of the ones on Boya. They wouldn't hurt them if they could avoid it, but if it came down to the line, then, well, Boya and Ninia would do what they had to do to survive.

Rome walked down the middle of the warehouse, his hands clasped behind his back, a sick smile plastered on his face.

The Banshee and the Pantue walked behind him. Helena bared her teeth, her white hair flying, eyes darting around the room rapidly. The Pantue walked with his head up. And his eyes straight. The look on his face said that this was all beneath him.

Rome came to stand before us. His gaze traveled from me, to Lin, to Ninia.

That feeling of needing to be closer to him was still there, but I was doing everything I could to temper it. "Brothers and sisters. I see that you got my invitation." He turned to the Banshee. "I guess we have Helena to thank for that." The woman beamed at his praise and I tried not to vomit.

He gestured toward the twins. "As well as Mitch and Misha. You played your parts well. Thank you." Though there was a spike in their body temperatures, neither twin moved a muscle.

Rome walked around Lin, Ninia, and me. He raised an index finger. "You know, you have to ask yourself why we allow the First Families to hold so much power, make all the rules." He waited for a response and when he got none, he continued. "I don't want to fight with you, my fellow Cubuses. I want you to join me. I want us to work together."

He watched our faces closely, no doubt trying to gauge our reaction. "I want to put the power in the hands of the people. Does that make sense?" He looked between us again, eyebrow raised.

The feeling to be close to him started to get stronger. So I bit my lip hard to get rid of it. His voice was like smooth wine. "Shouldn't we be in control of our own lives? That's all I'm asking." He made it sound so reasonable, but that way laid danger. I already knew that.

Waiting for us to agree and getting nothing, this time when

he spoke his voice came out hard and almost taunting. "There's been a big round of succubus killings. How long before the First Families bring down their gavel on both the innocent and guilty of our kind."

He looked from me to Ninia to Lin. "Doesn't it make you mad? To be held accountable for something you didn't do? What happens the next time or the time after that?"

He shook his head as if to say we just didn't get it, and if we could see things his way, then everything would be fine. "Why live in fear if we don't have to? That's all I'm asking."

My hands curled at my sides. It wasn't as simple as he made it out to be, and he knew that. "So you killed innocent humans just to put us on the defensive, thinking we'd come running into your arms and help your plot to take out the First Families?"

An almost amused look crossed his face as he stared at me. "No. Well, not at first. I told my disciples to kill anyone who got in their way."

"So Chris and Alley Hemsworth?"

He thought about it for a second before answering. "Saw their son using his newfound powers and wouldn't back down. He called, and asked what he should do, and so I told him." His grin was cocky and smug now, and the only thing I wanted was to wipe it off his face.

Ninia leaned her head to the side as if putting all the pieces together. "So because you gave the humans power, and you're an incubus, that's why it looked like a succubus or incubus did the killings, when all along it was just your super powered army of twenty."

He looked pleased that she'd come to that conclusion on her own. "I never meant for any Cubus to take the blame for this. When transferring powers, you never know what the end result will be. Some of your own power always leaks through."

He seemed a little too happy with himself, and I got the feeling that nothing snuck through unless he wanted it to. "Kind of unavoidable. No, I didn't intend for it to happen, but once it did, I saw an opportunity. I knew it wouldn't be long before the First Families brought down their hammer of justice. And after that...."

"You thought we'd be more likely to be on your side from fear of the First Families?" I tried to hold onto my patience just a little longer. "Sorry, but that's not going to happen." I let him know.

He nodded as if he'd expected as much and then launched into a long monolog of why he was really doing this. "My cousin Derik. He'd had too much to drink one night, thought he'd bust into Riverwalk and maybe air out a grievance or two."

His face tensed up and for the first time, I saw genuine emotion there. "They didn't ask questions. Didn't give him a chance to voice his concerns. They killed him, on the spot, because he dared invade their precious sanctuary." His voice went low and deadly on that last part, and I could clearly feel the force of his anger.

Then, as quickly as it had appeared, it was gone and he was back to that charming smile and "come-hither-vibe.

A shiver ran down my spine and sweat broke out on my forehead. I had to stay strong. I couldn't allow myself to get caught up in his bullshit. His cousin knew the risk going into Riverwalk uninvited. We all did.

"You know, you may have been able to make a case if you hadn't caused the murder of Chris and Alley Hemsworth, along with five other innocent humans. Or did you think we'd forget that little detail?" I asked.

Rome flicked his hand, not looking bothered by this at all. "You don't really believe we can do this without spilled blood do you, Kia?" Hearing my name on his lips had me inhaling sharply, trying to fight the desire that came naturally to both succubi and incubi alike.

I stilled myself and vowed not give in to him.

"Come on now, let us not play games." His chest swelled with, I don't know, pride. "There's so much power in this room. Just between the four of us."

He pointed to himself, Lin, Ninia, and me. "And your panther and dragon friends are encouraged to join us, of course. They too have been unfairly persecuted by the First Families. I remember when both groups were gathered up and taken away just because one panther or one dragon got out of control."

"I pass," Boya said, smoke coming out of his nose and mouth.

Iscca exhaled fire, angry dark smoke flew out and circled the room. "I pass as well."

Steva extended his claws and roared loudly, showing off his sharp teeth and fangs. "Pass."

Rome chuckled and looked undaunted, proving that he'd had no interest in them in the first place. He turned to those of us with Cubus blood. "They've made their decision. Have you made yours?"

I sent a blast of energy right by his head, missing him by only an inch. He looked completely unimpressed and simply turned his attention to Ninia and Lin. "So say you all?" I hadn't really tried to hit him, mostly just warn him off.

Ninia took the exact appearance of one of the humans circling her. The man jumped back, with a gasp as if shocked to see his own image standing before him. His mouth hung open, and his eyes said "how?"

She didn't answer. Instead, she flipped him over, while blasting the man beside him, sending him to his knees with a grunt. Misha sent her hurling across the room, probably hoping to keep her out of the way.

One of the men surrounding Lin jumped toward him, and with lighting fast speed Lin's hands transformed into sharp talons scraping the man across the face. The man screamed out in pain, while frantically holding his hands to his face trying to stop the blood loss. After that, all hell broke loose.

The three surrounding me lunged. I sensed it coming and dropped to a low spin, knocking two off their feet and throwing the other across the room.

Like three well-tuned jack-in-the-boxes, they bounced back immediately.

I released my claws and bared my fangs daring them to come at me again.

Lin's hands moved chaotically. Energy flew all around him

in a way that seemed undisciplined and loose but was completely controlled and measured.

A calculated blast directed at two of the super humans surrounding him split them in half. One man, he pulled close and whispered hellish nightmares in his ear. The man raked long nails down his eyes and ears at a supersonic speed, tearing his eyeballs out, and causing both ears to hang loosely from his head, both mangled and destroyed.

I invaded the mind of one of my assailants, searched out his worst fear, and then sent him rapid-fire images of it until he fell to the ground twitching and screaming.

Ninia burrowed her energy into one woman's body, ripping her chest out and crushing her heart.

I turned to the side just in time to receive a hard blow to my face. It rocked me off balance, and I stumbled back and fell to the ground.

My vision blurred, and I shook my head trying to clear it. Before I could get up, something hard and solid pressed down on my neck cutting off my air supply.

My pulse sped up and true fear shot through me. Panic. I was panicking and that wouldn't help, but I couldn't breathe.

I could hear myself gagging and gasping and nothing had ever sounded so horrific in my life. I tried to use my energy, my hands, anything to get it off me, but I couldn't move. My windpipe was being crushed and I couldn't fucking move.

The foot moved just a little, but it was enough for me to try and get a stronghold on it. I grabbed at it with my hand, but I was so weak that I couldn't get any kind of grip, and my arm slipped back to the floor.

I tried again, but before I could even make contact, a different human started a relentless assault, kicking me in my stomach and lower body.

It felt like I was being stomped by an elephant and there was nothing to insulate me from it. I had to just lay there and take it, which wasn't something I was good at.

Then the boot moved and the kicking stopped. Relieved, I tried to sit up, but a sharp knife across my right cheek knocked me back again.

I put a hand to my face, trying to stop the bleeding, but then the blade cut me again, slicing into my chest and stomach.

I could feel the blood leaking out, could feel myself losing consciousness. The pain was so intense that I actually lost my breath for a moment trying to get a handle on it.

I put my arms up to protect my face, but I was too weak to sustain it, and soon I was completely unprotected.

I needed to focus on healing myself. That's the thing about Cubus. We could partly heal ourselves, but it wasn't a hundred percent. Sex was the preferred method and a lot more efficient.

Doing it ourselves took too much out of us and gave little back. Right now, it was the only thing that could save me, so I had to give it a try.

I closed my eyes. I needed to gather up all the energy I had left. It floated above me and stretched to cover the length of my body. It wasn't much, but it was enough to act as a low-level shield against my assailants.

I still needed some of it to heal me, though. So without causing gaps in the protective layer, I pulled off bits and parts, sending it to my face, stomach, and legs. I felt a bit of relief as some of the wounds closed and the bleeding stopped.

From the corner of my eye, I could see Boya steadily destroying two of the humans that were on him.

He wrapped around the throat of one, choking him to the ground. He sent smoke into the mouth of another, exploding his lungs and dropping him to the floor.

Mitch, he just kept knocking to the floor, and kicking away, trying not to hurt the boy.

Steva had his claws out and was literally ripping his opponents apart. Iscca simply set fire to anyone who opposed him, he and Boya both putting out the flames as quickly as they started them.

My energy began to wane, and I knew it wouldn't be long before it dissipated altogether. I needed to force it outward because right now it was the only weapon I had.

It was a gamble, because if it wasn't strong enough to get them off me then I'd just lost the only protection that I had.

Still, I had to try. I closed my eyes and pushed every bit of it out. The super humans that were on me flew back and landed somewhere I couldn't see. I took a breath, hoping that meant the end of them.

Once I was sure they wouldn't be coming back, I got shakily to my feet. My legs wobbled and the unsteadiness in them meant I couldn't really stand straight, but I held my body rigid, trying to give the appearance of strength if nothing else.

Lin was still standing, barely. He had cut marks up and down his arms and torso, and large angry welts covering his whole body. His breath came in heavy gasps, his chest rising and falling from the strain of it.

Five bodies lay at his feet, but I could see the effort it'd taken for him to get them there.

Five humans still stood, Mitch and Misha thankfully among them. They were hurt, but still breathing. Both had burn and claw marks and neither seemed too steady on their feet.

Me, Ninia, Lin, Boya, Steva, and Iscca stood together. Blood ran from Ninia's side and neck. She had a hand over an open wound on her stomach and her breath was short and catchy.

I leaned over slightly so that we could keep each other upright.

We'd put up a good fight considering that our backup had never arrived. Then again, we hadn't waited like we were supposed to, so the chief probably hadn't even known where to find us. I sent out a signal letting them know what was going on.

My wounds were opening back up and I could feel the blood starting to seep out. I was almost depleted of energy and didn't know how long I could keep standing.

Rome walked over, clapping his hands, and smiling. "As was expected." He looked at us with some kind of deranged pride. "Now think about how freeing it would be to turn that same rage on the Riverwalk First Families." The Banshee and Pantue stood behind him, heads held high, eyes shining in his light. He had them. They were so caught up in his spell that they couldn't see through to the bullshit.

He looked between myself, Lin and Ninia as if waiting for our acquiescence.

I wanted to wipe that smug grin off his face, but my arm was screaming, and my stomach felt raw and open. The only thing I could do about it right then was lean on Ninia for support.

Lin wrapped his arm around my waist and I knew that was his way of keeping me standing.

Seeing that none of us were ready to join him, Rome smiled and pointed to Helena. "I'll just leave you with this. Give you something to think about."

He turned on his heels, the Pantue, and his five remaining followers right behind him.

Lin, Boya, and Ninia tried to give chase, and that's when the Banshee released the full fury of her rage. Her legs bent. Her arms fell to the side, and her mouth opened wider than any beings had a right to. She looked like something out of one of those horror movies that the humans were so fond of.

She let out a scream so shrill and bloodcurdling that it dropped us to the floor in an instant. I tried to cover my ears, as blood seeped from them as well as from my mouth and nose.

Steva and Boya made an attempt to join hands, but it was hard as both were bleeding profusely. Once connected they sent a double blast of fire straight to her face. She hissed and took a couple of steps back, but didn't stop that horrific screaming.

Ninia's face contorted in pain, her breathing hard and ragged. She still wouldn't give up, though, she didn't know how. It drove Steva insane, but had helped them out of some sticky situations.

From her position on the floor, she raised one hand, and followed up where the dragons had left off.

Lin took my hand, and together with Ninia, we sent out a blast while Boya and Steva let loose with more fire.

Our efforts combined, the Banshee spun on her heels, stumbled back, and then disappeared into thin air. I sagged against Lin for support, closing my eyes, glad I could finally breathe again.

SIX

I awoke sometime later. My stomach felt raw and my jaw and upper face ached. Someone had patched up my wounds, and so at least I wasn't bleeding anymore.

I was still hurt though, and I guessed Lin was as well. This meant we didn't have to wait weeks to be together. The fact that we'd both been hurt so badly meant that we started at zero.

Since we both needed healing energy, we could be together and heal at the same time.

I looked around a bit, trying to get a better clue of my surroundings. The bed under me was my own, and to one side of me was Boya, on the other side was Lin. Which meant the chief eventually found us and brought us home.

I sat up and rubbed tender fingers over my head. Something was coming back to me. I vaguely remembered the chief yelling as they loaded us into the med van; rescue workers doing what they could to keep us alive. An image of Steva, Iscca, and Ninia being carried to the same room once we'd made it home popped into my head, yet I had no clue if it was real or imagined.

Well someone had gotten it right because I needed Boya and Lin tonight as much as Ninia needed Steva and Iscca.

It was the only way to get better. Lin and I both needed Boya. There was an incredible trust there, between the three of us. There had to be, because it was more than just Boya healing us.

It was Lin and I both pouring so much healing energy into

Boya that we were almost incapacitated.

Yet he never took advantage. Never did anything we didn't want him to do. There was no one on this earth that either of us trusted more than Boya.

A touch to my thigh alerted me to the fact that Lin was now awake. He put his hand on my face and just stared, his features soft and inviting.

I stared back wanting to be as honest and as open as I could. Slowly he moved toward me. His hand tangled in my hair as he pulled me in for a slow tender kiss.

Boya in the meantime started a slow kiss on my back and neck. I leaned into his touch as Lin rose to his knees. Boya rose as well. They shared a long smoldering kiss and then Lin and I breathed energy into Boya.

The kiss from us would heal him, and then he, in turn, would heal us.

We all fell back onto the bed, and after that, it was a free for all. We tore into each other, loving hard and good, as only we knew how.

It was one of the best nights of my life, no matter what it'd taken for us to get there.

The next morning, I felt energized and refreshed. I walked into the kitchen and saw that Ninia looked as well as I felt. "See you had a good night," she said giving me a knowing grin.

"Backatcha." I raised a single eyebrow to let her know that I knew exactly what she'd been up to.

She smiled cheekily, completely unfazed. "We gotta do what we gotta do, right?"

I poured myself a cup of coffee and sat across from her smiling. "The life of a succubus is so hard," I whined.

She threw a piece of bacon at me and we both fell out laughing.

Later, once the others had joined, we talked about the night before.

The chief called and informed us that the First Families had called off their hit on us, satisfied that we'd provided enough proof of Rome's guilt.

Now that they knew who the guilty party was, they'd focus all their attention on finding him and leave the rest of us alone, which was a welcome relief to us all.

We went on to tell the others in the kitchen about Rome. I wanted the other agents to be on their guard, know what to look out for.

Rome was the real deal. We couldn't stress that enough. His allure was powerful and could theoretically draw any of us in. So they had to be ready.

Other succubi and incubi lived in this house. He couldn't get us to join him. No doubt he'd go after them next. I just wanted to make sure they'd be ready.

Steva put jelly on a piece of toast and bit into it. He talked, with a mouth full of food, not caring in the least about the disgusted groans around the table. "I don't think we'll see him again. Now that his little coup has failed."

Lin shook his head, his brows drawn together, his face hard. "It hasn't failed. We stalled it. He'll be back. Probably stronger than ever. We need to be ready."

He was right, of course. Guys like Rome didn't give up easily. The only thing in our favor was that we at least knew what we were dealing with now. "What about the twins?" I asked, knowing that he'd wanted to save them.

A pained look crossed his face, but he shook it off quickly. "We keep trying."

"We keep trying," I repeated, letting him know that I would stand with him as long as he needed me to.

Boya wrapped an arm around my waist and kissed my neck, mumbling a *good morning* for my ears only. He swatted me on the behind, and then turned to the others. "So, who's up for a game of spades?"

ABOUT THE AUTHOR

N.R. Hairston resides in Southern Virginia with her family. She enjoys writing, reading, cooking, and spending time with her family.

Please be on the lookout for upcoming books by N. R. Hairston.

If you enjoyed this book, please consider leaving a review.

Visit N. R. Hairston's website and subscribe to her newsletter to get exclusive short stories, and be the first to hear about deals and promotions! www.nrhairston.com

---

I hope you enjoyed reading this book. It really was a blast to write. If you have a favorite character or favorite story, I would love to hear about it! You can find me in these places:

Website – www.nrhairston.com
Twitter - twitter.com/nrdhairston
Tumblr - a-sharp-pen-world.tumblr.com

Also, I'd like to give a special thanks to my beta readers, and editors for making this book what it is. Thank You!